Douglas Lindsay was born in Scotland in 1964. He lives in eastern Europe with his wife and two children.

# The
# Haunting
# Of
# Barney
# Thomson

**Douglas Lindsay**

This edition published in Great Britain in 2007 by
Long Midnight Publishing
Suite 433
24 Station Square
Inverness IV1 1LD
e-mail: info@barney-thomson.com

# www.barney-thomson.com

*A catalogue record for this book is available
from the British Library*

ISBN 978 0 9541 387 6 9

Printed and bound in Great Britain by
Mckays of Chatham plc, Chatham, Kent

# The
# Haunting
# Of
# Barney
# Thomson

## Douglas Lindsay

This edition published in Great Britain in 2007 by
Long Midnight Publishing
Suite 433
24 Station Square
Inverness IV1 1LD
e-mail: info@barney-thomson.com

# www.barney-thomson.com

ISBN 978 0 9541 387 6 9

Printed and bound in Great Britain by
Mckays of Chatham plc, Chatham, Kent

for Kathryn

# Prologue

## Too Many Thieves

Late September, the summer still clinging to the islands in the Clyde estuary. A strange and alien mugginess to the evening after a still day of sun and cloud and no wind and flat seas. Even the seagulls were silent, perched on railings and white walls, faces turned to the south searching for a breeze.

The town had been listless all day. People huddled in cool doorways. Now the night was uncomfortable and the small room above the bar on Cardiff Street was warm and lazy.

There were ten of them sitting around the table. Two women, eight men. Each one of them in it for the money, not one with the slightest trust in any of the others. Squabbles and petty bickering.

Tonight had been slightly different, none of them seeming to have the energy to fight. There had been routine discussion, the usual arguments from the old woman, but for once no one had taken her up on any of her contentions.

Everything seemed normal, everything seemed to be continuing as it had now for three years. But nothing ever stays the same, nothing lasts forever, all things must pass...

He drummed his fingers on the table and looked around the room. Nine others. It was an absurd amount of people to have in on an operation such as this. It was flabby, and once the whole thing started to disintegrate, there would be too many people to talk and too many people trying to pick up the last of the pieces.

Too many people, not enough pieces.

The fruits of their ill-conceived labour were never going to increase, and so there was only one way to improve on his own personal profits. When the time was right, when it became apparent that everything was about to implode, then it would be time to start reducing the number of the group.

No honour amongst thieves.

'You want another drink?'

1

He looked at the young man to his right and smiled. Maybe not everyone needed to die.

'Aye, that'd be nice, thanks. A gin and tonic.'

The younger man stood and squeezed his shoulder, headed for the bar. He watched him for a second, letting his eyes stray down the length of his jeans. Then he turned back to the table, surveyed the others, and wondered which of them would be the first to go.

# Part I

# 1

## And Slowly,
## It Crept In From The Fog

*The first week in November. Now that the clocks have gone back, the evening seems to arrive in an unexpected rush and the mild breeze of early autumn has been usurped by a bitter wind whipping in cold off the sea.*

*It has been a troubled day out in the bay, a restless sea, agitated waves snapping at the few boats left buoyed on the shore side of the two small islands which shelter Newton beach. However, as the cold afternoon progressed, the wind died and now, as darkness begins to creep from the east and enclose the town of Millport in its sombre fist, a strange fog has settled over the town and the sea is still. The still of the grave.*

Barney Thomson turned away from the window of the barber shop. The fog was so thick he could barely see the ten yards across the road to the white painted promenade wall. He felt the chill of early evening, even though it was warm in the shop and it had been two hours since he'd last stepped outside to breathe in the remains of the day.

'It's a little flowery,' he said, 'although maybe you were getting away with it until the line about the grave.'

The young man sitting in the third barber's chair closed the lid on his laptop and smiled.

'It's totally cool,' said Keanu McPherson, a child of *Bill & Ted*, if ever there was one. 'You have to have something about the grave, man, you know. Grave's are like, so symbolic.'

'You think?'

'Totally.'

3

Barney smiled and glanced at the clock. Almost seven o'clock. He could have gone home two hours ago, but always there seemed to be someone else drifting into the shop for a late afternoon cut, or just for a chat or a piece of advice. And what was it that he was going home to exactly?

'You should head off,' he said, something he'd already said fourteen times.

The summer had been busy. Millport was changing again, people seemed to be coming back. Terrorism, the war in Iraq, airport queues, all-over body searches, the possibility of getting blown up in mid-air, the likelihood of getting held up at the airport for three days. People were staying home. Millport had had its best summer in two decades and Barney hadn't been able to keep up.

He'd advertised for an assistant and had had just four applications. One old fellow whose fingers were so arthritic he could barely hold a pair of scissors, but who had claimed that scissors were no longer necessary for today's barber. Another old guy who had fallen asleep while Barney was giving him his informal chat. A third old guy who had ranted incessantly during the informal chat, and who had clearly wanted to use the barber shop as a platform for his futuristic views on the deportation of all women to the kitchen. And Keanu McPherson, 21, who had actually been trained as a barber.

They'd had a good summer. Somewhere along the way he'd intended letting McPherson go, however it hadn't happened yet and now he wasn't sure if it would. The customers liked him, and what did Barney care if his workload was cut in half?

Keanu McPherson stood up, tucked the laptop under his arm, grabbed his jacket from the hook on the wall and held up a farewell hand.

'Adios, my old amigo,' he said.

'See you tomorrow,' said Barney.

The door opened, he felt the chill of the night sweep into the shop, and then it was closed again and the sound of McPherson's footsteps quickly vanished into the fog.

Silence.

4

He turned round and looked at the shop. Another day done. There hadn't been a real customer in over an hour and a half. What was it he was waiting for?

He now had a house round on Kames Bay, looking back over the town and beyond to the hills of Arran. He enjoyed the walk back after work, even now that it was dark. Feeling the sea in the air, the taste of salt on the wind. Sometimes he'd stop at the Crocodile Fryer and pick up a fish supper, so that he'd meander even more slowly back to his house. Sometimes he wouldn't stop at the house and he'd walk on round the island. Forming great philosophies or maybe just with a blank mind. Getting used to being settled again after years of wandering, becoming accustomed to Millport, the pace of the town, the people, knowing that at last he'd found the place he was going to stay.

The door opened. Barney turned quickly, surprised, trying to shake off the fright. There was an old fella standing just inside the door. An old green, wax coat, undone, a wool sweater underneath. A neat, grey beard. Grey hair, eyes the colour of the sea. Barney noticed his hands, a fisherman's hands, calloused, resilient.

'You gave me a fright,' said Barney, slightly disconcerted by the stare. In a town of old fellas, here was one who he didn't recognise.

The man smiled and removed his coat.

'Sorry, didn't mean to scare you. You got time to give an old man a haircut?'

Barney looked unnecessarily at the clock.

'Of course,' he said.

'Just a quick dash with a pair of scissors,' said the guy. 'In a bit of a rush, as I expect you are yourself.'

He slipped into the chair, Barney went about his business. Sorted out the cloak, the rubber hair-falling-down-neck shield, scissors, comb. Action.

'You here visiting?' asked Barney, once he had embarked on the cut. Hadn't needed to ask what was required. Here was a man who would clearly benefit from a Cary Grant.

The old guy was off, mind elsewhere. Finally he caught Barney's eye in the mirror and snapped back to the present.

5

'Just stopping at the pier for a couple of things. Got a small fishing vessel, the *Albatross*. Working out of Ullapool. Heading back out into the Kyles tonight.'

'In this fog?' asked Barney curiously.

The old guy glanced out the window, then he looked back at himself in the mirror. Face expressionless, as if the fog wasn't there.

'Needed to pick up food for Grudge.'

'Grudge?'

The man giggled, a strange but delightful sound from an old throat.

'My lab. He travels everywhere with us. He's a wee gem. Found him on a night just like this up at Tighnabruaich.'

Barney nodded and smiled. There was a beautiful serenity about the old man. Outside the evening was cold and grey, the clawing mist enveloping the town. The fisherman was like a warm and lazy summer's afternoon.

The quiet of an autumn day fell upon the shop. There was silence outside, and inside just the snip of the scissors, the occasional click of steel against the comb. Barney was on autopilot, the fisherman stared into the mirror.

Barney had to snap himself out of the reverie when he suddenly realised that he had finished. The Cary Grant was done. He removed the cape, brushed away the hairs which had escaped onto the old man's shoulders and nodded at him in the mirror.

The old fella stood up, admired himself in the mirror for a few seconds, then ambled across the shop and took his jacket from the peg. He turned and stared out at the fog as he slipped it over his shoulders, then he searched around in his pocket for something. Barney took a brush and started to sweep up, as ever giving the customer time to sort out the finances.

'I don't have any money,' said the old guy, a statement of fact delivered with no apology.

Barney looked quizzically at him. He was surprised but not at all bothered. There was something about the man that made it all right.

'How are you going to get food for Grudge?' he asked instead.

6

The old fella smiled and tapped his pocket.

'Already dealt with that. I'll drop the money by the next time I'm in town.'

Barney shrugged.

'Whenever.'

The fisherman looked away from Barney around the shop, taking in the white walls and the adverts for Gillette, the three large mirrors, the pictures of George Clooney and Brad Pitt, and the painting of Alan Rough, playing against Iran in 1978.

'Nice place,' he said. 'Bright.'

He looked at Barney, smiled again, and then walked out into the fog and the chill evening. Barney got the blast of cold as the door closed, and watched the green of the jacket slip away and disappear into the mist.

He shivered. Caught sight of his reflection in the window.

Barney Thomson, barber. Fifty-five and a half.

He stopped another shudder before it racked his spine any further, then he bent over the brush and finished off sweeping up the remains of the old fisherman's cut.

## 2

## If Death Was A Fish

The mist had cleared by the following morning, the day had the fresh beauty of mid-autumn. The air was crisp, the sea flat calm, there was a weak sun coming from over the mainland.

The forty-five foot yacht, *Cruachan*, was puttering along the coast of Bute, having spent the night nestled away from the fog in Rothesay Bay. Headed down the firth in search of a wind, three men were sitting on deck, looking over at the Isle of Cumbrae, enjoying the stillness of a calm day at sea. Bacon sandwiches, tea. The surrounding hills were green, the mountains of Arran bathed in a beautiful light. They had been disappointed to awake to no wind and the prospect of a day running on the engine, but the glory of the surroundings more than made up for it.

Up ahead, coming round the head of Little Cumbrae, they could see a medium-sized tanker heading towards them. The only other boat present was a small fishing vessel, sitting dead in the water near the shore on Kilchattan Bay. No movement on board, the three men had been keeping an eye on it for the previous few minutes, waiting for some sign of life.

It was just before eight-thirty when they came to the bay, and the small trawler was a hundred yards across the calm water.

'Cut the engine,' said one of the three men.

The man at the engine followed the other's gaze to the fishing vessel. Nothing out of place, no sign of trauma. And yet there was an air about it. Maybe it came from the silence of the morning, maybe from the lack of movement on the boat. Perhaps it was just the peculiarity of a fishing vessel sitting in this place at this time. He cut the power and they steered the boat round directly towards the fishing vessel.

As they drew up alongside they could see the name written in white down the side. The *Bitter Wind*. MPT908. Light blue lines, red in the lower half. The boat was running light. Not a new vessel, but well kept.

'Hello!' one of the men shouted.

'Ahoy!' called another.

*Cruachan* drifted lazily up beside the *Bitter Wind*, then the two boats bumped side by side. Such was the stillness of the water and the slow approach of the yacht, they were able to grab the side of the fishing vessel so that they stayed alongside.

*Cruachan* nestled a couple of feet lower than the *Bitter Wind*, and they looked warily onto the deck and into the cabin.

'Hello! Everyone ok in there?'

A metal chain clanked against a bar. The boats nuzzled together, gentle bumping noises. One of the men looked up at the clear blue sky, feeling a shiver of trepidation.

'No seagulls,' he said.

'Come on, you've got ten years on us. You can climb aboard.'

The youngest of the three men looked rueful, then put his feet up on the railing of their yacht, put his hands on the side of the *Bitter Wind* and hoisted himself up and into the fishing vessel.

Safely aboard he stopped and looked around. Everything in order, the boat had not been worked since the last time it had left port. The nets were packed away at the side, ropes neatly stored, the deck uncluttered. It was as if the owners had been wanting to sell the vessel and they'd been paid a visit by the Boat Doctor.

'Hello,' he said, looking into the cabin. Still expected three or four angry fishermen to suddenly appear brandishing machine guns, accusing him of being a pirate.

That kind of thing happens on the Clyde.

'Go into the cabin,' said one of the others.

'Get the log,' said the other.

The man on the fishing vessel nodded and walked forward.

'Hello?' he ventured again, but he knew that there was going to be no one there. At least, no one who was going to answer him.

As he reached the door he got the first hint of death. Not a smell, nothing tangible. He could just feel it. He hesitated, stopped himself glancing back at his crewmates. *I don't want to go in because it doesn't feel right...*

He ducked down through the door and entered the small cabin. Stopped, took it in. Nothing out of the ordinary. A chart of the firth of Clyde and Kyles of Bute laid out on a small table. An empty mug, its insides tea-stained, set beside it. Three macks hung on the pegs on the back wall, two yellow, one green. A hat on another peg. Chair in the corner, a newspaper on top. From the headline, *America Invades Itself As President Confuses Iowa With Iran*, he knew that it was a couple of days old.

From outside he could hear a radio playing. His friends must have turned it on, he thought. Break the stillness. What was the music? Mahler? Maybe it was Mahler, he wasn't sure.

He made himself approach the doorway at the back. A small space behind. As soon as he changed his angle, however, he could see the feet, propped up, in a pair of well-used boots. Not sailing boots. An old-fashioned pair of hiking boots.

He paused, then finally made himself look in through the doorway.

The body was sitting up against a wall, head slumped down over the chest. The eyes were open, dead grey eyes, staring. The legs were straight out in front, propped on a coiled rope. It wasn't obvious how he'd died. There might have been bruising around the neck, but in the dim light of the cabin, he couldn't be sure.

He turned away and stepped quickly out onto the deck and breathed in the sea air, his eyes squinting against the sun.

He stared at the low green hills rising in front of him up from the bay, and remembered scout camps from forty years earlier. Happy days.

The thought of the corpse in the hold suddenly drenched back over him and he turned and looked at his two friends. One of them held his hand out to help him back down onto the boat. The other was already on the radio to the coastguard.

10

# 3

## The Storyteller's Tale

*The sky is brilliant, a sheer blue that almost defies colour. It is as if iridescent blue angels had collected in heaven and were advancing across the sky in one great, striking mélange of blue. This is blue as must have been defined by the gods when they drew up the colours. This is a blue which would defy any paint chart. This is blue as warmth not cold, blue as exuberance not apathy. Just to look at it is to make one's heart soar and one's eyes to reflect in the giant blueness, turning all those who gaze upon it into other-worldly Paul Newmans.*

'What d'you think, chief?'

Barney stared at Keanu, then glanced out at the blue sky, which was very blue, right enough. The door to the shop opened and Igor, Barney's deaf, mute hunchbacked assistant entered, carrying some fresh rolls and a packet of bacon.

They'd been open for just under an hour, the customers had been non-existent, and so he'd sent Igor out to get something interesting for breakfast.

'Blue sky,' said Barney.

Igor smiled, said something that, no matter what was intended, sounded like *arf*, held aloft the bacon and walked into the back room to get on with the job.

'Maybe I haven't emphasised the blue quite enough, you know,' said Keanu, looking back at the laptop.

Barney glanced at him, Keanu with his unruly blonde hair over his face as he bent down over that morning's blog.

'You're probably right,' said Barney, not one to curtail creativity. 'Perhaps you could compare it to other well-known blues. The sea around Pacific atolls, the blue in blue cheese.'

Keanu nodded, the spark of inspiration having been struck.

'Cool,' he said, and immediately his fingers began to whizz over the keyboard. Barney smiled, then rose, deciding that he'd kill the time he had between now and the arrival of his bacon sandwich by standing at the door and enjoying the cold of a beautiful November morning. Under a particularly blue sky.

The door burst open, no warning, and they were confronted by Rusty Brown, one of the old fellas of the island, looking flushed around the chops, his hair still well cropped from his cut three days previously. The man wasn't here for a haircut.

'You hear the news?' he asked breathlessly.

Barney and Keanu looked at each other.

'Hold the front page,' said Barney.

'Something's actually happened in this dead end town?' said Keanu. 'Awesome.'

'They've found the *Bitter Wind* adrift in Kilchattan Bay,' said Brown, the words shooting out like they'd been fired from a whale gun.

'Crew?' asked Barney.

There were three of a crew, all of whom lived in Millport. Barney had cut the hair of Ally Deuchar the previous week. Colin Waites was another regular. Only Craig Brown had never been into the shop, and that was because he remained irresolutely shaggy, rather than the fact that he took his business elsewhere.

'They found Ally's body on the boat. Dead. The rumour is his head had been cut clean off, he'd been disembowelled, and the head was sitting in his stomach, his penis stuffed in the mouth.'

Keanu was open mouthed. Barney raised the universal eyebrow of scepticism.

'You made some of that up yourself, didn't you?'

Brown finally came down from the frenetic high of being self-appointed, door-to-door town crier, and looked a bit sheepish.

'The story may have grown in the telling,' he muttered, unused to anyone questioning the tale.

'Tell us what you've been told,' said Barney. 'No frills. These are people we know.'

The seventy-eight year-old Brown, the look of the scolded child about him, held his flat cap in his hands. Somehow alerted to the stramash out front, Igor appeared at the back door.

'Three guys out sailing this morning came across the boat. Everything looked normal, no sign of fuss, no sign of anything having gone amiss. But she was drifting. They called out, one of the fellas went aboard, found Ally dead. And to be fair to the lad me, I don't actually know yet if they've even worked out how it happened. Could have been bird flu.'

'Wow, that's way less exciting,' said Keanu.

'What about the other two?' asked Barney quickly.

'No sign,' said Brown. 'It was like the *Mary Celeste*.'

He said the last two words very slowly and let them hang in the air. A silence came upon the shop, and the four men looked at each other.

'Arf,' said Igor.

'There were no dead bodies on the *Mary Celeste*,' said Barney.

'I thought it was the *Marie Celeste*?' said Keanu.

'Mary,' said Barney. 'Conan Doyle wrote a story about it twenty years after it happened, he called it the *Marie Celeste* in his story, and it stuck. But it was really Mary.'

'Cool,' said Keanu. 'The power of fiction.'

'Are they bringing the boat back here or taking it into a harbour on Bute?' asked Barney.

'Here I believe,' said Brown. 'Right, I'd better get going, there are others who'll be wanting to know.'

'Keep it straight,' said Barney.

Brown hesitated at the door, gave Barney a salute, pulled on the flat cap and headed out into the fine November morning. The door closed behind him, the shop came upon silence.

Barney stared at Igor and Keanu. The Three Amigos.

'Cool,' said Keanu.

'Arf,' muttered Igor from the back of the shop.

'You know,' said Keanu, 'I'm still not picking up on them. What did he say?'

Barney looked back out at the day, as the first hint of wind out at sea began to break the tranquillity of the flat calm.

'The police will be coming,' said Barney.

Keanu smiled curiously at Igor, nodding his head. There was going to be an actual police investigation on his doorstep. How cool was that? Maybe they'd even want to interview him.

He had been the last person to cut the hair of one of the crew members after all.

'And the press,' added Barney, with some melancholy. 'They'll be round here like flies round...' and he let the sentence drift off.

A pause. Stillness. The possibility of murder had once again crept into Barney Thomson's life. He sat back, his heart sinking like an anchor.

It wasn't about him, he wasn't involved, he didn't need to take it personally. Yet, here he was, Miss flippin' Marple, and everywhere he went, someone was guaranteed to get murdered sooner or later.

'...overripe fruit?' said Keanu.

✂

The police from Glasgow arrived within the hour. There had been some initial confusion in Strathclyde Police about who would take charge of the investigation, because on the face of it all they had so far was a missing persons and a not-yet-confirmed-as-suspicious death. There was a minor struggle between the police in Largs and their superiors in Glasgow, and it seemed the only person who didn't want to protect his corner and was more than willing to give up as much authority as he could, was the resident policeman on the island of Cumbrae, Constable Thaddæus Gainsborough.

In the end, the constabulary in Glasgow had won the battle, as had been immediately inevitable. This was partly as the Chief Constable had wanted to justify the use of the extra helicopter he'd manage to finagle out of that year's budget, and so had sent four police officers down to the scene of the crime by the quickest means possible.

As the Sea King HAS6, bought for a snip from a downsizing Royal Navy, came in to land on the helicopter pad in the middle of a small field just across the road from the Millerston Hotel on the west side of the island, the *Bitter Wind* was just being towed to the pier at Millport, as its home port, barely quarter of a mile along the shore.

Constable Gainsborough was there to meet them, as the helicopter thunderously landed, disgorged its passengers, and then immediately whizzed off back up into the blue sky of a perfect autumnal day. Almost as if it had other things to do.

Gainsborough stood on the edge of the grass waiting for the noise to die down, before coming forward to introduce himself to the three men and one woman who had come to the island.

The four visitors stood and watched the helicopter, as it turned north and began to head back up the Clyde. For all of them it had been their first helicopter trip. Once it had finally become a dot on the horizon, they turned towards Gainsborough and made their way off the grass.

'Welcome to Millport,' said Gainsborough.

The man at the head of the four looked at the gloriously picturesque scene around them – nuclear power station notwithstanding – and said, 'Aren't you supposed to say that after we've found a pit full of dead bodies or we've been in a shoot-out with fourteen masked bank robbers?'

Gainsborough looked a little nonplussed.

'We don't usually get that kind of thing on Millport, Sir.'

'But you do get abandoned fishing boats with dead bodies on board.'

The man held Gainsborough's gaze to see which way he would crumble. Gainsborough shrugged.

'So it seems,' he said.

The police officer walked past him and looked up and down the road. A few cars parked, no moving traffic. An old guy on a bike heading towards them. The gardens of the large Victorian houses all looking neat, tidied for the winter.

'I'm DCI Frankenstein,' he said. 'Any jibes about the name, I'll have heard them before, and I'll break your legs.'

Gainsborough looked at him and then glanced at the other three, as if looking for someone normal to talk to. The woman smiled at him, deciding it was time to put him out of his misery.

'Hi,' she said. 'I'm Detective Sergeant Proudfoot, this is Watkins and Peters, our SOCO's for this job. They'll give the boat the full going over, and then be gone for the time being. The professor and I will stay around for a while, see what we can dig up.'

15

Frankenstein turned and looked at his sergeant.

'You know I hate it when you say that,' he said.

'You stop threatening to break peoples' legs,' she said, 'and I'll think about it.'

She turned her back on him and looked along the road towards the town, the sweep of Kames Bay in the distance behind it. A scene which would not have looked too different had she been standing there a hundred years earlier.

'As you can see we're a happy bunch,' said Frankenstein to Gainsborough in a low voice. 'Where's you car?' he added abruptly.

Gainsborough pointed towards the white Land Rover, sitting outside the police station, quarter of a mile along the road. Frankenstein followed his gaze.

'I walked,' said Gainsborough, unnecessarily.

Proudfoot smiled and started walking along the road towards town, the two SOCO's following.

'God's sake,' muttered Frankenstein as he fell into line behind Gainsborough.

'Nice day for a walk,' said Proudfoot, looking out over the blue sea to the island of Little Cumbrae.

'Nice day to find a dead body in a fishing boat at the arse end of the fucking Clyde,' muttered Frankenstein.

# 4

## Three Men In A Boat

As with all small towns up and down the coast of Scotland, there had once been a thriving fishing fleet working out of Millport. However, in time it had dwindled and died, until finally the last trawler had gone out of business and the fishermen had moved on. Then, in the previous year, Ally Deuchar, a local man trained in the arts of crisis loans and job centre applications, had managed to acquire for himself a business plan, a grant from Ayrshire Enterprise and a fishing boat, and had started making short trips out of Millport searching for whatever fish he could find off the coast of Ayrshire and Argyll.

It was a small business, but after initially thinking of the whole enterprise as some sort of scam to acquire business grants, he had discovered a love of the sea and a talent for finding fish when others couldn't. Then one episode of watching Rick Stein charge about Britain meeting people who make garlic toffee and honeyed mince had persuaded him that there was a niche market for the iconoclastic fisherman. He had begun to sell himself as some sort of localised Jamie Oliver to the rich business widows in Helensburgh and to the hotels on Loch Fyne and on down the coast. He still worked out of Millport but had begun to think that maybe it was time to move to somewhere that was a bit more of a hub. Had also begun to think of a bigger boat and more crew.

And now Ally Deuchar was dead.

His girlfriend, Seattle Henderson, discovered the news when Rusty Brown burst into Mapes toy shop and bicycle hire, full of renewed enthusiasm for an extravagant tale, and said, 'Have you heard the news?'

Seattle Henderson, preparing the shop for another sleepy November day, looked up from a small display of Top Trumps cards.

'I know,' she said.

Rusty stopped in his tracks, suddenly realising who he was speaking to, and deciding that the new post-Barney tale that he'd begun telling – of the giant eight-foot lizard which had been discovered on board, dismembered limbs strewn around the cabin, the monster having choked on the head of one of the crew – probably wouldn't be appropriate.

'You know?' he said weakly.

'Yeah,' said Seattle Henderson, 'Britney's pregnant again. I mean, like, what is she doing?'

Rusty Brown wasn't the quickest.

'Britney…?'

'Duh,' said Seattle.

'Not that,' said Rusty Brown. 'The *Bitter Wind*.'

The enthusiasm had completely gone from his voice. Despite the telling off from Barney, he had carried on expanding the story where he saw fit. But now he was about to tell an innocent young child of a girl that her boyfriend, her true love, was dead.

'The *Bitter Wind*?' said Seattle. 'The trawler?'

'Aye,' said Rusty Brown.

Cap in hand again, a solemn look on his face, he took a further few strides into the shop, almost knocking over the *Lord Of The Rings* crossbow, which had been propped against a pillar, un-bought, for five years now.

'She's been found at sea. Deserted.'

Seattle Henderson stopped wiping the dust off the Buzz and Woody models which had gone un-bought for eight years now.

'You mean, like the *Marie Celeste*?' she asked.

'Mary,' said Rusty Brown.

'Whatever,' she said, looking away from him and returning to the dust.

'Well, the ship wasn't completely deserted. There was one of the crew on board. Dead. I'm not sure which one,' he lied.

Seattle Henderson brushed away at the dust on Woody's brown waistcoat.

'So Ally's missing, maybe dead?' she asked.

'Aye.'

18

'I mean,' she said, looking up again, 'how many times did I say to him that the whole fishing thing was stupid? How many times? He's such a muppet.'

Rusty took a step or two back.

'I expect he'll turn up,' she continued, turning and placing Woody high up on a shelf. 'If he doesn't, it'll free me up to have a go at Dougie, 'cause he's going to be right pissed off at Britney for getting up the duff.'

'Ah, I thought you meant Britney, you know, *the* Britney.'

'Naw, wee Britney from up the road.'

Rusty Brown nodded sagely. Here he was, the storyteller, getting told the news.

'She's pregnant?' he said. 'Hardly seems old enough.'

'Duh,' said Seattle, 'she's like fifteen. Like, how old did you think you had to be?'

Rusty Brown felt safe to put his flat cap back in place. He waited for Seattle Henderson to look at him, realised it wasn't going to happen, and then turned and walked slowly out of the shop.

Colin Waites' ex-wife lived in Gourock, and so was not within Rusty Brown's sphere of influence. Craig Brown had a dark and somewhat mysterious background, which did not include anyone who would need to be immediately informed of his disappearance.

Rusty Brown could return to telling elaborate tales to dispassionate parties.

19

## The Notebook Guy

Early afternoon. The man from the Largs & Millport Chronicle had arrived. No one from the Glasgow press seemed interested yet. There was a man from the Evening Times on his way, but he had been waylaid at the Holy Friar just after the Largs turnoff on the Beith road. The others were for now working from a brief report that had gone out on Reuters, a report which had stuck to the facts, made the story sound as uninteresting as possible, and had failed to mention murder, decapitation or haddock wars.

Barney Thomson stood at the white promenade wall and looked along at the pier. He'd come out for a walk, fresh sea air, a quiet morning in the shop. He'd had one customer – an elaborate but ultimately unfulfilling Simon Le Bon *Rio* – while his creative assistant, Keanu, had been quiet all day. Every now and again the lad had gone out to try to find out more details on the *Bitter Wind*, but had come up with little other than absurd gossip, much of which he had presented to Barney as truth.

Now it was Barney's turn to take a stroll along the promenade. Igor was having lunch with his intended, the town lawyer Garrett Carmichael. Keanu was writing up the latest wild speculation for his blog, in the hope that something major would happen and he might become some sort of a thing, while holding down the fort in case there were any haircutting emergencies.

The crowd on the pier was dwindling. What with it being another slow day in Millport in November, a small assembly had gathered to watch the police investigation. Gainsborough had initially cordoned off the entire pier, but eventually his friends in the audience – and he had known virtually everyone there – had persuaded him to move the rope closer and closer, until the crowd was within about ten feet of the boat. In the end it had more or less turned into a spectator sport. Like watching CSI live.

Frankenstein had watched the throng get closer and closer, but was of the opinion that if a crime had been committed here, then there was a good chance that the perpetrator would be back to take a look.

However, police investigation doesn't really reward long-term viewing, so after the spectators began to realise that no murderers were going to be uncovered that day on the pier, and that a murder might not even have been committed, the crowd had dropped off, back to whatever mundane aspect of life it was which held them on this sleepy November day.

Barney walked past the small clock tower at the pier entrance. He nodded at a couple of old guys who wandered by – Barney knew all the men on the island, not so many of the women.

'Nothing to see,' said old Tom Brady.

'Took the body away two hours ago,' said old Tom Ramsay. 'By now it'll have been sliced apart like the Rangers defence against Juventus in 1995.' He giggled.

'Away you and shite,' said Brady. 'Rangers defence in '95. At least we were in the Champions' League, what were you in? The Idiots' League. The Losers' League?'

'I've had enough of your pish.'

'My pish? What about your pish? Enough to flood the Loire valley...'

The cut and thrust of radical argument drifted off into the day as they disappeared from the pier. Barney smiled and walked on to the edge of the cordoned-off area. There were only three people left standing now, two still fascinated by events, one leaning against a pole, making notes in a small book.

There were two men working on the boat that Barney could see. One on deck, rummaging carefully through nets, the other bent down inside the cabin, his back turned. Barney watched them for a second and then approached the man with the notebook.

The swell had started to get up and the sea was becoming a little boisterous beneath the pier, sucking noises and the sound of water being drawn between wood.

'What's the latest?' asked Barney.

21

The notebook guy gave Barney the once over, a classical head to foot glance, taking everything in.

'You're the town barber?' he asked.

Barney didn't even begin to wonder.

'Barney Thomson,' he said, extending his hand, knowing that this wasn't a guy whose hair he'd cut in the past.

'William Deco,' said the notebook guy.

'Your friends call you Art?' ventured Barney.

'Tell me about it,' he replied grimly. 'Might as well have Art stamped on my forehead.'

'What's with the notebook?'

'Largs & Millport Chronicle.'

'William Deco,' said Barney, nodding. 'Of course. I read you every week.'

'You're the one.'

'Always presumed that it was a made-up name. Wondered why you didn't just call yourself Arthur Deco or Artimus Deco.'

'I come from a long line of Decos,' said Deco.

'Your family left Spain in 1646?'

'It was '54 to be precise. We did all right in this country until Charles Rennie Macintosh.'

The guy rummaging through the nets finally stood up and stretched. Looked out to sea, then started wandering around the deck poking at things with a small stick.

'You can't have many abandoned fishing boats to report,' said Barney.

'First one,' said Deco, 'and I've been on the job for thirty-three years.'

'Thirty-three years working for the Largs & Millport Chronicle?'

'Used to think I was going to be someone. The Herald. The Scotsman. Commentary on Good Morning Scotland. Maybe even make the London Times or Newsweek. Used to imagine my by-line in the Herald Tribune, being read and ignored by people on aeroplanes and in big international chain hotels.'

He paused, he let out a heavy sigh, filled with all the weariness of the years.

'Suppose I was right. I am someone. I'm someone who's been writing for the Largs & Millport Chronicle for thirty-three years.'

'You've got your story at last,' said Barney.

'Maybe,' said Deco, 'maybe not.'

'What's the latest?' asked Barney again, having first ventured the question seemingly hours earlier.

'They took the body away zipped up in a bag. None of us saw it. Word is there was no obvious cause of death. These two comedians have been on the boat gathering evidence. They're what we call Scenes of Crime Officers, although everyone just calls them CSI now 'cause of the tv show.'

Barney was familiar with the work of Scenes of Crime Officers, but he wasn't immediately going to fill a reporter in on his background.

'There are two other police here at the moment, they've gone off with the local plod to talk to people, find things out. Two crew members missing, all three of them lived on the island. The trawler was discovered by three old guys out on a yacht. They came in with the boat, gave statements and they're gone. At least they'll have a tale to tell at dinner for the next few weeks.'

Deco paused and looked through his notebook, seeing if there was anything else of note. Face a blank, then a small nod.

'The boat only usually went out for one night at a time, got that from a guy who was standing where you are right now, but it had been gone three nights this time. They'd reported in that they'd be away longer, but no one knows why. Least, no one who I've spoken to yet.'

Barney looked back along the front of the town, Stuart Street quiet in the early afternoon sun. Along the promenade, the Garrison building, newly refurbished and gleaming, past Newton Beach and the crocodile rock, and beyond to Kames Bay, where he could see his house, sitting in amongst the neat row of large Victorian homes at the east end of the town. The seagulls dipped and swooped and cried, the sea showed increasing signs of life.

'When do you have to file?' asked Barney.

'Three days,' said Deco.

'Plenty of time for things to develop.'

Deco muttered something low and dismal.

'Maybe your editor will want to bring out a special *Millport Trawler Mystery* edition,' said Barney.

Deco wrote something else down in his notebook, as if Barney had just given him an idea, the pages turned away so that Barney couldn't see what he was writing.

'I am the editor,' said Deco darkly.

Barney smiled, turned away from the *Bitter Wind* and began walking slowly back down the pier.

✂

Detective Chief Inspector Frankenstein had removed himself from the hands-on investigation and ridden off on a bike. Wanted to get a feel for the town and the island, as he suspected that he was about to be spending the next few days, if not weeks, mired in the place. Nothing concrete yet to say there had even been a crime committed, but he had a feeling.

They'd been told on arrival that riding a bike round the island was what everyone did. He'd scoffed, he'd muttered, he'd stared darkly along the road...and then he'd hired a bike from Mapes and set off on the ten and a half mile island circumference tour. Kames Bay, Farlane Point, the Aquarium and Keppel Pier, the lion rock, the wishing well, the sailing club, the ferry ramp... For all that he moaned and curmudgeoned his way through life, he was a good detective. Took it all in.

He reached the far side of the island from the town of Millport, where there is a small obelisk set off the road, just above the rocky shoreline. There were four bikes already leaning against the grey stone, the riders sitting on the grass, looking north up the Clyde estuary, towards Wemyss Bay and beyond. A large dog lay on the grass beside them, stretched out, sleeping. Frankenstein slowed his bike, deciding it was time to get some local knowledge. Or visitor's knowledge.

He laid the bike down on the grass verge and stopped for a second. The day was still beautiful, seagulls spiralling through a sky which had clung on to the astonishing blue which had so captivated Keanu MacPherson. In the distance, the mountains of Argyll were stark in the clear light. He could see the Rothesay ferry heading back to the mainland; a small cargo vessel to his left making swift progress towards the Irish Sea.

He caught the eye of a couple of the cyclists and nodded.

'All right, friend?' said one of them.

Frankenstein grunted in reply. Looked away, smelled the breeze. The Rothesay ferry didn't seem to be moving. Even allowing for perspective. What do I know about perspective, he thought.

'You visiting the island?' asked Frankenstein.

The one who'd already spoken turned and nodded.

'Like, kind of a work team bonding session. You police?'

Frankenstein cursed, an undistinguishable single syllable that still managed to sound incredibly vulgar.

'You're probably here for the *Mary Celeste*,' said one of the two women, without turning.

Frankenstein nodded. Some police officer. Five seconds' conversation and they had him pegged, and he still didn't have a clue. Work team bonding session?

'What work?' he asked gruffly. He usually needed Sergeant Proudfoot with him to ameliorate his complete lack of social skills.

'MI6,' said the guy who had yet to say anything.

The four of them looked out to sea. No further comment. Frankenstein gave them the once over.

'You came all the way up here from London?' he asked.

'Based in Edinburgh,' said two of them at once. Synchronised lying.

'Bullshit,' said Frankenstein. 'What are MI6 doing in Edinburgh? Isn't that MI5's job?' For some reason, he felt stupid.

'Like you don't think they have foreign nationals in Edinburgh?' said the other woman.

That was why I felt stupid, he thought. He grumbled and found himself looking at some indistinct spot on the water at which they were all staring.

'So,' he went on, thinking that he might as well try to achieve what he had stopped here for, regardless of how annoyed these people were making him, 'are you really here team building, or are you investigating the trawler?'

Another pause. Frankenstein was disarmed by these people, which he hated. He really ought to just get back on his bike. He noticed a family of swans mincing through the water not too far from the shore. Felt small.

'Maybe,' said one of them.

'Could be.'

'We're so secretive, even we don't know what we're doing most of the time.'

'Of course,' said the fourth monkey, 'we've been on the island for three days, so that would have been showing a remarkable amount of prescience, don't you think?'

Frankenstein lifted his bike and clumsily swung his leg over the bar. Three days? If it was true, maybe they would have something to tell him. Not that he was about to ask.

'MI6,' he grumbled under his breath, when he was a good few yards along the road. 'They're probably advertising executives.' As he rode off he heard one of them say, 'Pass the corn chips.'

And once he was out of earshot, the four people lying on the grass by the small obelisk could go back to discussing the international diamond smuggling operation that had brought them to the west coast of Scotland in the first place.

# 6

## Creep

A few more people arrived in the town during the day. Some police, some media, some curiosity seekers. There wasn't much to do and less to find out. The police took a small shop unit along the front and set up an incident room. It had once been a short-lived antique French furniture store, but there hadn't been much call for antique French furniture in Millport, and after a couple of months the place had folded and the owner had legged it with what was left of the local enterprise money he'd pocketed. Now the police were in. The antique French furniture had already been removed, the windows were dirty, the floor covered in dust. Spiders looked down from corners.

The police incident room was next door to the barbershop, separated by two feet of one hundred and thirty-five year-old stone wall.

The men of the barber shop were idle once again. A long winter beckoned. Barney stood at the window, looking out over the sea. Igor brushed slowly at the floor around the chairs, although no hair had fallen for more than an hour. Keanu had fallen into torpor. The sun had dipped behind the Arran hills and darkness was on its way.

'Going to be stormy tonight,' said Barney from nowhere. 'You can feel it. Once darkness comes.'

Igor leant on his brush and looked outside. Keanu glanced up from his laptop, at which he had been staring with ever more glazed eyes, and looked out at the darkening skies.

'Looks pretty clear,' he said.

Silence. Walls too heavy and thick to get even a trace of the activity next door, which wasn't exactly frenetic in any case. The hands of the clock on the wall moved silently. A car drove past in hushed tranquillity.

Barney looked out the window. Seemed to spend his life doing just that. Didn't mind. The others followed his gaze now, Igor leaning on his brush, Keanu, head resting on fist.

27

The sky seemed to darken as they watched. Clouds were gathering from somewhere, the first of the day.

'This is kind of weird,' said Keanu eventually.

'Arf?' asked Igor. Barney didn't turn.

'You know, like, we're sitting here looking out of a window at absolutely nothing. I mean, nothing at all. And yet, it's like, really cool. I'm so chilled. It's like some weird, transcendental drug. I'm tripping on silence and introspection. What is that all about?'

Igor smiled and looked back at the window. A cyclist passed the shop front, panniers stuffed full of shopping; the local road sweeper, Morgan Rembrandt. He threw a wave at the shop as he went, without turning. Barney and Igor nodded in reply. The rear wheel disappeared out of sight.

A seagull landed on the white promenade wall opposite. Cocked its head to the side, squawked. Seemed to look into the shop.

The door opened. Garrett Carmichael, the lawyer. Auburn hair, newly in curls. Lips full, eyes sparkling. Brown suit, knee-length skirt, pale blouse, two buttons undone. Pearls around her neck. Barney and Keanu stared, smiled. She wasn't for them.

'Hi guys,' she said. 'Another busy one?'

'November,' said Barney casually.

Igor leant on his brush. She kissed him on the cheek, stole another quick kiss on the lips, he blushed. A year and a half in. He still blushed.

Garrett Carmichael sat down on the old bench which ran the length of the shop and laid her bag beside her.

'I've had the same kind of day. It's like the place is shutting down early. Usually not this bad until January.'

'You hear about the boat mystery?' said Keanu.

'All about it,' she said. 'Read your blog. Cool.'

'Thanks!'

'You nailed the colour of the sky.'

Keanu nodded and looked mildly sheepish. Barney smiled.

'I'm off home to get the kids,' she said. 'Can I drag Igor away from you?'

'Of course,' said Barney. Probably for the next six months, he thought. But the place wouldn't be the same without the wee fella, so he wouldn't want it even if she tried.

She stood up, Igor muddled into the back room to get his coat, Keanu let himself stare at her for a while. Wished there were more women on the island like Garrett Carmichael.

'Why don't you close for the day?' she said. Looked at the clock. Almost five.

Barney shrugged.

'You're getting a reputation,' she said. 'Sad lonely Barney, spends all his time in the shop, waiting for customers that don't come.'

He gave her a look.

'Well, ok, I made that up. But you know, won't be long, people will start talking.'

Igor appeared back in the shop, she smiled.

'Had a guy in here for a cut past seven last night,' said Barney, annoyed that he felt the need to defend himself. Maybe she was right. Barney the loner. Barney the loser.

'One of the old guys who felt sorry for you?' she said, smiling. Playing a game, wondering if it was really getting to him.

Igor pulled on his coat, waved at Keanu. Keanu saluted.

'A fisherman,' said Barney. 'Old guy right enough. Said he was just stopping off for supplies.'

He hadn't thought about it all day. Just saying it now, though, it sounded strange.

'A fisherman?' she asked. 'From a trawler?'

'That's what he said,' replied Barney. Felt the shiver work its way down his spine. He'd believed him. Why not? Maybe it had just been some old guy with a story to spin. But what difference did it make? The guy had blagged a free haircut. No big deal. Why the shiver? 'Said he was heading off again last night.'

'In that fog?' said Carmichael. 'Sounds pretty weird. D'you tell the police?'

Barney turned and looked at her, as if at last fully engaging the conversation.

'They haven't been in here.'

'They're next door.'

'What am I going to tell them? It was some old guy, it wasn't any of our three from the boat.'

'Barney,' she said, tone starting to drift into the one she used with her kids, 'one guy's dead, two missing, and you get a mysterious fisherman on a dark and foggy night, looking for a haircut at seven o'clock in the evening.'

'Seven-thirty,' said Barney, mind wandering back to the night before. She was right. Why hadn't he thought to go to the police?

There'd been something about the old guy that had made him want to file the thought of him away, to relegate him to some dark recess of his mind and leave the thought to stagnate.

'Seven-thirty,' she repeated. 'Whatever. When you found out about the *Bitter Wind* this morning, didn't it set some little bell ringing? Are you scared of the police or something?'

Barney looked at the floor, rummaging through his head, trying to work out what it had been that had stopped him from making the connection.

'I don't know,' he said eventually, looking up. 'I didn't make the call, that's all. Just a guy getting a haircut.'

She puffed out her cheeks and shrugged. Glanced at Igor, who was feeling a little excluded.

'You'll go to them now, though,' she said.

Barney held his hands out in a conciliatory gesture. 'Sure.'

'Men are such muppets some times,' she said, giving her bag an unnecessary hoik over the shoulder.

'Arf,' said Igor, with raised eyebrow.

'Yes,' she said, 'you 'n all.'

She opened the door, Igor in tow, and turned back to the others.

'See you, guys. Go to the police.'

Keanu saluted again. Barney nodded.

'Did the old guy give a name at all?' she said, leaning on the door frame. Igor hovered at the exit.

'No name,' said Barney, shaking his head, 'though he said the boat was called the *Albatross*. Seemed an odd name for a boat.'

She stepped forward, Igor giving her room. Igor was eager to leave.

'I thought the albatross was bad luck for that lot,' continued Barney.

'Isn't it like, if you see an albatross your boat explodes?' ventured Keanu from the sidelines.

'Something like that,' said Barney.

'Or you get eaten by a giant sea serpent.'

'There's only ever been one boat called the *Albatross* around here,' said Carmichael, cutting through the banter.

Barney shrugged. 'Makes sense. You know the old guy then?'

'The *Albatross* was a trawler working out of Millport,' she said. Her tone was peculiar and the light-heartedness that Barney had felt from his short exchange with Keanu left him.

'And he moved to Ullapool,' said Barney. What was it that was making his stomach crawl?

The silence from outside seemed to creep into the shop. Keanu leant forward, getting the vibe. Igor shivered under his hump and stared at the ground. He knew what was coming.

'The *Albatross* was captained by a man called Judah Bennington. He worked out of Millport, but he'd had a couple of bad years around here and he decided to move to Ullapool. Three days after he left, his boat was found deserted at sea. All hands missing. Except for a small dog.'

'When?' said Barney.

'Over a hundred years ago,' she said. '1895 or thereabouts.'

Barney shrugged, a movement which suggested he was much more relaxed than he actually felt.

'Must be another *Albatross*,' he said.

'Come on,' said Igor, shuffling towards the door, 'we should go.' Although, sadly, it came out as *arf!*

Carmichael nodded, pulling her jacket more tightly around herself. Feeling the chill of a darkening late afternoon in November.

'There's usually an explanation,' said Barney.

Carmichael smiled weakly and held the door open for Igor, who threw a farewell hand at the others and walked out into the dusk. She exchanged a glance with Barney and then headed out into the cold.

Barney watched them go and then turned to look at Keanu, who was leaning forward, his elbows on his knees.

'Pretty creepy, man' he said.

Barney looked at the clock and decided that it was time to shut up shop for the night. Not yet five, but what did it matter? And he could see the police in the morning. What exactly was he going to tell them now that would make any sense?

'There'll be something,' he said. 'Nothing's ever truly interesting in life. Always something mundane.'

Keanu nodded and drummed his fingers on top of his laptop. Thinking of how this might read on the blog, although he was slowly realising, like an overwhelming majority of bloggers, that he was wasting his time.

'Like a guy in a mask,' said Barney without conviction.

'We've all seen Scooby Doo,' said Keanu.

'Exactly,' said Barney, walking to the rear of the shop to close up the back room.

'Of course,' said Keanu, standing up and making for his jacket, 'that would mean there was some kind of smuggling operation going on. And it won't be drugs, it'll be gold or diamonds or something. That'd be really cool.'

Barney stared at him for a second, then shook his head.

'No,' he said simply.

Keanu stood at the door, jacket on, laptop under his arm, ready to rock 'n roll.

'Yeah, you're probably right,' he said. 'Likely just some dumb-ass ghost or other.'

He saluted, opened the door and was on his way.

Barney watched him go and then stood alone in the shop. Felt the silence of the empty workplace. It was a feeling he had always enjoyed, but not this afternoon. Suddenly felt something very uncomfortable, a feeling that could only have been fear.

Nothing scared him, not after all he'd been through, not after all the death and bloody carnage that he'd been witness to in his life. That's what he'd thought these last few years. Too cool, or maybe just too old and tired to be afraid.

He pulled on his jacket, opened the door, turned off the lights and walked quickly out of the shop. A glance along the street, the smell of the sea. Locked the door, turned and looked out at the waves and the darkness coming in quickly from the east.

He could see the Arran ferry in the distance, moving silently and slowly towards Ardrossan. Another small boat, indistinguishable in the dark, was coming round the headland of Little Cumbrae.

Barney Thomson turned to his right, and decided that tonight he'd eat his dinner in the Incidental Mermaid halfway up Cardiff Street. Maybe he'd talk to Carrington for a while if he was in, and maybe he'd spend the evening watching whatever European football happened to be showing on the tv.

# 7

## The Frankenstein
## Forensics Phobia

Erin Proudfoot hit the off-switch on the computer, then took her feet down off the desk. An incident room for one dead and two missing fishermen. She hated incident rooms. The very fact of one being there suggesting the seriousness of the incident which had preceded it. You didn't get an incident room for non-payment of parking tickets.

'Still in the wrong job,' she muttered, as she shuffled a couple of pieces of paper, inadvertently glancing at notes she'd made from the investigation so far. A day of talking to islanders who knew nothing, or at least, nothing that might be of use. Lots of detail on the lives of the crew members, nothing that would even remotely point to a reason for their disappearance.

The door at the back opened and Frankenstein walked out. She'd heard him on the phone, the low drone of his voice, talking to someone in Glasgow. She thought maybe the pathologist. He looked miserable, but then he always looked miserable.

'Where are you going?' he said.

'I want some dinner,' she replied. 'It's late.'

He glanced at the clock. 7.30.

'Don't say it,' she said. '*I* think it's late. There's nothing else doing for the night. I'm hungry. You should eat something,' she added. 'Come on. You can tell me your favourite jokes.'

'Just spoke to pathology,' he said. 'Had a long chat.'

'Go on,' she said. 'After twelve hours of searching for the cause of death they found a knife in his back?'

Frankenstein settled back against the edge of a desk. Proudfoot recognised that he wasn't happy with what he was about to tell her.

'They say he died of fright,' muttered Frankenstein grudgingly.

Proudfoot stared at the floor and then smiled.

34

'That's, em, very Sherlock Holmes,' she said.

'It's Scooby fucking Doo,' said Frankenstein, 'that's what it is.'

'No one ever dies in Scooby Doo.'

'Whatever.'

'How did they come to that conclusion?' she asked, enjoying the look of cantankerous gloom which was rampaging across her boss's face.

Frankenstein shook his head and grumbled some more.

'Jesus knows,' he said. 'Jesus knows how that lot ever come to any of their decisions. Some baloney about how the heart had stopped, the constriction of his blood vessels, the muscles in his face. Bullshit, but I never understand these guys. They're all a bunch of weirdoes, even Semester. I mean, he looks like an ok guy, but really, who grows up thinking that when they're older they want to work with dead bodies? Is that a sane person? Seriously. Nutjobs the lot of them. So how did they decide he'd died of fright? God knows. I don't understand anything they do, and they don't understand how I manage to live a normal life without cutting into putrid flesh with a scalpel every day.'

'They have any idea of what time the dying of fright might have taken place?'

He thrust his hands into his pockets and grumbled some more.

'Between seven and nine last night, that's their best offer. Try and pin 'em down, and before you know it they've run off claiming they have to dissect another fifty stiffs in the name of forensics.'

'I have this theory that you used to go out with a forensics student and she dumped you.'

Frankenstein raised himself from the desk intending to rise to the bait, and then shook his head and walked towards the door.

'Weren't there like fifty constables in here earlier?'

'There were three. The two from Largs who you sent home for the night, and the local guy, Gainsborough, who's out and about still. We've got them and another eight coming down from Glasgow tomorrow.'

35

'Eight?' said Frankenstein incredulously. 'Fuck's sake. Eight. I presume from that, the press have started taking a bit more of an interest?'

'Right again,' she said. 'You've got the chief pegged.'

'He's a complete twat 'n all. Let's go and eat.'

He opened the door, pulling the collar of his jacket tight as he did so.

'Bloody freezing. And you can bet the locals will probably all shut up the minute we walk into the bar. We're not the ones who are weird,' he muttered, as he wandered off along the road, although the end of his romantic soliloquy was lost on Proudfoot. Smiling, she brought up the rear, closed and locked the door. Then she fell in a few paces behind him and looked out at the dark sea, a single light shining on a small boat out beyond Little Cumbrae.

## 8

# The Tempest

The storm came up out of nowhere, sudden and violent. After the calm of the day, the night had welcomed an edgier sea. Still, there had been no sign of the brutality of the squall which rose up and attacked the island at some time after two o'clock the following morning. The winds hurtled up the Clyde from the south, the sea rose up in anger, and the island of Cumbrae was battered by the most brutal storm in memory, living or otherwise.

Trees were levelled. Anything lighter than a car was lifted up and thrown against a wall or through a window. Roofs creaked, slates tumbled. The cover on the small beach shelter at Kames Bay was blown off, ending up lodged in the front window of Thomas Peterson's Victorian semi, a hundred yards along the road from Barney Thomson's house. The few boats anchored in Newton Bay were all wrecked and battered. The boats in the yard round by the Millerston and the helicopter pad did not fare much better. High seas battering the coast and a wind that wreaked havoc. A road sign, which had been hanging loose for three months, flew through the stained glass window at the bottom end of the cathedral.

And the boat which was tied up at the pier, the cause of all the attention, and which was due to be towed up the Clyde to Glasgow the following morning, was utterly laid waste. Thrown against the pier, the slender ropes and chains twisted and broken, the shattered remnants of the vessel blown out to sea and lost to the swirling waves and crashing tempest.

The *Bitter Wind* was gone, finally lost to its namesake.

✂

Old Ward Bracken, 74, widowed, part of the great ageing male Millport collective, tossed and tumbled in his bed, unwilling to rise and face the storm. Worried about what damage might be getting done to his roof and his garden, but too scared to go and check. Had the absurd security of lying inert under his duvet, the quilt pulled in tight at his neck.

Ward Bracken had not lived long on the island of Cumbrae, but on his arrival a couple of years previously he had blended in seamlessly, just another old face in an old town. But not by chance had he come to Millport.

He lay under the protection of an Ikea feather duvet, one of the few men on the island with some idea of why the old trawler *Bitter Wind* might have come upon tragedy at sea. That knowledge, and the storm, chilled him to the core.

There was a sudden loud bang in the sitting room downstairs. A window crashed open. A tumult of noise as lamps and books were knocked over. Bracken sat bolt upright in bed. Heart thumping, breath coming in gulps.

'The wind,' he breathed. 'Just the wind.'

He shuddered. The window continued to bang downstairs, back and forth, clattering off the wall. Bracken began to whimper. Glanced at the digital clock. Not yet three a.m. He couldn't let the window crash all night. He had to stop being so silly, cut off his imagination and go down the stairs. Put on a couple of lights, make himself some hot milk. Horlicks, maybe. Turn on the tv, watch some of that American sport Channel 5 always showed in the middle of the night.

He finally extracted himself from bed, to the soundtrack of continuing banging down the stairs. He'd likely have the neighbours round if he didn't stop the racket. Slid his feet into his slippers, wrapped his old dressing gown around him. Stepped out into the hall, fumbled for the light switch in the half-dark. He flicked the switch, the light didn't come on.

'Shite,' he muttered. Tried to keep his composure, but the fear had returned.

The window clattered against the wall again, a double bang, swung back, whacked noisily into the frame.

Bracken stepped down the stairs, steeling himself against the fear, gripping the banister. Into the hall on the ground floor, tried the light switch, again nothing. The wind must have taken out the electrics, he thought. Mind on the prosaic. Not a big deal. No tv, he thought, trying to keep his mind straight, but he could still heat some milk on the stove. Light a couple of candles. Do some sudoku.

As he put his hand to the door into the living room, suddenly the noise stopped. Silence. The window was still, all that was left of the whirl of the wind was from outside.

Bracken felt the fear creep up his body, like he was being frozen solid from the feet up. He stood still in front of the door, petrified. Mouth slightly open. Barely breathing.

The door to the sitting room opened slowly. A tiny squeal from the hinge. Bracken was immobile, his body was capable of no more fear.

He looked at the man who had just opened the door. He looked at the latex mask pulled tight over his face, then at the axe held high above his head. And the short phrase 'oh my fuck' escaped Ward Bracken's inert lips.

'Power,' said the lisping voice from behind the mask, 'is given only to him who dares to stoop and take it....one must have the courage to dare.'

Bracken looked confused.

The axe fell.

✂

Barney Thomson woke up at just after six o'clock. It was still dark, the very beginning of the dawn of the day lost in the hill behind him. He looked out over the bay, past the town and beyond, to Bute and Arran. The sea still churned, every few seconds spray being thrown up from the rocks just down in front of him. The street lights were out along his stretch of road, all the way round Kames Bay, but they still shone along Glasgow Road and Stuart Street.

He had not slept through the storm. Standing by the window on restless feet, he had watched it unfold, listening to the sounds of persistent destruction. Wondering if anyone would be harmed, watching the few people who dared venture out into the storm to try to rescue something, including two police officers wrestling with the ropes of the *Bitter Wind*, as if that might possibly make any difference. They had been a long way off at the other end of the town, but he could see them struggling and floundering on the edge of the pier, waiting for one or both of them to disappear into the water.

Gradually, its job seemingly accomplished, the storm had subsided, the sea had stopped snapping so angrily at the land,

and only then had the rain started, a heavy downpour to add water and misery to the desolate town.

Barney had gone back to bed at just before four, but had not slept well. Now finally he forced himself out of bed, shivering, aware that the heating had gone off with the rest of the electricity in the house, and sat down by the window, to watch the town wake up. Wondering how much damage had been done to the shop, hoping there would be enough hot water in the heater for him to have a shower, fearful of how many of the townspeople might have died in the storm.

This, after all, was what happened to him. Wherever he went, whenever he arrived in a town, some time, sooner or later, people started dying. As the grey light of early morning began to slither over the town Barney went downstairs to the kitchen and, thankful that he had a gas hob, boiled a small pot of water to make himself his first cup, of what was to be a long day.

## 9

# Early Morning Town Blues

Barney walked slowly around to the shop, meeting a lot of stoicism along the way. Storms happen. Everyone he met seemed to be all right, no one knew of anyone who had been hurt. People had got up and were already getting on with it. Damage was being assessed, lists written out, phone calls made.

He arrived to find Keanu and Igor standing across the road from the shop, looking up at the roof. The rain had eased but was still a steady downpour. Keanu was in long shorts and a Chicago Bears hoodie under an umbrella. Igor, like Barney, hidden under a thick rain jacket. All around shop owners from along the front were making the same assessment.

'Arf,' said Igor ruefully as Barney came alongside.

Barney put his hands on Igor's shoulders. He would have phoned him earlier, but the lines were down, his mobile's battery was flat...and Igor couldn't answer the phone anyway.

'Garrett and the kids all right?' he asked.

Igor smiled and nodded, asking the same question about Barney with his eyebrows.

'I'm cool,' said Barney. 'Keanu?'

'Immense,' he said. 'Totally immense.'

Barney smiled. 'What's the damage?' he asked.

Barney had had a cup of tea, a cup of coffee, two slices of toast done under the grill, no major damage to his house.

'Well,' said Keanu, pointing at what Barney had seen from far along the road, 'the window's cracked. Doubt it would survive a couple of drunk guys stumbling against it, but it's holding firm for the moment. A few tiles off the roof, but it's not a show stopper, and I don't believe it's our responsibility anyway.'

'Arf.'

'Fair comment. The back garden's a bit of a mess, that small Douglas fir in the back corner snapped like a...yeah, well, I'm not going to say it. It's broken. That's about it. Nobody's talking about deaths around the town. However, the big newsflash, the *Bitter Wind* was lost. Every last scrap of that haunted vessel, like washed out to sea.'

Barney and Igor looked at each other. Keanu stared idly up the road.

'Almost as if the storm just came up to get rid of it. Kind of creepy.'

He smiled. He had meant it jokingly, but the thought had already crept into the bones of Barney Thomson and his able sidekick, Igor.

'It's amazing, isn't it?' said Keanu, waving an arm along the road at the bustle of activity.

'The power of nature?' said Barney.

'Human spirit,' said Keanu. 'We, you know, like, in the west, we live this pampered existence. Blame culture, everything done for us, celebrity-driven society, everyone wants to be on tv, no one wants to lay bricks or paint walls. We're the most sheltered, extravagant, pampered society ever in the history of mankind. Yet, when the chips are down, when the wind blows and slates come in through the windows, we don't fall apart. We knuckle down, we work together, backs to the wall and we keep going until it's fixed and back to the way it's supposed to be. Then we have a latté and watch *Celebrity Dump My Boyfriend!*'

An old guy had stopped to listen to Keanu's exhortations on behalf of mankind.

'Apart from the looters,' he added as postscript.

'There were looters?' said Keanu.

'Well, you know, not here, in Millport. But generally, in life, when bad stuff happens, while I concede that a majority of people bend their backs and get on with it, there are also those who seek to exploit the situation. To take advantage of the weak. To steal.'

Keanu shrugged. Barney nodded. Igor looked suspiciously along the road.

'And then,' said the old guy, 'there are also those kinds of guys who would, for example, murder their wife, bury her body in the back garden, and then say to the police, well she

42

just stepped outside when the storm was at its peak to bring her pants in off the line. Never saw her again. Terrible tragedy.'

He giggled, the other three gave him a sideways glance. Then the old guy chewed some air and looked quizzically at Barney.

'So are you just going to stand around out here all day, or is there any chance of a haircut?'

The three men from the barbershop looked at each other, although of course the decision was all Barney's.

'Sure,' he said. 'We're open for business.'

'Fine,' said the old fella, 'I'll have my usual George Peppard *Breakfast At Tiffany's*.'

And off he strode across the road. They watched him go and then started walking slowly after him.

Barney got a sense of her first, before noticing the woman leaning against the door frame in the next shop along. The police incident room. She was standing in the rain in a long brown overcoat, her hair uncovered and soaking. She'd been watching Barney since he'd arrived outside the shop, and only now as he neared his door did he notice her.

He stopped, still staring at the ground, visited by another feeling of unease, another ghost walking across his grave. He lifted his head, stared at her. The look of curiosity on her face, the water dripping from her nose. He pulled the hood away from his eyes and it fell back, so that his head was immediately soaked.

'Hi,' she said simply. Giving herself time. Trying to remember why she knew the face. Although the dark period from which she knew Barney Thomson was one which she had ignored, challenged, fought off and finally faced a thousand times in therapy. She twitched inside as the memory of it tried to squeeze itself to the surface.

Barney stared at her, struggling with his own memories. There was enough in his life which he had tried to forget, but faces rarely left him. A policewoman.

'Barney Thomson,' she said slowly, her head shaking. 'Jesus, I thought you were dead. You're dead aren't you?'

Barney held his hands out at his sides.

'I think I tried,' he said, and both of them knew that he hadn't meant suicide.

She glanced round at the shop, then looked back at him.

'Still cutting hair,' she said.

'Sgt Proudfoot,' said Barney, and she nodded. 'It's been a while,' he added, still surprised and not entirely sure what to say.

She smiled weakly, they stared at each other. Standing in the pouring rain, the moment seemed almost romantic, yet there had never been any love between them. What they had shared had been a couple of stressful and bloody encounters with serial killers. There was no way that Barney was about to say that they should get out of the rain and for Proudfoot to respond that she hadn't noticed it was still raining. None of that rubbish.

'Come on, Big Man,' came a voice from within the shop, 'quit hitting on the police skirt and get in here and cut my hair!'

She smiled again, and Barney shrugged.

'I'll come in for a chat later,' she said, although even as she said it she was thinking that maybe she would delegate the barber shop to someone else.

'Sure,' said Barney, thinking that maybe he would close the shop down for a couple of weeks and go to the Dominican Republic on holiday.

Not that they didn't want to talk to each other. It was their common past they did not want to face. A last look, and then he turned and walked into the shop, closing the door on the torrential rain.

Proudfoot watched him go, and then looked back along the road at the beginning of the day, as the town went about in the pouring rain, putting itself back on its feet. She had listened to Keanu from across the road, heard his cry on behalf of the human spirit. However, she was a policewoman, it had been many years since she'd been able to have the view of humanity that he had championed.

Footsteps beside her, and then she was confronted by DCI Frankenstein, who had minced along from the George Hotel, where he had just enjoyed a full Scottish and enough toast to build another wall at the border. He felt fat, still had crumbs on his left cheek.

'Sergeant,' he said, standing next to her under a dark blue and gold umbrella which he'd picked up while doing duty at the G8 in Gleneagles, 'what are you doing standing out here in the pishing rain?'

'Just, I don't know,' she shuffled. 'Getting wet, I guess.'

'Why?' he asked, and then waved a hand to tell her that he wasn't interested in her answer, and turned into the small office which they had arranged the day before.

Erin Proudfoot looked out over the busy sea and felt the rain as it finally worked its way through her four layers of clothing to touch her cold, pale skin. Barney Thomson was back in her life, and the nightmare which had woken her in the middle of the night, to the thunder of wind and the breaking of glass, had now been explained.

# 10

## Rats

'They say a rat can last longer without water than a camel.'

Barney Thomson and Keanu MacPherson were both cutting hair, which was rare for November. In fact, it was the first time since just after three o'clock on the afternoon of the fourteenth of October that they'd had two customers in the shop at the same time. It had been a relatively busy morning, as if the people had decided that they had to face adversity with good hair.

Barney caught the eye of the old fella whose hair he was cutting. An Arnold Palmer *Troon '67*.

'That's a load of pish,' said the other old guy under the scissors in the next door chair. A Dean Martin *Slumped In His Dinner*. 'Where'd you hear that?'

'Read it on the back of a Penguin,' said Arnold Palmer. Dean Martin scoffed. 'You know, I mean a biscuit wrapper, not a bird. Although I was in Antarctica once right enough.'

'Away and shite,' said Dean Martin, 'you've never even been to Aberdeen. When were you in Antarctica?'

'There used to be rainforest in Antarctica,' Keanu chipped in.

'Aye,' said Arnold Palmer, 'the rainforest is disappearing from everywhere. Soon there'll be none left in the Amazon.'

'I expect you were in the Amazon 'n all,' muttered Dean Martin.

'Only when I worked as cinematographer on the motion picture event *Medicine Man*,' replied Arnold with a chuckle. 'Sir Sean personally requested that I get involved.'

Barney smiled, Dean Martin choked on his Fisherman's Friend.

'Wasn't Medicine Man the one with Dustin Hoffman as an old Indian geezer?' ventured Keanu.

'You're thinking of *Little Big Man*,' said Barney.

'Aye,' said Dean Martin, 'the one about Custer.'

'Custard!' barked Arnold Palmer. 'The guy's name was Custard. That's where the dessert comes from.'

'Arf!'

'You don't half talk some amount of pish,' said Dean Martin, but Arnold Palmer had glazed over, the look of an old man reminiscing about the good old days.

'Jings,' he said, 'I used to make a rare old custard, you know, way back, years ago before I had my colostomy bag fitted. Haven't felt much like cooking since then.'

The four other men in the shop stopped for a second, unwelcome thoughts having been conjured up in their heads, and then they slowly went about their business. The discussion, which had never really attained any great intellectual heights, was over.

✂

Next door things were getting rough. The room which had been more than big enough the day before, was now jumping with officers, a minibus load having just turned up from Glasgow. DCI Frankenstein hadn't been prepared, even though he'd known they were coming. He'd left the office the evening before thinking that he needed to sort things out for their arrival, but then hadn't managed to get around to any of it.

The eight policemen from Glasgow, along with the two from Largs from the day before and Constable Gainsborough, were hanging out in the incident room, eating doughnuts and drinking coffee. Some talk of the missing trawler, mostly the discussion centring around the forthcoming Old Firm game. Celtic already fifteen points ahead in the league, Rangers wilting, restless natives. Both teams still in Europe, for the first time since 1972.

The door to the rear opened and Frankenstein and Proudfoot emerged. A couple of the guys wondered if they'd been having sex, though only the ones who didn't know either of them. The crowd quietened down, Proudfoot folded her arms and looked at the floor. Frankenstein rested against a desk and looked around his squad. Seven men, four women. He nodded.

'Welcome to Millport,' he said.

A few of them mumbled back, most of them presumed he was being sardonic.

'It's a sleepy dump,' he said, 'I've been here a night and I don't want to stay much longer. We need results quickly or I'm going to fester into a big bag of rotting flesh, and if that happens I'm taking you lot down with me. So we need to get out there and find out what happened to this stupid boat. Today. *Capiche*?'

There was an odd mutter. Proudfoot looked up.

'Did you just say *capiche*?' said someone from the back.

Someone else giggled. Frankenstein rolled his eyes and silently lamented that things weren't how they used to be.

'We have four main areas of enquiry,' said Frankenstein. 'Sgt Proudfoot is going to go through it, split you into teams.'

He looked at Proudfoot, he looked back at the crowd.

'Right,' he said, 'I'm going for a coffee. Someone's got to do some thinking.'

The crowd parted as he headed towards the door, a couple of them catching his eye, most of them staring at the floor. He shuffled out the room, closed the door behind, stood out on the street for a second breathing in the morning sea air. Might have enjoyed it if he'd ever allowed himself that sort of positive thought, and then walked slowly away to his right, along towards the pier. Or, more specifically, the Ritz Café. Thinking that he might have a bacon roll along with his coffee. Or maybe sausage.

The room turned back restlessly to Proudfoot. Now that the investigation was afoot, they were keen to get on with it. Preferable to be out there, rather than stuck in a small room, no room to breathe or think.

'Ok,' she said, 'let's crack on. For those of you who don't already know, we lost the trawler in the storm last night. It'd been due to be moved up to Glasgow this morning. Fate, divine providence, call it what you will, it's gone. So, firstly, and this might be a complete wild goose chase, but two of you will go out on the police boat and see if you can find anything from the trawler floating out at sea.'

'Police boat?' said Gainsborough.

'You don't have a police boat?' she said. 'You live on an island and you don't have a boat?'

'Cutbacks,' muttered someone else from within the crowd, and Gainsborough nodded.

'Of course,' she said. 'Constable, can you source another boat? Thank you. Second, we continue the house to house. Constable Gainsborough will take overall charge of that as he knows what areas we covered yesterday. Thirdly, we need to look more specifically into the lives of the three trawlermen. There has to be some explanation as to why those men went missing from their trawler in the middle of a calm night, as opposed to anyone else. Lastly, I need someone to leave the island and start tracing back the movements of the trawler before it reached Kilchattan Bay. And I don't just mean on this last voyage, I mean its last six months. A year if needs be. Keep going until you find something. We have the log here, you don't have to go swimming for it.'

She stopped and looked around the crowd. They were engaged, it was an interesting case to get their teeth into.

'Good,' she said. 'Let's, you know, get out there and get on with it.'

As the words passed her lips, she winced slightly. She'd always wanted a really good catchphrase for that moment, but everything seemed so derivative. She'd tried, 'Hey, let's not fuck up today,' for a while, but it hadn't exactly been a crowd pleaser. 'Be big, be bold, let's win one for the good guys!' had just been laughed at, and 'Forget heroics, forget subtlety, forget flamboyance, let's just put the ball in the back of the net with no fancy stuff,' had been too long-winded.

And so, with another thought of regret at the inadequacy of 'get out there and get on with it,' Sgt Proudfoot went about the business of splitting up her team and delegating responsibility.

## 11

## Bruce Willis

Not long after two-fifteen in the afternoon. The shop was quiet, no customers. Igor had gone off for the afternoon, brought into service as husband and father-to-be to collect the gently vomiting Ella Carmichael from school. Barney and Keanu had sat in silence for a while, occasionally breaking into sporadic bouts of curiosity about life and the day, before Barney had offered Keanu the chance to head out into the afternoon to do a little bit of investigative journalism himself. Search around, see what he could find out about the missing trawlermen.

Barney was on his own. The day outside was cold, the shop was warm. He had been sitting in the middle chair looking out at the day, then the quiet of the afternoon and the warmth of the shop had begun to insinuate itself into his lazy bones, and slowly he'd drifted off into a comfortable afternoon snooze.

Two-seventeen. The door to the shop opened and Barney was brought suddenly from his slumber, his head snapping up to the side. So instant it looked like he'd been sat poised, waiting for the next customer.

He stared at the man for a second. A young guy, mid-twenties maybe, head mostly obscured by a great mass of brown hair and beard, which made it slightly harder to tell his age. Barney still had that peculiar sensation of being drawn suddenly from deep sleep, not entirely sure where he was, not entirely sure what was going to come next. Vague look of confusion.

'Haircut?' asked the guy.

Barney shook his head, the cobwebs washed away. Sudden, instant clarity and the benefit of twenty minutes' power sleep. He practically leapt out of his chair.

'Of course,' he said. He smiled. 'You, eh, look like you could do with it.'

The guy laughed, a lovely gentle sound. He removed his jacket and sat down in the warm chair that Barney had just vacated.

'Toasty,' he said.

Barney flung the cape around the lad, with a glance outside at the day through the broken window pane. The glazier booked for the following morning. The afternoon still dull grey, the colour of his dreams.

'What would you like?' he asked.

The man hesitated then shrugged.

'I was looking for a Bruce Willis *Die Hard*. What d'you think?'

Barney caught his eye in the mirror.

'That's a bit of a departure from the general prevailing shagginess that you've got going on here,' he said.

Bruce Willis smiled.

'It's just, well, you know...this might sound stupid.'

'Go on,' said Barney. 'I'm no judge.'

'I've been at sea for a while, but I'm done with that now. I just want, you know, a new life, you know what I'm saying? I want everything to be different, a new start, that whole bag.'

Barney felt the shimmer of foreboding. Across his shoulders, the back of his neck. Although Millport was on a small island, it was not a seafaring community. He had gone a year and a half in this place without coming across anyone who worked their living from the sea, with the exception of Deuchar and his lads.

'I know what you're thinking,' said Bruce, 'I'm just like one of those women who get dumped by their boyfriend. First thing they do is head down to the hairdressers and get their napper cut into a bob. I know, that's what it looks like, but it's different. Really. And it's not about women.'

Barney started running his hands through the guy's hair, gauging the thickness, working out where he was going to start.

'What's it about then?' asked Barney.

Looked into the guy's eyes again. Dark, blue-grey.

Bruce Willis lowered his eyes. He stretched his fingers out and stared at his hands.

51

'You ever want to walk away from the past?' he said. 'Forget things you've done. Not sins necessarily. I'm not talking about divine misdeeds. Sometimes, though, you just want to run away.'

Bruce Willis was still studying his hands. Barney looked at his own hands. Soft skin, slowly aging. Short nails, but neat, a couple of tiny strands of hair stuck beneath them. He flexed his fingers, studying the skin as it tightened and relaxed.

Suddenly he felt the need to wash his hands. Was it just the hairs under the nails, or was there something else he needed to wash away?

'It's what's inside that matters, isn't it?' said Barney distractedly.

Bruce Willis glanced up and caught Barney looking at his fingers.

'There's no escaping that,' he said.

'No,' said Barney, 'I don't suppose there is.'

He dragged himself away from his hands, looked Bruce Willis in the eye.

'However,' said Bruce, 'you make the illusion of change, and sometimes the illusion, if you try hard enough, can impact on the reality. So, I'll have my Bruce Willis *Die Hard* and see if it makes me feel any different when I walk out of the shop.'

'Ok,' said Barney. 'I take it then that you also want to lose the beard?'

'Go for it. I might ask you to shave it down to a bit of a goatee, see how that looks, but more than likely that'll just be getting off the train along the way to take a look, before getting back on again and completing the journey.'

'I hear you,' said Barney. 'I'm no fan of sculpted facial hair, I have to admit, although I am occasionally obliged to administer it. Mostly to women of course.'

They smiled at the joke, Barney ran his hand down the side of the guy's beard to scope the job. He was going to need heavy barbetorial equipment, the likes of which he didn't usually keep out front.

'You're going to look pretty baby-faced once it comes off,' he said.

Bruce Willis shrugged.

'Not for long. And maybe that's part of the whole bag. Take a few years off me, like I can imagine they never happened.'

Another look exchanged, Barney felt the shiver again, stronger this time.

'I just need to go and get the lawnmower,' said Barney, the joke having been on his mind before the return to whatever peculiarity of conversation it was that haunted him about this man.

Bruce Willis nodded and scratched his beard.

'I was expecting you to charge me triple,' he said, smile disarming.

The conversation seemed all over the place and Barney couldn't pin it down. He turned away and walked towards the back of the shop. Did he really need anything in the other room, or was he just going in there to break the spell? To wash his hands.

'You ever kill a man, Barney?'

Barney froze. Felt the words as much as heard them, and then felt the very real, violent shudder which racked his body. He turned quickly.

Outside the shop, a single gull cried mournfully, the doleful sound cutting through the silence, a lament to the sins of Barney Thomson's past. Inside, the shop was empty. Empty, save for Barney Thomson, barber, looking lost and confused. The seat was empty, the customer was gone. Gone, that is, if he had ever been there in the first place.

## 12

## Shoes

The police officers who had been roped in to the investigation were about their duties. A couple out on the choppy water, a couple currently heading up the craggy coasts of Argyll in search of the movements of the *Bitter Wind*. The rest were in the town, chasing up the lives of the three crew members, one dead, two missing.

Proudfoot had headed out beyond the boatyard, to the rocky beaches out at the west bay, which she had been informed were a likely resting place for flotsam and jetsam, particularly after a bad storm. Along the way she had picked up Frankenstein, upon whom she had stumbled while he was out walking. And thinking.

They stepped across a broken piece of fence, down some rocks and onto a small stretch of stony beach, Frankenstein watching every step. Nearly slipped a couple of times, felt safe on the beach. The sea surged sporadically onto the rocks, the hills of Arran were lost in cloud, already the dying of the day seemed evident, even though it was still a couple of hours away.

'I'm not dressed for this crap,' he muttered. 'You spend two hundred quid on a pair of shoes, you don't want to be walking around fucking beaches.'

'You should've brought a pair of boots,' she said.

He looked at her boots and shook his head.

'How did you know to bring boots?' he muttered. 'I came down here thinking we'd be five minutes. You, on the other hand, probably brought your whole wardrobe.'

She smiled, bending down to rummage through a matted pile of seaweed and rubbish.

'Seriously,' said Frankenstein, 'how many pairs of shoes did you bring with you? Women can't leave the front room without enough shoes to last them until they die.'

Proudfoot examined a sea-ravaged grey plimsole, then tossed it aside.

'Five,' she said, straightening up and moving on. She had come along here on a whim, but was already wondering if this was something which should be getting done by fifteen officers, collecting and cataloguing everything they found. Just in case. They just didn't have the resources for that, not any more.

'Five! Jesus suffering fuck! I mean, seriously, didn't you think you were just coming down here for one night?'

She stopped and shrugged, then moved on.

'Yeah,' she said. 'If I'd known it was going to be longer I'd have brought more.'

Frankenstein muttered several dark expletives and watched where he put his feet.

Proudfoot bent down and raked through another small tangle of seaweed and detritus. With the exception of making sure he didn't slip over, Frankenstein was paying no attention whatsoever to what might be lying on the beach. With Proudfoot kneeling down, he looked over her back, out across the water to Kilchattan Bay, where the trawler had been discovered the previous morning. He was trying to stay distant from the investigation, insomuch as he could being the lead investigating officer, and he knew inside that it was because he had such a bad feeling about it. The *Bitter Wind* may have been becalmed when it was found, but it had been surrounded by an ill wind that Frankenstein could feel in his soul. This thing, he knew, went much beyond missing persons and possible murder. Deeper, darker, murkier waters.

'Bad news,' said Proudfoot standing up.

'You leave your pedal-pushers in Glasgow?' quipped Frankenstein.

She stared at him.

'Was that supposed to be a joke about shoes?'

'It *was* a joke about shoes.'

'Pedal-pushers aren't shoes.'

'They're not?'

'Cut-off trousers, tight to the calf.'

'Why would you push pedals with your trousers?'

'You're such an old man sometimes.'

55

'I always thought they were shoes, long pointy bits at the front.'

'Can we talk about the case now?'

'What d'you call those kinds of shoes then? You women have a name for everything.'

'There's a torch here,' she said insistently, holding up a long, thin, green torch.

'Why is that bad news?'

'It's from the *Bitter Wind*, I remember it from yesterday. Which means that however the storm blew last night, it didn't just carry the remnants of the ship away out to the Irish Sea. If it brought the torch here, then it might well have brought something else.'

'You'd better get looking then,' he said, rolling his eyes. Knew what she was saying, didn't want to think about it. This investigation was just going to keep getting bigger and bigger.

'You know we need to get a team on this. A thorough search along this area of coastline, we're looking at eight to ten guys, at least. Come on, you need to make some calls.'

Frankenstein muttered miserably, bent down, picked up a stone and hurled it at the water. The tide being out, he fell several yards short. He looked out to the grey sea and at the darkening skies, and knew that this was something which he should have organised properly for the full extent of daylight. Not a thing to rush into an hour and a half before it got dark.

'I wish you wouldn't be so bloody right all the time, it's pissing me off. We'll never get it going for today. You and I'd better look now while we've got the chance, I'll get something cranked up for tomorrow.'

Erin Proudfoot nodded, followed his gaze out across the cold water to the masked hills of Arran, and then once more lowered her head and began walking slowly along the beach.

✂

'You ever kill a man, Barney?'

The words still clung to the walls, as if they were being repeated, over and over. The chair was empty, the door had neither opened nor closed. The man was gone. Vanished.

Barney felt the chill, the cold draught of the presence which had infested the room. Had he known when the guy was sitting there? Had he known when he'd put his hand into his hair? He tried to think back, but even though it was only thirty seconds previously, he couldn't remember it, couldn't recapture the sensation of standing there with this thing in front of him.

'You ever kill a man, Barney?'

He walked to the door of the shop, opened it and stepped outside into the cold. Looked along the street, but knew that he wasn't going to see the tall, shaggy figure marching off along Stuart Street, having changed his mind about the image adjustment. Felt the cold, rubbed his arms, turned and looked back into the shop. Bright and warm. But did he want to go back in there?

'Out looking for customers?' said a smiling voice.

Barney turned. Keanu, laptop tucked under his arm, rubbing his hands together, walked past him into the shop. Barney followed, closing the door behind him.

'I could murder a cup of tea,' said Keanu. 'Get you one?'

Did you ever kill a man? Yes, he thought. But not murder. I never murdered anyone.

'Ok,' said Barney, vaguely. 'Tea would be good thanks. I need it.'

Keanu laid the computer down on the counter and slung his jacket on the coat rack.

'Cool,' he said. 'You must've been busy.'

Barney watched him retreat into the back room, then turned and looked in the mirror, standing behind the chair in the usual position. Tired face, needing to shave, a mouth that seemed long, lips which had long forgotten how to smile. And eyes that were beginning to look haunted.

## 13

## Chicken Head

The two police officers from Rutherglen had been doing the rounds all day and they were fed up. They'd started with the right amount of enthusiasm, but six and a half hours of listening to small town gossip had just about done for them. They were glad that the deal was for them to travel home every night, and that they wouldn't have to stay in Millport for the duration of the investigation. Two more houses to go, along the bottom end of George Street, round behind Kames, and then they'd be done. Report back to Proudfoot, tell her the little which they had to hand over, and they could be on the 5.15 back to Largs.

'Still make it home in time for the Celtic game,' said Constable Gemmill.

Constable Seymour stopped at the pink door and checked his notes.

'Not watching it,' he said.

'How come?'

'Alison wants to go out for dinner. Just the two of us, you know.'

Seymour lifted his hand to ring the bell, Gemmill caught his finger before he could press.

'Celtic are playing Benfica tonight. You're going out for dinner with the missus?'

Seymour shrugged.

'Yep,' he said. 'That's about the sum of it. She wants to talk.'

'Jesus,' muttered Gemmill, as Seymour pressed the bell. 'You've been married for twelve years. What can there be to talk about?'

Seymour shrugged.

'Women...' he said plaintively.

The door opened. An old woman stared at them suspiciously, looking them both up and down, inspecting every button on the two uniforms.

'The pair of you can just bugger off,' she said. 'I'm not paying.'

Gemmill stopped himself laughing. Rolled his eyes instead.

'We're conducting enquiries regarding the fishing vessel which was found abandoned off Kilchattan Bay yesterday morning.'

'Oh,' she muttered. 'Well, you'se had better come in then.'

And she turned, leaving the two policemen standing at the door.

✂

They sat in an old lounge on rugged sofas. Frayed floral carpets, wooden furniture, pill boxes and pottery, mirrors on the walls and pictures of young men on hay bales. Nelly Johnson was making the tea, Gemmill and Seymour were looking at their watches.

'We're going to miss that ferry if the old bag doesnae hurry her arse.'

Seymour glanced at his watch, then took a look at the old clock on the mantleshelf. He was close enough to read the small inscription on the clock face. *Allison Clockmakers, Paisley, 1936*. The room smelled of apples and pipe smoke. They wondered where Mr Johnson was.

Nelly bustled back into the room, carrying a laden tray. Five different types of cake, shortbread and mince pies. A large pot of tea.

'You'll have something to eat,' she said. An instruction rather than an offer.

Gemmill and Seymour started to tuck in, Nelly watched them approvingly.

'Mince pies,' said Gemmill, putting two on his place. 'Haven't had one of them since…well, since last Christmas I suppose.'

'It's a piece of shite,' said Nelly. Gemmill and Seymour were both drawn to look at the rich, mousse-like chocolate cake sitting grandly in the middle of the tray.

'What is?' asked Seymour.

'Mince pies and the tyranny of the supermarkets,' said Nelly. 'I mean to fuck, try and get a mince pie on the 26th December and you'll have more luck finding a Fenian at

59

Ibrox. Christmas over, they're gone. Just like that. I mean to fuck, mince pies are a year round treat, they're not just for Christmas.'

Gemmill and Seymour were staring at her, Gemmill with a mouth full of mince pie. She could see it churning around in his teeth as he gawped.

'They should do adverts. I mean, like they do with dogs. They could have a dog eating a mince pie in June, or some shite like that, then you get one of they famous bastards off the tele to say something like, *dogs aren't just for Christmas...and neither are mince fucking pies.*'

Gemmill and Seymour were still taciturn on the subject.

'Couldn't you lot do something about it?' she said. 'I mean, what do you do all day anyway?'

'Can I be blunt, Mrs Johnson?' said Gemmill. His name was Norman, but everyone called him Archie.

'Nelly,' she said. 'I hate anyone using that dead bastard's name. Been stuck with it all these years.'

'Nelly, let me be blunt.'

'What? About mince pies?'

'Not mince pies. I'm not here to talk about mince pies.'

'Neglecting your responsibilities...'

'Mince pies are not the responsibility of the police.'

'Fine, if that's...

'You said when we came in, and to be honest, it's kind of the only reason we're still here, despite the delicious tea and the entertaining conversation about Christmas cakes...'

'Mince pies aren't cakes.'

'Whatever...'

'To be honest they're not technically a pie either, not really, and obviously it's not like they're a fucking biscuit. I like to call them fancies. A Christmas fancy.'

'You said you knew something about the fishermen,' snapped Seymour, as he could sense that Gemmill had lost control.

Nelly Johnson stared at them from over the top of the mince pie from which she'd just taken a bite. Eyes narrowed. Seymour could imagine them turning red.

'Very well,' she said coldly. 'It's about old Stan Koppen, lives in one of those little holiday homes, round past the Westbourne.'

The policemen shook their heads.

'No one else mentioned old Stan Koppen to you?'

Another shrug. Gemmill checked his notebook, although it was entirely for show. No one had mentioned anything. She smiled. Loose tongue. She didn't owe Stan Koppen anything, even if he thought she did.

No honour among thieves.

'Everyone's too scared to open their mouths, but not me,' she muttered. 'Stan Koppen comes round here looking for trouble, he'll get a toe in the nuts from my size 6 Rosa Klebs.'

'Tell us about Stan Koppen,' said Gemmill, writing the name Stan Koppen in his book, wondering if this was them finally getting somewhere and if it was going to ultimately keep him from watching the football. Although, deep down, he presumed that she was about to tell them that Stan Koppen preferred almond slices to mince pies and therefore was a total idiot.

'Used to run a fishing boat out of the harbour. Did all right for himself, but you know, that was back in the days when there were fish in the sea, wasn't it? Nowadays, well God knows how they catch anything. It's all because of the Icelandics. And the Spanish.'

'He lost his boat?' asked Seymour.

'His wife died. Margaret. Stomach cancer. They seemed miserable as shite the two of them, but when she went he just went to pieces. He'd always been a drinker, but without her there to pour his hidden bottles of vodka down the drain, he turned into a walking vat of 100% proof. Gave the boat up before he lost it.'

'Who did he give the boat to?'

She stuffed the rest of the mince pie in her mouth and lifted a mug of tea.

'Ally Deuchar,' said Seymour.

'No,' replied Nelly Johnson through a mouthful of mincemeat. 'Went to a firm in Campbeltown. But since you mentioned Ally Deuchar. Comes a time when old Stan ends up in hospital with the drinking. The doctor gives him the usual spiel, you know the routine, if you don't stop drinking you're going to be pushing up the fucking tulips in two months, all the while Stan's swigging the fucking booze from a brown paper bag under the covers, 'cause he's a stupid old cunt. Then one day some bunch of religious weirdoes is doing the rounds, Jehovah's or born agains or Christ knows what. And you know, I mean fucking hell, who would've seen it coming, but old Stan fell for it. He fell for it! Hook, line and stinker. Next thing you know he's out of hospital telling every other bastard about the dangers of drinking and debauchery. What a plantpot.'

'Ally Deuchar?' asked Gemmill. One day, he was thinking, the old girl might actually get around to telling us something relevant. But it's highly unlikely.

'I'm getting there, for pity's sake,' she said, starting on another mince pie. 'Last year, part of the old bastard's thing, now that he was fit again and up and at 'em, ready for business, was wanting to get back out to sea. Course, he's got no money, and even though it's been only a few years since he left, the industry has crumbled in his absence. No eejit is willing to lend him the money to get another boat, and so the old bastard, the born again Christian, starts coveting the only boat left operating out of the town.'

'The *Bitter Wind*...'

'Exactamundo. The *Bitter fucking Wind*. Ally, of course, tells him to take a hike, and I think it was all a bit of a joke at first. Eventually though, when Stan the Man starts leaving headless chickens and shite like that outside Ally's house, Ally starts getting pissed off.'

'Headless chickens?' said Gemmill. For some reason felt the hairs rise on his neck. Pavlov's dog.

'All that kind of shite,' she said. 'Got to be quite a thing. A big town dispute. I mean, none of us actually knew what old Stan wanted. Did the big eejit really think that Ally was just going to give him the stupid boat?'

She stared at the two of them, as if expecting an answer to the rhetorical question.

'Well, it's too late now, in't it?' she added.

Gemmill finished scribbling in his notepad.

'And we'll find Mr Koppen round at one of the small chalets on the west side of the island?' asked Seymour.

'Aye,' she said. 'If you're brave enough to go there. The muppet'll probably put a curse on you, or some shite like yon.'

'That doesn't sound very Christian,' muttered Gemmill, grabbing another piece of cake and thinking that it might be time to take their leave.

'Religion,' said Nelly Johnson, 'we all make of it what we choose.'

Seymour snaffled another biscuit and stood up. Gemmill did the same, his mouth crammed with cake, and folded his notebook into his pocket. Nelly Johnson gave them the benefit of her eyebrow, and decided not to tell them all the other information which she would have happily divulged about the town if only they'd been prepared to wait and ask.

✂

It was around this time that a lone yachtsman upon the Irish Sea, a man who had endured a hellish night of storms, and who had spent the day repairing what he could of his boat on the hoof, thought he saw something floating in the water, fifty or sixty yards to starboard. However, by the time he had manoeuvred his yacht in that direction, whatever it was had been dragged under by some current, or washed further away and out of sight. He searched for a short while, but finally gave up and turned back on his heading south.

And the further he got away from the point on the map where he had stopped to search, the more he persuaded himself that he didn't need to contact any authorities and that he really hadn't seen a headless body floating on the waves.

## 14

# The Return Of
# The Fantastic Five

End of the day, the returns were coming in. Items from the *Bitter Wind* found on the beach, a few found out at sea. The love lives of the dead and missing, some gossip some scandal, but nothing to pin an investigation on. Gemmill and Seymour presented their story from Nelly Johnson, and no one else had anything with which to corroborate the tale. A few stories from up the coast, of womanising and late night card games, but nothing of note. No gambling debts, no drugs, no enraged husbands, no vendettas, no human trafficking.

Frankenstein was perched on the edge of a desk, Proudfoot was standing by the whiteboard, where she had been noting down points of interest. The whiteboard remained almost entirely white.

'So,' said Frankenstein, when the last of his team had finished, 'we've got an old, mentally-deranged, chicken-obsessed religious nutjob to speak to, and even that's based on the testimony of some fruitcake old asylum-case who couldn't be trusted to report back on the weather.'

Proudfoot glanced at the board. She had recovered a large number of items along the beach, but it hadn't been an act of looking for clues. She had only been recovering what had already been noted and then lost.

'I spoke to Mr Koppen yesterday,' said Gainsborough.

Frankenstein lifted his head.

'So he wasn't confessing to anything then?' he said.

'I've spoken to him before, you know, but there's nothing...I don't know, he's a bit weird. Comes into the station every now and again trying to give me a Bible. Wants me to help sinners to repent. Thinks there should be a Bible in every cell. I told him, we have someone in that cell once every three years. Go and stick your Bible in the public toilets at the pier.'

'You know of any connection between him and the trawler or its crew?'

'You know, I've thought about it, but it's like, you know, the guy was a fisherman, although before my time, and now he's just a guy who seems to have gone a bit senile. No one to look after him, to keep him in check, and he's away off on his God-kick and all that chicken stuff. Just a bit mental.'

Frankenstein stared at him intently, face deadpan.

'And, so, any connection between him and the trawler or its crew?' he repeated.

Gainsborough looked at the floor, thinking that he'd just answered that.

'No,' he said.

'How did he seem when you interviewed him? Evasive in any way? Did he hurry you out? Was he quite happy to talk about it?'

Gainsborough shrugged.

'Really, nothing exceptional. Didn't seem to care, really, and when I mentioned the guys, he just started going on about how we'll all be judged by God, and all that kind of malarkey. Like, you know, whatever.'

Gainsborough took a long drink of tea and laid the mug down on a desk. Frankenstein looked round at Proudfoot.

'It seems, Sergeant, that we have a list of one thing to do,' he said, then he turned and looked out at the day turned dark. Almost seven o'clock, the roundup, despite its paucity of information, having taken much longer than expected.

'I guess you lot can go for the evening, wherever that is,' he said. 'I want you back here tomorrow at eight. We've got beaches to sweep and....' The thought drifted off.

'Come on, Sergeant,' he said, 'no time like the present.'

And the men and women of the Millport Incident Room began looking at watches and putting on coats and wondering, in some cases, how much of the football they were going to miss.

✂

Barney Thomson was out walking around the west side of the island. Had gone as far as the new war memorial and turned back, by Deadman's Bay. A dark night, but the memory of

65

the shaggy guy who had disappeared from his shop had gone. Or at least, the fear of it had gone. In his head it had become just another unexplained episode that there was no use thinking about, no point in agonising over and, by extension, nothing to be afraid of.

A damp night, the rain not actually falling, but the air itself wet. The sea had finally settled to a moderate swell and the first signs of a mist had begun to develop over the firth. From where he walked, Barney could not see the lights in Kilchattan bay.

He was just coming to the point which is called on the old maps Sheriff's Port, when the first car in over quarter of an hour came round the far bend, its small round headlights infiltrating the dark night. Barney stepped off the road onto the grass verge and saw a bench, facing out to sea, north-west, looking across and up the firth. As the vehicle approached he sat down and watched the movement of the light of the headlamps as it swung over the grass and rocks.

The noise of the engine lowered, Barney thought it was slowing down to an unnecessary degree for the corner. He turned. Not a car, he noticed, an old white van. It turned off the road and parked on the grass next to where Barney was sitting. More ghosts he wondered, although he felt no trepidation or fear.

The doors opened and out piled two men, two women and a dog. The crew whom Frankenstein had met the previous day. Team building. MI6.

'Hey,' said one of the guys casually.

'Hi,' said Barney.

'Kind of a creepy night.'

'Like yeah,' said the other guy. 'Spooky.'

Barney glanced at him and then looked back out to sea. It had, he thought, been a little bit creepy until you lot turned up. The creepiness had gone, along with the solitude and the beautiful peace and quiet.

The dog came and sniffed at Barney's feet. Barney clapped his ears but it didn't seem too interested. It stopped for a second, momentarily enjoyed the ear scratch, and then bowed its head and moved on, smelling the grass.

'Nice dog,' said Barney. 'What's his name?'

'He doesn't have a name,' said one of the girls, the one with a short black bob. 'The Dog With No Name.'

Barney looked round at them. They were all standing still, staring out into the mist. They looked less friendly now. They seemed to be working. Maybe they were part of the police investigation, the island was full of them. Not that they looked like the police.

Barney followed their gaze out to sea.

'Police?' he asked.

'MI6,' said the bloke who had spoken to him first.

Barney nodded. In the distance he could just make out the lights of a small vessel, barely visible in the mist.

'Isn't that supposed to be a secret?' asked Barney, not taking his eyes off the light out in the firth.

'Full disclosure these days, my trusty amigo.'

'Yeah?'

'Too many lawsuits from people claiming entrapment. We're the security services for crying out loud! Anyway, the lawyers tell us that these days we have to declare ourselves to everyone we speak to.'

'Shop assistants?'

'Yep,' said one of the women.

Barney was still watching the distant dim light.

'I'm Fred,' said the guy who had been doing most of the talking, 'this is Deidre, Selma and Bernard.' He pronounced Bernard with the emphasise on the second syllable, so that it sounded American.

A few nods.

'Like, hi,' said Bernard.

Barney turned and nodded. Bernard was now scanning the foggy sea with a large pair of binoculars.

'And a dog with no name,' said Barney.

They were silent, intent on looking out over the water. Barney turned back round and relaxed into the seat. The dog was sniffing frantically around, searching for something that no one else seemed interested in.

Silence fell again, a hush that grew every time they stepped back and allowed it in. Barney pulled his coat closer to him.

Shivered, but it was from the cold. Took a quick glance back, wondering if one of these times he'd look round and they'd be gone. Yet he didn't get that feeling with these four. And their dog. Maybe because of their dog.

The vessel was becoming more distinct as it emerged from the fog. A small fishing trawler. No sense of peculiarity or danger, but Barney was not surprised. Life sometimes gets on a roll, the no-bus-for-an-hour-and-then-three-in-five-minutes syndrome. If that happens anymore. Fishing vessels, fishermen everywhere. Haunted.

He lost himself in the fog, thoughts meandering. The man from that afternoon came back to him. Had he dreamt him, the shaggy guy who had disappeared in a turn of the head? He had been sleeping just before it, maybe he had slept all the way through it.

The quiet crept over them, no sound but the lick of the waves against the rocks. The trawler moved silently through the fog.

Barney felt a tap at the shoulder and he turned quickly, drawn back to the misty night. Bernard was holding the binoculars out to him.

'Here, pal, like take a quick look before the thing gets shrouded in mist again.'

'This sure is a creepy night,' said Selma.

Barney took the binoculars from Bernard with some uncertainty, wondering why he was being drawn into their gang.

He looked through the binoculars into the mist, searching for the trawler. Found it eventually, although it took him a while. The mist was swirling around it, almost like it had targeted the boat and was closing in from behind. He focused the binoculars and got his first good close look at the vessel before the mist completely descended.

Somehow he wasn't surprised by what he saw, even though it should never have been out there. The mist swirled round, the boat moved silently through the water midway out in the firth, and then suddenly it was gone, once more enveloped in the thick soup of the har.

68

Barney kept the binoculars up for another few seconds, wondering if it would reappear, and then he lowered them slowly and looked round at the gang. He held out the binoculars for Bernard who took them back. The dog with no name sat in front of them and started barking, a few rough shouts at the fog.

'Just the same as last night,' said Deirdre.

'I think I need a burger,' said Bernard. 'With fries on the side, and pickle and ketchup and more cheese than you can shake a stick at.'

Barney turned round and looked at Fred.

'The *Bitter Wind...*' he said.

Fred nodded. 'We had reports that it was seen out here last night as well, thought we'd come and take a look.'

'Funny how you arrived just as it appeared,' said Barney.

They exchanged a glance. Fred put a hand on his shoulder.

'We're MI6 my friend,' he said, 'a lot of things about us are funny.'

Barney looked back out at the mist, wondering if the answer to this mystery was prosaic or supernatural.

'Another trawler with the name daubed on?' he asked, 'although I have no idea why anyone would do that.'

Selma had taken a small box from her bag and was now using it to scan the firth.

'Jings,' she said, 'if it was that, it's disappeared awful quickly.'

'No sign of it?' said Fred.

'No sign,' said Selma.

They all looked out at the sea and the fog and wondered.

'Looks like we might have found ourselves a fully-fledged ghost ship,' said Deidre.

'Zoiks!' said Bernard. 'Come on, Dog With No Name, let's get out of here.'

Fully-fledged ghost ship...

The possibility put into words, Barney finally felt the shiver that the sinister night and the eerie vision of the trawler demanded. He stood and turned, as the gang of four and a dog clambered back into their van. Fred climbed into the driver's seat, then wound down the window and leant on the door.

'We'd offer you a lift back into town, friend, but it's a bit cramped back here.' He saluted.

Barney nodded. Wouldn't have taken it anyway. Found himself returning the salute, and then the van reversed out onto the road and disappeared on the short drive back into town.

## 15

## The Ways Of The Lord

Proudfoot knocked on the door of the small wooden chalet. Frankenstein was waiting at the bottom of the stairs. Six little huts in a semi-circle. Holiday homes. Only one of the other six appeared to be currently occupied.

Frankenstein turned and looked out at the misty sea. Noticed the lights of the small vessel out in the fog. Felt the fleeting flicker of uncertainty, but didn't want to know the feeling, so turned back to the house. The door opened and a man in his eighties stood framed against the light, staring angrily out into the night.

'What?' he said.

'Mr Koppen?' asked Proudfoot.

'I'd like to deny it,' he said, 'but I suppose I can't. Police?'

'Detective Sergeant Proudfoot, this is Detective Chief Inspector Frankenstein.'

The two men took each other in, neither liking what they saw. People with something to hide never liked staring at Frankenstein. He had a quality which made them think that he could see right through them. And he usually could. For his part, Frankenstein never liked anyone he went to interview in connection with a case.

'You're his monster, are you?' asked Koppen, without looking at Proudfoot. Eyes locked on the man he could see as his adversary.

'I've never heard that before,' said Proudfoot dryly. 'You're funny. This is the part where you invite us in.'

Koppen looked back at her, glanced over his shoulder, shrugged and then stood back to let them walk past him. Proudfoot led the way, they walked into the cabin, Koppen closed the door. Inside, the cabin had the feel of a mobile home which is on display in the caravan park. Immaculately tidy and clean. A small sitting room with a kitchen, two bedrooms and a bathroom leading off. Everything that a single man would need. He had eaten his dinner sitting in front of the television, but all that remained on the small table was an unfinished bottle of Lipton's Green Ice Tea. There was a copy of the Bible sitting on the table. Over the back of the slender sofa was a throw depicting Jesus the shepherd in gaudy Technicolor.

There was porn showing on the tv. Explicit. Three men, one woman. Proudfoot glanced at it, looked away in disgust, then she caught sight of the Jesus throw. Frankenstein folded his arms and watched the tv for a few seconds. Koppen sat down and made no attempt to turn the television off.

'Feeling lonely, Mr Koppen?' asked Frankenstein.

'It's a free country,' he said.

'For the moment,' Frankenstein muttered in reply.

'A life of piety?' said Proudfoot.

'Tell me which one of the Lord's blessed commandments I'm breaking and I'll turn it off,' said Koppen.

'It's a moot point,' said Frankenstein, glancing at the tv as the woman was rammed forcibly from behind, 'since I'm turning the damn thing off anyway, but from where I stand it looks like you're doing a fair amount of ass coveting.'

Koppen grunted, Frankenstein leant forward and turned the television off. The moaning was gone. Silence. Frankenstein re-folded his arms, intent on standing throughout. Proudfoot perched herself on the edge of a seat, not really wanting to give herself fully to furniture that Stan Koppen had anything to do with.

'Where d'you keep the chickens?' asked Frankenstein sharply.

'Watch therefore: for ye know not what hour your Lord doth come,' said Koppen, who was used to hiding behind biblical quotes in a tight spot.

'Depends when he's been watching his porn movies,' quipped Proudfoot, and then winced at the fact that it was her who had just said that.

Frankenstein stifled the laugh. 'Chickens, Mr Koppen, where do you keep them?'

Koppen stared ruefully at him.

'In the freezer,' he said.

'You and Ally Deuchar,' said Proudfoot, 'tell us everything.'

Koppen looked annoyed, stared at the floor. Squeezed his fingers together, let them all linger there in silence for a while. Frankenstein and Proudfoot let him stew, waiting for information or waiting for a lie. Koppen leant forward and picked the Bible off the table. He didn't open it, just leant forward tapping it between his fingers.

'For the Lord seeth not as man seeth: for man looketh on the outward appearance, but the Lord looketh on the heart.'

'Enough of the mumbo, big guy,' said Frankenstein.

'And how is your heart, Mr Koppen?' said Proudfoot, before her boss could descend any further into name-calling.

'I have nothing to hide,' he said meekly, still looking at the carpet.

'Is your god forgiving of lies?' asked Proudfoot softly.

Koppen straightened up, not looking her in the eye. Staring at a point somewhere on her left shoulder.

'I wanted the boat, that's no secret. I thought I made him decent terms. It's no life for a young man, the fishing, not anymore. No future in it. So, to be honest, I was thinking of him, his crew. It was more for their benefit than mine. The Lord teaches us that we must put others first.'

'Very charitable,' said Frankenstein.

'What were the terms?' asked Proudfoot. 'You don't seem to have much that you could offer them.'

It was always the same. They didn't operate on a good cop, bad cop basis, it was more of a competent cop, comedy-grumpy cop routine.

'I had my own terms,' he said. No tone.

'And I'm asking you what they were.'

He glanced at her, a quick, shifty look, then started turning the Bible over in his hands.

'Business is business,' he said eventually. 'I don't have to tell you nothing I don't want to.' Particularly when it related to the illegal sideline of the gang of ten who occasionally met in the room above the Incidental Mermaid.

'Anything,' growled Frankenstein.

'What?'

73

'You don't have to tell us *anything* you don't want to, not nothing. Why can't people speak properly anymore? I mean, how fucking hard can it be?'

'When was the last time you spoke to Mr Deuchar about the *Bitter Wind*?' asked Proudfoot, trying to stay on track.

Koppen stared at Frankenstein, trying to work the man out. He was doomed to failure, something he had already realised, and so he could feel another quote coming on. However, for some reason when it came out, all he could think of at the time was, 'My little finger shall be thicker than my father's loins.' He held the bible aloft as he said it to give the quotation some extra gravitas.

'If you think you're getting the porn back on,' said Frankenstein, 'you can fuck off.'

'I'll stick the kettle on,' said Proudfoot. 'Coffee.'

She walked into the kitchenette. Frankenstein stared loathingly at Koppen. Koppen randomly opened the Bible, finding himself at Isaiah chapter 28. *We have made a covenant with death, and with hell are we at agreement*.

He raised his eyes, made some sort of contact with Frankenstein, and then looked back at the well thumbed pages of the Bible which he'd had since his Christening day in 1925.

✂

Frankenstein and Proudfoot were walking slowly past the Westbourne on their way back to town. An hour later. They had extracted little, if any, further information from Koppen in that time. Frankenstein took it all in, though, all the verbal feints and misinformation and bluster. He never failed to impress Proudfoot with the way he could drag up some piece of knowledge which had seemed completely trivial and unimportant at the time.

'I'm guessing,' said Frankenstein, 'that it's going to contravene some sort of human rights directive if we just nick the bastard and feed him a truth serum.'

'You think?'

'And all that Bible shite. Didn't believe a word of it. He's not a religious nutter, he's just a lying bag of crap.'

Proudfoot looked out into the mist as they walked. She hadn't thought that the man's tale of religious conversion had been credible, but neither did she suspect him of complicity in the deaths and disappearance of the crew of the *Bitter Wind*.

'You know who he is?' she said.

'I'm all ears,' said Frankenstein.

'He's like the mean looking guy in Scooby Doo. The guy who's rude to the kids and looks like he's got a lot to hide. He's grumpy, usually tells a tall tale about the local ghost. But you know, he never turns out to be the guy under the mask at the end. It's always the mild-mannered puny student who thinks he's going to inherit a million dollars.'

Frankenstein scuffed his shoes, grunted. Checked his watch, relieved to see that there was still plenty of time to have a pint.

'I can see your point,' he said. 'But for every episode like that, there's a *Gold Paw*, where the mean guy's also the bad guy.'

She regarded him with new respect. '*Gold Paw*?'

'Don't look at me in that way, Sergeant,' he said.

'What?'

'You're looking at me like, *cool, he's an old fucking geezer and yet he has a full and deep understanding of Scooby Doo as a cultural reference*. Piss off. Condescending bastard.'

She laughed. They reached the thirty mile an hour sign signifying the start of the town.

'As my line manager, are you allowed to call me a condescending bastard?'

He shook his head. Cider, maybe he'd have a pint of cider.

'Think I'll bring a complaint of harassment against you,' she said, still smiling.

'You can fuck right off.'

They walked on, Proudfoot laughing lightly.

## 16

## The Paintbrush
## For The Defence

Nelly Johnson was painting. Everyone should have a hobby. Just before eleven-thirty. Nelly didn't do mornings, working to a different clock from most people. Up at two in the afternoon, retreated to bed around six a.m. Eight hours sleep. Nelly was old, never sure that she needed that much, but usually found it hard to get up to face the day. In winter she saw two hours of light. Her daughter, who lived in Kilmarnock, thought her mother was weird. Used to smoke rolled up newspaper. Had thought about getting her committed. Really she just wanted to sell the house and take the money. Hoped that her mother would die soon and save her the effort of having her put away.

She was about to get her wish, although Nelly's will would be ultimately disappointing for her.

There was a noise in the kitchen, a stumble, the low whisper of a curse. Nelly looked round. She was in her front room, bathed in artificial light, painting a curious scene of Gothic depravity. Goblins, blood, naked witches, witches' brew…

Nelly pursed her lips. Intruder. No skip of the heart, although she did briefly wonder if she should open the curtains in the room she was sitting in, so that whatever was about to happen would be in full view of the road. Not that there would be too many people abroad on George Street at this time in the evening.

The kitchen door creaked, Nelly gripped her paint brush. Doesn't sound like much, but bury one in your eye and see how much it'll upset your equilibrium. She had a thought, the sort of thought which it didn't take much for her to have. Stuck the second and third fingers on her right hand into the red paint and drew two lines on either cheek. Next into the blue and then she had a purplish streak across her forehead.

Footsteps in the hall. She contemplated a brush in each hand, decided to stick with just the one. *A free hand is worth a thousand swords*, isn't that what the ancients used to say? Probably not, but it's the kind of thing the ancients in Nelly's world would have said.

She looked at her painting and noticed a tiny detail amiss in amongst her epic triangular exposition of Sapphic batcave death rock.

'Nelly?'

She didn't recognise the voice. Muffled. She leant forward and touched up the small area of dark grey in amongst the tangle of arms and legs. The door to the sitting room was pushed open and a man walked into the room. Stopped in the doorway. Nelly looked round from behind her painting.

An old man dressed all in black. Absurd hair, thin on top, long down to his neck. A long, thin beard. She shuddered for a second, thinking that it might be Mr Johnson returned from the grave, then she realised that for a kick-off he didn't look anything like Mr Johnson, and secondly, it was a mask. Just a guy in a mask. More or less what she had been expecting, from the moment she had heard the noise in the kitchen. Consequently, what with her face made up in the manner of a regulation 1950's Hollywood Red Indian, the intruder got more of a fright than Nelly.

'Bloody hell,' he muttered through the latex, before managing to compose himself.

'Who the fuck are you?' demanded Nelly, clutching her paintbrush, but not rising from her chair. 'Are you from the government? Here about the mince pies?'

'Nelly,' said the guy. Holes for the eyes and mouth. He was clutching an axe, the same brute of a weapon which had done for the still undiscovered Ward Bracken the previous evening.

'Big fucking brains on you,' said Nelly. 'Bugger off.'

The guy moved forward. Still, strangely, there seemed nothing particularly menacing about him. Despite the axe.

'What's with the mask?' said Nelly. 'You look like a drooling old gipper, all incontinence pants and falling asleep in your soup.'

'You'd know about that,' he said.

Nelly was getting mad, not scared. She stood up and raised the paint brush above her head. Lips curled in a snarl. The old man hesitated before the kill.

'Are you going to say what this is about before you kill me, or are you too pusillanimous even for that, you stupid prick?'

Took aim at his right eye.

'I wanted to murder for my own satisfaction,' said the old man, and she could sense the smile and the sweat behind the plastic.

'Oh for God's sake,' muttered Nelly, 'here we go, quoting Russian literature pish. Well you can go and stick your Dos...'

The axe fell swiftly, moving through the air with the romantic swoosh of a cricket bat swinging through the line of the ball and hitting a beautiful boundary back over the bowler's head.

Nelly's head spun into the air, blood spraying in a mathematically precise parabola around the room, bounced off the painting and fell with a thump onto the floor. Eyes open, still angry. Her body stayed inert in the seat for a second, then the arm fell to the side and the movement toppled the body over and it fell heavily onto the floor beside the head.

He stood over her body. Making sure she was dead. You never knew with Nelly. Then he straightened up, chest thumping with the excitement of the kill. Wiped the blade of the axe on the curtains. Then, almost as an afterthought, he walked quickly across the room, turned out the light, and then back and pulled the curtains to the side. Wanted the body to be discovered in the morning. Still a little disappointed that his first work of atrocity had not yet been spotted. He wanted the town to get on with the business of being in ferment and turmoil.

Another few seconds, a last glance around the room in the dim light from the street, and then he turned and walked quickly back through the house to the kitchen.

## 17

# I'm Dead, Get
# Me Out Of Here!

A grim morning. Low clouds but no rain, an edgy sea. News of the death of Nelly Johnson had spread quickly around the town.

It had happened as the killer had supposed, at dawn's first light. A little before eight o'clock, Jacob Ecclesiastics had been meandering slowly along that end of George Street, looking in windows, staring at bushes. On his way to work at a small garage behind Kames Bay, taking his time, not wanting to get there. Wishing he was still in bed, dreaming of a canal boat holiday in Norfolk, being that that was what he thought about when his mind was not required to be engaged on anything else.

He had looked in Nelly Johnson's window, the scene had registered but not been computed, he had walked on. Ten slow yards, and then he'd turned back. When he'd had a good look, and realised that he was looking at what he thought he was looking at, he had been fascinated rather than nauseated. And it was going to mean that he would have to take the morning off work.

✂

'This,' said Frankenstein, waving a hand over the scene of grotesque murder, 'this never happened on Scooby Doo.'

Proudfoot glanced round at Frankenstein. Almost allowed herself to smile at the stupidity of the remark, but something about the decapitated head kept the smile from her face.

Nelly Johnson's house was awash with police, scenes of crime officers, photographers and the bloody remnants of her fastidious slaying. George Street was closed off, the press and public amassed a short distance from Nelly's house. Several of the town's people were there, hoping to catch a glimpse of Nelly dead. Just to make sure.

'He's in the kitchen?' said Frankenstein.

'Who?' asked Proudfoot, recognising one of those moments when Frankenstein was thinking too fast for his mouth.

'The guy who found......this.'

Proudfoot nodded.

'If you're going to speak to him, I think I'll join you,' she said. 'I've seen enough of this kind of thing before.'

Frankenstein gave her a quick glance and then picked his way between the blood spatters and forensics crew back out the room. Proudfoot followed, eyes down, watching where she was putting her feet, trying not to think about what she was in the middle of.

It had been long enough for her to forget, long enough for the psychiatry sessions to have been effective. She always knew, however, that the bandage over the wound had been slight.

There were four people in the small kitchen. Two forensics officers methodically clue searching, another constable standing guard on Jacob Ecclesiastics, and the witness himself, looking quite happy, sitting back, drinking a cup of tea. Proudfoot leant against the fridge, Frankenstein folded his arms. Ecclesiastics looked over the rim of his plain, white Ikea mug.

'You're the guy who discovered the body?' said Frankenstein.

'Aye.'

Frankenstein held his gaze for a few seconds and then glanced at his notebook.

'Jacob Ecclesiastics? What the fuck kind of name is that?'

Frankenstein usually only asked that question of people who he thought didn't know that he was named after a mythical, mad German scientist.

'That's good coming from you,' said Ecclesiastics.

There was, of course, no one on the island who didn't already know that there was a Detective Chief Inspector Frankenstein on the loose in the town.

'Whatever. You discovered the body and then proceeded to call several of your friends to come and see before you called the police, is that right?'

Ecclesiastics smiled, the smile mostly directed at Proudfoot. He winked at her. Proudfoot's face was blank.

'What was your thought process exactly?' said Frankenstein. 'You imagined we'd be happy for you to do that?''

Ecclesiastics thought about it for a while and then shrugged.

'It's just life, you know. Life, life itself, I mean actual life, is a reality tv show. It's all just, like, you know, for entertainment purposes. And let's face it, she was dead anyway, right? There was no business of rushing her to hospital to try to put her head back on. Dead.'

'What if the killer had still been on the premises?' snapped Proudfoot, annoyed by his flippancy. 'What if there had been some time-critical piece of evidence?'

Ecclesiastics sipped his tea, staring at Proudfoot's shoes. Finally he shrugged again.

'Don't know,' he said. 'But you can see my point, though, eh? Here we have this rancid old bag, the most hated woman in the town, put to the slaughter in brutal fashion. I know that the second you lot are round, wham, the place is closed off. But I also know my mates are going to want to have a gander at it, maybe take a few shots on the old mobiles. Seriously, what do you expect a lad to do? Eh?'

'Hated?' said Frankenstein.

Proudfoot looked away, eyes drifting around the room. A callous attitude, but it was what they found all the time now, no matter the crime. No one cared anymore. Life was, as he had said, a reality show, played out for the entertainment of others.

'I care,' she mumbled, too low for the others to hear, eyes having settled on an old jar of Bisto that looked like it had been sitting in the same spot on the same shelf for thirty years.

'What?' said Ecclesiastics.

'Why was she the most hated?' asked Frankenstein.

'Couldn't shut up,' replied Ecclesiastics quickly. 'Told every bastard what she thought of them. Had that old persons thing, you know the one, where they think they can say what they like, think that they won't offend people, or don't care if they do. *I'm some old geezer, I drank condensed milk during the war, I'm entitled to my opinions.* You know what they're like, and there're hundreds of them in the town. She was just a bit more vocal than all the others. And nastier.'

Frankenstein looked round at Proudfoot. Knew that Ecclesiastics had already been interviewed at length and that he didn't really have much of interest to contribute.

'We have a town of suspects, Sergeant,' he said, 'although one glaringly obvious one. Come on.'

'You mean old Stan Koppen?' said Ecclesiastics. 'That's a fair point, after Nelly in there fingered him to you lot last night.'

Proudfoot looked at the lad and then turned and walked quickly out of the house. They did have plenty of people to see, but she knew who it was that she should go and see first. A man she should have visited already, a man she should have been talking to the second she realised he was on the island. A man who she knew had previously been involved in brutal murder.

Barney Thomson.

'You,' said Frankenstein to Ecclesiastics, 'can fuck off. Constable, we're done with him. Escort him off the premises.'

Frankenstein walked away, following Proudfoot from the house. When he got outside, out into the dull, bleak morning, he was surprised to see that his sergeant was already walking quickly away along George Street, heading back towards the centre of the town. As the shouts from the gathered press started up and immediately gained urgency and resolve, Frankenstein cursed under his breath, watched her for a few more seconds, and then turned to face the multitude.

## 18

## Onion

'You know what I hate?' said Keanu MacPherson. The rest of the guys in the shop kept schtum, respecting the rhetorical nature of the question. 'Burning the roof of my mouth, so that it's sore and tender for three or four days. I do it all the time, usually with sausage. Roll 'n sausage first thing in the morning...... you know it's going to be hot, you say to yourself, as the King said, fools rush in, just take your time, blow on it a little, don't rush, and then the smell of the sausage hits you and you just bite massively into that wee fella, and boom! The next second you're screaming in agony because you've torched the roof of your mouth.'

The glazier had come and gone, the window had been repaired, the shop was returned to normal. And full. Two customers. William Deco, fearless reporter of the locality, had decided that although he didn't really need his hair cut so much, the barbershop might be a good place to come to pick up some gossip. He'd already visited the latest crime scene, gathered everything useful he thought was likely to come his way, left his sidekick, Robin, waiting outside in the melee of reporters, and gone wandering through the town searching for inspiration and investigative insight. The other customer, Rusty Brown, now just five days removed from his most recent haircut, was there for more or less the same reason. It wasn't like his hair needed anything doing to it, but five pounds fifty bought so much more than hair that was already so short it was indistinguishable from an out and out baldy napper. Of course, he was just looking for scandalous gossip about the trawler and hoping that someone might repeat some rumour that he himself had started a couple of days previously. That would at least represent some achievement.

Inevitably, neither Rusty Brown's nor William Deco's conversational needs were being met by Keanu's lengthy thesis on the perils of the morning sausage.

Rusty Brown, in an effort to bring the exchange over the hazards of breakfast to a swift conclusion, suddenly produced the set of false teeth from his mouth and held them up to let Keanu get a good look. Keanu, who was cutting Rusty's hair at the time, reeled, and studied them from a safe distance.

'These'll protect the roof of your mouth,' he said, before slipping them back in. 'Of course, in the long run, your palette becomes soft and unable to stand heat and if you don't have your falsers in, you can't drink lukewarm tea without ending up in casualty.'

He caught Keanu's eye in the mirror. Keanu nodded and then tentatively moved back in to continue the nugatory scissor work. Barney and Deco looked at Brown with suspicion – no one likes it when someone starts brandishing their false teeth in a seditious manner.

'The real tragedy, the broader, bigger picture,' said William Deco, suddenly deciding that what was required was for someone to grab the bull by the horns and start riding round the mountain with it, 'is the death of the fishing industry itself, not just the apparent loss of three of its sons.'

Before Barney, Keanu or Igor could even attempt a penetrative spearhead across the front lines and into the trenches of the conversation, Rusty Brown had pounced on the discussion with extraordinary zeal and verve, leaving the other three straggling at the back with the generals and the catering staff.

'You know, at the moment,' said Rusty, 'I don't think the plight of the fishing industry represents a bigger picture here in Millport than the trawler mystery and now the decapitation of Nelly Johnson. It reminds me of Arnhem. Was there a bigger picture, sheesh, of course there was. There were four hundred thousand guys floating through the air getting shot up the arse, for goodness sake, that's a pretty big bloody picture, you know. But when you get down to the.....'

'You know, I think,' said Barney, recognising that if you didn't interrupt Rusty Brown early on, he was liable to still be talking fifteen years later, 'that Rusty's right. Every story has many layers, but here, the basic story, that foundation layer, is for Brussels and the business sections of the broadsheets. The more intimate story of the crew of the *Bitter Wind* is of much greater immediate interest.'

'Exactly,' said Brown.

'Hmm,' said Deco. Had not had the courage of his original conviction, had just been looking to start the discussion. 'Fair point. And so the question is, who in the town would have wanted to get rid of the crew? All this talk of old man Koppen wanting the boat, but he only had to waste Ally Deuchar for that, not the three of them.'

'Arf,' said Igor.

'Totally,' said Keanu, although as usual he hadn't picked up the nuance. 'Who knows or dares to say what goes on in the minds of men?'

'You're saying that anybody in this town could have had a motive that the rest of us will never know?'

'Yep,' said Keanu. 'Anybody. Look at Igor, for example. The poor wee fella's a hideous, deaf, mute hunchbacked little guy in a white coat. There's nothing sinister about him at all. But who knows what goes on underneath that crop of weird black hair? And Barney, back there brandishing a pair of scissors. Seems mild-mannered and harmless enough. Switched on, reasonably cool guy, if slightly tending towards grumpy old man status. But you know, he's turned up in Millport in his mid-50's, and does anyone know what he's been up to in the past? Could be nothing, could be all sorts of things. The story of your life's a blank page, Barney, and only you know how to fill it in, eh?'

Barney was staring at Keanu, the weight of his life dragging at his face. Art Deco stared at him strangely in the mirror. Keanu suddenly felt the burden of Barney Thomson's past and he smiled to try to shrug it away.

'Only messing, Barney,' he said. 'Life, you know, it's just one big gigantic bag. You stick your hand in and you never know what you'll pull out. Might be nothing, might be covered in slime, might be chocolate cake...'

'Now you're just talking pish, son,' said Rusty Brown, a man so proficient in that himself that he easily recognised it in others.

85

Barney shivered and turned back to the head in front of him. William Deco, sitting there receiving a patient Hugh Laurie *House*. Nearly finished. Barney breathed heavily and resumed the careful scissor work. Keanu hadn't meant anything, he didn't know anything, and he hadn't even been fishing for something which he thought might be out there, but he had wrapped him up in accusation all the same and suddenly Barney felt smothered.

'Are you a man with a past, Barney?' asked Deco. He was a reporter after all.

'Everyone's got a past,' replied Barney dourly.

'Arf?' muttered Igor, and Barney shook his head. *Thanks, Igor, but I don't need you to pan the guy's napper in with a broom.*

The weight of gloom emanating from Barney suddenly sat heavily on the shop and a stillness descended. An uneasy tranquillity. The click of scissors, the shuffle of feet, the smooth and repetitive swoosh of a brush.

Barney was just wrapping up when he shivered again, the feeling of someone walking on his grave. He turned to the door, even before it opened. He waited and then the door clicked, and Detective Sergeant Proudfoot was inside, unzipping her coat against the lazy warmth of the shop.

'This a good time, Mr Thomson?' she asked.

Barney glanced down at the beautifully coiffed head before him. It was such a perfect Hugh Laurie *House* that William Deco was probably going to start limping.

'I guess I'm done here,' he said.

He brushed away the hair from Deco's shoulders, whisked off the cape and stood back. Brain buzzing. Forgot the regulation move of displaying the rear of the customer's head in the mirror, but then Deco was so suddenly grabbed by the scent of a story that he didn't even notice.

He was a man on a mission. Barney Thomson, barber.

He fished around for some money and handed over a ten pound note, so engrossed with his sudden investigative energy that he waved away Barney's attempts at getting him change. Grabbed his coat and grabbed his cap, marginally stopped short of licking the end of his pencil. Took a final glance in the mirror.

'Nice job,' he said. 'Thanks.'

Barney was on to him. Could smell trouble.

'No problem,' said Barney.

William Deco nodded, glanced suspiciously at Detective Sergeant Erin Proudfoot, and then opened the door and walked quickly from the shop, displaying, for those who might have looked closely, a bit of a hobble.

They watched him go, the five people in the shop, and then slowly the normality of a quiet afternoon in a barbershop on a small island on the west coast of Scotland returned.

'He seemed in a hurry all of a sudden,' said Rusty Brown. 'Probably dying for a pish.'

'Arf!'

Igor bent to his work, sweeping up after William Deco. Barney and Proudfoot looked at each other, both finally facing up to the inevitable.

'Time for a coffee?' she asked.

Barney nodded. He clapped Igor on the shoulder, a familiar and yet strangely final gesture, and pulled on his coat.

'I'll be a while,' he said to Keanu. 'Keep the fires burning.'

'Sure, boss,' said Keanu.

The door opened and Barney and Proudfoot disappeared out into the cold of the morning. The others watched briefly, and then they were gone and the shop was bereft of conversation and authority, and Keanu was left alone with Rusty Brown and the continuing sullen and quiet presence of Igor.

'There's something funny going off,' said Rusty Brown eventually.

'Aye,' said Keanu after a while. 'There usually is.'

## 19

# The Remains Of
# The Morning

Secretly Detective Chief Inspector Frankenstein was delighted. In fact, it wasn't even that much of a secret. There were too many things about the *Bitter Wind* which he didn't like, too many imponderables. Cases which weren't open and shut were one thing, he could handle a little peculiarity, some uncertainty. But all his senses told him that this was a case which threatened to lurch horribly over into the supernatural, and it made him feel uneasy. Now, however, everything had changed. They had a simple and straightforward bloody case of murder. Brutal maybe, but plain and obvious murder all the same. This he could deal with.

He pointed to a large man at the back of the press horde, a guy he didn't recognise from the usual collective who plagued the police station on these occasion.

'Big Man?' said Frankenstein.

'Yeah, like hi,' said the big fella. 'Dan Watson from DC Thomson.'

'The Sunday Post?' said Frankenstein incredulously. 'Your mob are actually acknowledging that murders happen? That won't sit well with the knitting patterns and recipes for fruit scones.'

'Nah,' said Watson, 'I'm actually covering the Scooby Doo-type angle for the Dandy and Beano.'

'Ah,' said Frankenstein. That, at least, made more sense. 'You're on to plums, though, eh, Chief? I can see the whole conspiracy, men-in-masks possibilities from the case up until now, but this? A decapitated woman? A sickening blood-splattered front room? Hello? That ain't Scooby Doo.'

'Well,' said Watson, encouraged by the detective's use of phrases such as *sickening blood-splattered front room*, which made great press, if not exactly for the Beano, 'you're forgetting the more recent Scooby feature length animated films, where the monsters aren't always men in masks, and there is an acknowledgement of the existence of the supernatural. Look at *Witch's Ghost*, for example.'

'Fair point,' said Frankenstein. 'However, while that particular episode is filled with ironic nods to the earlier series, and in the end the ghost herself turns out to be a genuine four hundred year old malevolent spirit with authentic evil powers, here's the thing... No one gets hurt! There's an actual old woman in there who will never wake up again. Her head has been completely severed. Blood on the walls, blood on the curtains, blood on the carpet. You going to tell that to your five year-old readership, bud?'

Watson was writing furiously, jealous of all the guys around him holding up a wide variety of recording devices.

'Well, I think children today are far more sophisticated than you give them credit for, and they're also desensitised to violence, but then again, you may have a point. Still, it might have been a man in a mask who chopped her head off? Can you comment on that?'

Frankenstein shrugged.

'That it might have been a man in a mask? Sure, I can comment on that. Here's my comment. Who the fuck knows? It could have been a monkey in a mask.'

The press conference did not last much longer.

The headline in that evening's newspaper: *Police Search For Genetically Modified Masked Killer Monkey.*

✂

From where they were sitting they could look back along the front at Millport. A cold morning, the town still showing the remnants of the ravaging by the storm. They had picked up a coffee each and were sitting on a bench up by the pier, a few yards from where the *Bitter Wind* had been swept away. The pier itself had been given at least a surface clean up, so that it took closer inspection to notice the underlying storm damage.

'So, tell me everything?' said Barney. They'd been sitting in silence for a few minutes, enjoying the peace, watching the world go by. The slowly changing artwork of small town life.

'Me?' she said, surprised that he'd even think to ask. She had been waiting to strike up the conversation about him. 'You care?'

Barney smiled.

'Sure,' he said. 'You did me a favour once. That, and you're one of the few people on the planet that I actually recognise from my past. Whatever life that was before all this insanity started.'

She nodded. Not everyone in this modern day is self-obsessed, she thought.

'Not much to tell,' she said. 'The last time I saw you I was lying in a pool of blood. Nearly died, somehow managed to hang on. Took a year out from the police, recuperated. A few months in bed, spent a few months walking in the foothills of the Himalayas.'

'Meditation and all that sort of thing?'

'Nah. Mostly internet café hopping, but it was fun. Got me back on my feet. Joel came with me.'

'The detective guy, your sidekick?'

'Yeah. We got married in Singapore at the end of it all. He left the police, I was going to, but they were really good to me during the whole thing, and, well, here I am. Been back in a few years. This is my first murder since back then. Guess they've been keeping me away from it.'

A seagull landed on the railing not far from them and inspected them for signs of food. Barney lifted his coffee cup to show that they were packing caffeine and no crumbs. The seagull moved its head to the side and then turned and flew off.

'How are you coping?' he asked.

'Denial,' she said quickly. 'Denial. Been three years since my last therapy. Maybe I'll need to go back.'

'What's Mulholland doing now?' said Barney.

'You remember him?' she asked, surprised.

'Everything from back then seems kind of vague, but yes, it's in there somewhere.'

'He works for the Forestry Commission. You remember the Wolf in *Pulp Fiction*?'

Barney smiled and nodded.

'That's Joel. He's the Wolf of forestry.'

They drank their coffee, they looked at the skies and the sea. An elegiac moment, the small bay stretching before them.

90

'Your turn,' said Proudfoot eventually, and Barney stared at the ground in front of him. 'The last I heard, whereas I nearly died, you did the job properly. Dead at the foot of a cliff, thanks to old man Blizzard.'

'Well,' said Barney, quickly, 'he didn't push me, I just slipped. Although, to be fair to the lad Blizzard, maybe he'd have pushed me if he'd had to. So then, what happened next...? Back from the dead. Hard to explain.'

He paused, sipped on his cup of joe.

'Presumably though, you must have some explanation,' she said, amused by his reticence. No impatience, just a lazy cup of coffee on a cool autumnal day by the sea. She could sit here all day, take nothing else to do with the investigation, talk to Barney Thomson, chew the fat, wait a few days to return to her own personal Wolf.

'Well, you know, Sergeant,' said Barney Thomson, 'I'm not sure that I can. I was never, to be honest, personally aware of being dead. No light at the end of a tunnel, no Heaven, no Hell, no deity-like figure casting doubts over my presence in his house, no red, bearded, long-tailed sneak, waiting to whack me over the head with a steaming iron bar, before sending me into the caves for an eternity of back-breaking, soul-crushing penance. Nothing. I fell off a cliff, woke up some time later in a bed, having been employed with the First Minister.'

She looked at him. There was a story there that she had studiously avoided at the time, since murder had been involved.

'You were the personal barber, when all those cabinet murders were being committed?'

''Fraid so.'

'Jeez, that's pretty funky. Murder has followed you around'

Barney smiled. Never a truer word...

'I'm Jessica whatshername from *Murder She Wrote*,' he said.

'Miss Marple,' she added.

'Poirot.'

'Hannibal Lectar.'

He laughed, she smiled with him.

'Cheeky sod. That's a bit different.'

'So how'd you find yourself here?' she asked.

'Came here a lot as a kid. Every year. Forgot about it over time. Then after the First Minister thing, I walked off into the sunset. Thought I'd walk the earth and get in adventures. But you know, that's just the movies. I went from town to town, never got into any adventures. On the one hand I was seeking the quiet life, on the other, it was too damn quiet. Remembered this place, don't know why especially. Came here, it felt like home. Stayed.'

She had almost stopped hearing what he said. Not bored, just letting the sound of his voice sweep over her, blending with the sea and the breeze and the chill of morning. She could listen to him talk for a long time, didn't really matter what he was saying. There had been a time when the name Barney Thomson had scared her. Now, however, the Barney Thomson who sat next to her, talking honestly and softly, was like an old friend.

'You're like a different person,' she said.

'Getting killed will do that to you.'

She smiled. She looked out at the grey sea, the waves chopping against the small islands in the bay. The beach, still showing evidence of the storm. Her eyes wandered back along the promenade, along the front of the town. Drawn further along, until they came to the shop front of the police incident room. A hunched figure in a long black coat, shoulders stooped against the cold, was opening the door and going inside. Frankenstein.

And with that the wistful air was gone, and the vision of Nelly Johnson's front room suddenly seared through her head. Blood.

'What's he like?' said Barney. He too had felt the seismic shift in mood. She knew who he meant.

'Classical grumpy old man. Miserable as hell, misanthropic, moans constantly, complains about everything. I love him.'

Barney laughed, but he wasn't really in the mood for laughing. They were back on to the subject of death and he knew the obvious question was coming.

'So, here you are again, in a small town and people are dying.'

92

He took a sip of coffee, had to tip the cup almost vertical to get the last of it. He could take another. Maybe, after she'd gone back to work – and who was he fooling with that thought, as she was working now – he'd get another coffee and go for a long walk along the front, round Kames, past the aquarium, keep on going. And what if he didn't stop? Small town island life… he'd end up back where he started.

'You think I'm involved?' he asked.

'Not for a second. I think, however, that there are plenty of people who would think you were involved if they knew you were here.'

'What about Frankenstein?'

She kept her eyes on the door of the police office, as if that might help her see into the mind of the misanthrope.

'He'd jump to the obvious conclusion. He'd want to speak to you, he'd bring you in. But for all the bluster and general haranguing of the planet that he so dedicates his life to, he's a good policeman. He'd know you weren't implicated. He'd be a bad policeman not to talk to you, just as he'd be a bad one to draw the wrong conclusion.'

'Tell him I'm here,' he said quickly.

She looked at Barney for the first time in a while. The serene face, the lines of age, greying hair. Wearing well. Bit of the Sean Connery about him. Not the man she had known. Then she looked out across the bay, back towards oblivion. The investigation of a brutal murder to be continued. Life went on. If not for Nelly Johnson.

She tapped him on the knee and stood up. 'I should get back to the grind. Walk me round.'

Barney didn't rise. Felt the chill of the day for the first time since they'd sat down, but didn't feel like moving just yet.

'I'm just going to sit here for a while,' he said. 'Keanu can take care of the shop. The day can take care of itself.'

Detective Sergeant Proudfoot looked down at Barney. A long gaze between them, she smiled weakly, and then turned and walked off the pier, back past the George. Barney watched for a short while and then turned his head away and looked out to sea.

'I've got nothing to hide,' he said to himself.

If only that had been true.

✂

William Deco left the barber shop and headed straight back to his Largs office. Got down to work. Barney Thomson. The name had rung a bell, and when he checked the files, it all came back. Of course the name had rung a bell. Barney Thomson had been the most notorious serial killer of his day, and the day hadn't been that long ago. It was as if the nation had collectively absolved him of all blame for the crimes of which he'd been accused, and in doing so had chosen to forget about him, embarrassed that they had so quickly leapt to the wrong conclusion.

Maybe they'd been right, however, that's what William Deco wondered as he read the back story. Maybe they'd all been right.

And as he read, he decided that the Millport mystery, which had begun with the disappearance of the crew of a small fishing trawler out on the firth, and had picked up with a sudden decapitation, had just become even more interesting. It was time for a special murder edition of the newspaper.

William Deco, Art to his friends, finally had a story to get his teeth into.

## Part II

## 1

## The Fantastic Five
## Have A Cunning Plan

*Murder has come to town, and now fear hangs in the air like the putrid stench of burning cattle flesh. A pall hangs over us all, as we wait in terror behind locked doors. The streets are deserted, windows are shuttered, there is not a soul who does not wait with horror, wondering where the executioner's axe might next fall...*

'What d'you think?' asked Keanu, looking up from his laptop.

Igor glanced out at the sky, cloudy but still bright. A mother and her two young children walked past, the kids giggling and eating ice cream, the mum doing a funny walk to make them laugh. Old Thomas Peterson rode past on his bike. The waves fluttered in the bay.

'Arf,' said Igor.

Keanu had followed his gaze outside and nodded sombrely.

'Haven't quite caught the mood of the town, eh?' he said sadly.

✂

Barney went for his long walk. Didn't even stop in the shop to tell Keanu that he was in charge for the rest of the day. It wasn't like the kid wouldn't be able to work it out for himself. And, if it looked like he might still be out walking when it was getting dark, he could call him and get him to close up. Minimum responsibility.

Instead of walking along the front, he strolled up the hill, down along the back way to the cathedral and then up through the farm, to the highest point. It was cold up there, deserted. Not a day for tourists. He looked all around, low visibility. Cloud and mist had descended. Couldn't see the hills of Argyll that are so glorious on a sunny and clear day. Clutching his jacket close to him, he moved on, walking down the other side of the hill, swinging back round towards the town. But he was still in a mood for walking and thinking, not yet ready to return to the shop.

Three days ago it had been his place of refuge, but now, now that he had been visited there by ghosts and portents, the shop represented a haunted place for him. He wanted to stay away, and so he walked on, wondering what was left for him in this town if he could never shake the feeling. He knew, however, that there was some reckoning which had to be faced, and not until then would he know where his future lay. If he had a future.

At Kames he took another left, round the bay and out towards the aquarium. When he reached the corner at the far end of the bay, however, he turned off the main road, onto the small path which leads out towards Farland Point. A deserted rocky corner, for fishermen and the occasional seal. A perfect view of the nuclear power station just over a mile across the water.

Walking down the muddy path, past fading long autumnal grasses, he heard voices a short distance away, down by the water. Did he want human contact? Maybe, after a couple of hours of relentless solitude, his thoughts naturally getting nowhere, tied up as they were in a morass of old guilts and demons. A fair chance that whoever was down here was going to be one of his regular customers. Familiarity, perhaps that was all that was required.

He stepped off the path, through the grass and past a lone bramble bush. There were four people down by the water, working with a small boat which was tied to a short, disused jetty, sticking out into the sea, all rusted columns and broken wooden planks. Four people and a dog. The MI6 gang, if that's who they really worked for.

As Barney got closer, they turned towards him and stopped what they were doing. The Dog With No Name stopped sniffing around in the grass and approached to say hello.

'Hi there, Mr Thomson,' said Fred, the blond haired leader of the gang. 'We wondered when you'd get here.'

Barney smiled. 'You knew?'

'We've been watching you,' said Selma. 'You were at the pier, you walked up past the church and the school, up to the highest point, and now you're here. Our paths would eventually cross.'

'Satellite?' said Barney.

Bernard held up a pair of binoculars.

'So, what are you doing?' asked Barney.

Fred turned and looked at the boat which they had tied to the dilapidated jetty. A rowing boat, laden with five barrels.

'We're setting a trap,' said Fred.

Barney almost turned away but decided that he really needed to stand here and find out what was going on. When constantly presenting yourself with the reality of your past, perhaps it was best to break it up with the complete surrealism of the present.

'To catch the killer,' said Deidre, aware of the sceptical look on Barney's face. 'We haven't decided yet whether to call him the Trawler Fiend or The Incredible Captain Death.'

'The Trawler Fiend?'

'Sure,' said Selma. 'Tonight, after dark, Bernard and the Dog With No Name will pretend to be fishermen. They'll work down here at the boat, until the killer comes along.'

'The Incredible Captain Death,' said Fred.

'Exactly,' said Selma.

'That's insane,' said Barney. 'The guy who killed Nelly Johnson chopped her head off. It was horrible. Why give him this silly nickname? You make him sound like a character out of a kid's tv show. Some mad old fool, goofily searching for his grandfather's treasure. He's a killer'

'Like, that's why he's got Death in his name!' said Bernard.

'Or Fiend,' added Deirdre.

Barney looked quizzically around the gang. Shook his head, shrugged.

'You were telling me your brilliant plan,' he said, deadpan.

'How do we know that you're not The Incredible Captain Death disguised as a mild-mannered barber?' said Deirdre.

The Dog With No Name sat at Barney's feet, looking up, tongue out.

'You do have a bit of a history after all,' said Fred.

'What?' said Barney.

The wind had changed. Colder, coming down from the north, over the island, sneaking up coolly on Millport from behind. The small, barrel-laden boat bobbed against the jetty. The skies had grown darker as Barney had walked, but he had been so absorbed in entangling his mind in knots of remorse and introspection, that he hadn't noticed.

He felt the chill now, however. The wind, the sea, the murky skies.

'Like, we know all about you, friend,' said Bernard. 'The manslaughter, the death, the bodies in your mother's freezer, all those groovy dead monks, Murderer's Anonymous. It's totally whacked, man. Like we're never seen anything like it, have we Dog With No Name?'

The dog barked.

Barney was aware of the beating of his heart, but it didn't crash and thrash and threaten to burst through his chest. He could feel it slow down, settle into a declining rhythm, as if it might be eventually going to stop. And as it slowed down, it seemed to rise in his chest. A slow ascent up his throat. Not leaping into his mouth, just slowly working its way out, so that it would soon lie dead on the floor.

His past wasn't coming back to haunt him; the past was three hundred thousand orcs at the gates of Helm's Deep, and Barney was alone on the walls.

Fred clapped him on the shoulder.

'Don't be alarmed, Barney old buddy, we're MI6. We know all kinds of shit.'

'Sure we do,' said Bernard. 'What we don't know is, like, where's the best place on this island to get a fried banana burger with mayonnaise and chocolate sauce?'

The dog barked again, wagging its tail with gastronomic excitement.

'There are no secrets,' said Fred, his hand still squeezing Barney's shoulder, 'only certain things that we don't know about each other. We were checking you out last night, with our trawler in the mist ruse. That was all a scam. We're full of them. Hey, maybe if you don't get killed on this gig, you might want to think about coming to work for us.'

Barney's heart had begun to speed up again, had begun the slow crawl back into position. There are no secrets, only certain things that we don't know about each other... How many times had he heard that one in the shop? Well, essentially, none, but that level of absurd tangential gobbledygook was commonplace.

'I'm going to go,' he said slowly. 'Still got a lot of walking to do. Thinking.'

Fred let go of his shoulder and took a step back.

'Sure, friend,' he said, 'but you don't need to worry. We won't tell anyone, we can keep a secret.'

'Yep'

'Sure.'

'Like, totally.'

Barney looked at them all and then turned slowly and walked back through the long grass, back up onto the path. He still had a long way to go, and the journey would take him much further than the ten and a half mile walk around the island. When he was a few yards away, he stopped and looked back at Bernard.

'Try the Ritz. They might make you your burger.'

'Like, thanks, pal!'

## 2

# Up The Graveyard

Proudfoot didn't go straight back to the police incident room either, although she didn't go for as long a walk as Barney Thomson. Almost at the door, and then she had a sudden vision of her chat with Frankenstein and having to explain where she'd been and to whom she'd been talking. She didn't need that.

She turned abruptly and walked back along the front and up the hill. Working on something in between a whim and a hunch. A whunch. She thought of the word as she passed the farm. A whunch. Made her smile. She could use it to Frankenstein and it would be something else to cover up her absence. Particularly when her whunch came to nought and she was returning to the station empty handed.

She reached the graveyard and turned in through the gate. Stopped for a second to look back down the hill; the island of Little Cumbrae, the sea and the mainland, Arran and Bute. It was beautiful, the starkest of contrasts to what she had had to endure that morning in Nelly Johnson's front room.

She thought of the photograph she'd seen of Bill Johnson. Bill on a boat, about to cast off from one of the endless small jetties which dotted the coast of the island, and which no one ever used any more. Except MI6. Bill grimacing at the camera. Trying to smile? Annoyed at the photographer for taking the picture? Had there been a story about the late Bill Johnson, that was what she was wondering.

As it happened, the story of Bill was brief and insignificant. A minor part in the diamond smuggling ring, then his place in the operation, such as it was, gratuitously grabbed by Nelly upon his death from heart failure the previous April.

Proudfoot walked along the main path of the cemetery, looking up and down neat rows of headstones, the simple, unadorned remembrances of the dead typical of the people. Nothing elaborate, no one trying to outdo the next grave along. Austere, minimal, honest.

She took her time, glancing along the lines, reading the epitaphs on some of the end-of-the-row headstones. *Margaret Patterson, Born 1856, Died 1893. Much missed mother of seven.* At the bottom end of the cemetery, near the far fence, there was a man standing by one of the gravestones. From the overalls and heavy yellow coat she knew that it would be the gravekeeper, or a council worker with some similar designation, rather than a family member visiting a Dead Relative.

She wandered slowly over in his direction, past Mary Martin, a dear friend and mother, and David McTaggart, much beloved son and father. She came round the last row of stones and immediately saw what was keeping him standing still, staring.

He was a few feet back from a grave, so as not to be standing over the body. Assuming it was in there. The headstone was a plain granite rectangle. On the ground beside it there were some weathered and beaten flowers, which had been sitting forlornly in the same vase for six months. Stabbed into the ground in front of the grave was a simple wooden cross, on top of which a chicken had been impaled. Whether the chicken had still been alive when it had been skewered onto the top spike of the cross, it was impossible to tell. Either way, the chicken had not died with a smile on its face. Across the engraving on the headstone, words had been splashed in red paint: *Reap the Bitter Wind.*

Nelly's killer had been intent on doing a thorough job.

Proudfoot approached and stood beside him, looking down at the grave of Bill Johnson. The words, *Here lies William Johnson, No Longer Alive, But Never Dead*, had not been completely obscured by the paint. The guy didn't seem to have noticed Proudfoot's approach, yet he showed no sign of surprise at her arrival.

'Do you think it's paint or blood?' he asked, his voice deadpan.

'It's not blood,' she said quietly.

'How d'you know?' he asked, finally giving her a glance, and then he made another little noise and nodded. 'The policewoman. You've seen blood before.'

'Too often,' she said. 'You're the gravedigger?'

'Oh, you can't say that. Not allowed to use the word grave.'

'No?'

'It implies that the worker himself might be grave in some way. You know, sombre and unsmiling. Some of us Cemetery Earth Reallocation Employees are quite cheerful. I mean, obviously not me, I'm as miserable as shite, me, but that's what the directive said. The union held out for it, you know. It was a big thing. There was a paragraph in the Herald.'

'Right,' she said. 'What's your name?'

'Headstone Harmison,' he replied. A pause. She gave him a glance. 'Obviously I wasn't Christened Headstone, I mean, my mum and dad would have had to be showing some amount of prescience for that, although of course, if they had Christened me Headstone, then you could never know if I'd drifted into this line of work because they'd pointed me in that direction. My real name's Morris. Everyone knows me as Headstone. You have to accept it in this line of work. And when your second name starts with an H, you're an absolute sitting duck for the alliterative aspect. It's like my mate up in Clarkston, Graveyard Gillingham.'

He paused briefly and Proudfoot made the rookie error of not jumping in when she had the chance.

'Then again, there's the fella over in Largs. Sam Tarrantino. You'd think they'd call him Tombstone, but everyone knows him as Mr Brown. Don't get it myself, but he's not really a friend of mine anyway. When I see him I usually call him Sammy. A bit over familiar, but that's one of my things. Over familiarity. Puts some people off, but I always say that you just have to take people as you get them. I am what I am.'

'When did you find the chicken?' asked Proudfoot, taking a leap at a millisecond of clear air.

'The chicken?' said Headstone, seemingly surprised that she'd want to ask about it. 'About half an hour ago. It wasn't here this morning. I was going to lunch, managed to fit in a half hour break sometime after twelve. Must have been done then. Like, I was just sitting in the shed, but my back was turned, head down in the trough, tv on, the whole distraction thing, it's not like I'm paid to guard this place, you know, and

102

then after that I was working down at the other end, the new section over there, where we put the urns and stuff, nothing specific just general maintenance, then I got a call from Tully Banta down at the Kendall, and he said about Nelly Johnson. Bit of a shock, but it wasn't like there wasn't a queue. So I got to thinking about old Bill, and wondering what kind of state his plot was in, and if there was space beside it for Nelly, you know, how it's going to work. I mean, it's not like I don't know all these graves by heart, and Bill's not been in the ground all that long, but I came up here just to have a look anyway, and as I was walking up I thought to myself, here, is that a chicken? That is, that is a chicken!...'

He talked on. Proudfoot switched off. She had a few more questions to ask, but essentially she knew there was nothing much else that Headstone Harmison would likely be able to tell her. She brought her phone from her pocket and took a few quick photos of the headstone and the chicken, and then she took a photo of Headstone himself as he seemed keen for it to happen.

She turned away from the little scene of demonic indulgence and looked back down the hill and out to sea. Suddenly felt the chill of the graveyard, and the chill of the absurdity of someone who would kill a chicken to leave a warning, and who would scrawl a catchphrase in fake blood on a tombstone. Headstone's voice drifted in and our of her head, a dreary monotone, his conversation a continual polemic never destined to reach any destination or conclusion. '...made out of granite, because that's what most of them did, but of course these days people are stretching the boundaries because that's what they do and last week I heard someone talking about kicking the dead whale up the beach, but to be perfectly honest I had no idea what they were talking about...'

Eventually, although no gap in his conversation ever really appeared, Proudfoot patted Headstone on the arm and began to walk slowly away from the grave. Shook her head at her own forgetfulness, stopped and held a hand up for him to take a breath. He looked at her expectantly, surprised that anyone would want him to stop talking.

'We'll need to get a couple of guys up here, forensics, that kind of thing. They'll be here in a few minutes. Don't touch this thing, don't tidy it up. Close the graveyard, don't let anyone in before the police arrive.'

'Well, that's all very well saying that Detective, but there are some, like you know, Mrs Waverley, who comes up here every single aft...'

'Headstone,' she said firmly, 'I'm telling you, don't let anyone in. That's it. I could call it in and wait, but I feel like walking back down the hill. I'm trusting you here. If it helps, imagine that I'm making you my deputy. Until reinforcements arrive, you're in charge of the crime scene.' She reached forward and gripped his shoulder. 'Deputy Harmison, secure the area.'

Headstone Harmison saluted.

'Yes, ma'am,' he said. The poor lad had been watching a few too many American movies.

'Thank you,' said Proudfoot, then she turned and walked slowly back through the graveyard. Away from the desecrated grave of Bill Johnson. As she walked, she smiled at the thought of Headstone Harmison, but slowly the smiled died. Just like all the poor souls who lay beneath the ground in this, the latest crime scene in her career. Couldn't stop herself glancing at the graves as she passed.

*Agnes Desmond, A Faithful Wife, Died Mar 1923. Charles Bergemot, Died September 1902, Gone But Not Forgotten.*

## 3

## Snack Time

'Where the fuck have you been?'

Proudfoot stopped just inside the door. She smiled. The whole of the incident room looked at her, based on Frankenstein's bark from the rear of the room.

She walked over to one of the desks, where a geeky youth of a constable, newly arrived from Greenock, was sitting at a computer terminal. She took out her phone, found a lead lying in amongst the stramash of electrical equipment on the desk, attached her phone to the computer and then leant across the constable to work at the keyboard. Constable Corrigan, confronted with Detective Sergeant Proudfoot's left breast in his face, fought the urge not to move and then finally pushed his chair back.

By what she considered a small miracle, she managed to get the pictures downloaded in seconds, almost as if she was in an advert for the computer or phone company. It really is that simple! She straightened up and indicated for Frankenstein to come and look.

'This is where the fuck I've been. The grave of Nelly Johnson's husband. I had a whunch.'

Frankenstein looked dubious, and then he walked round and looked at the pictures. She flicked through them slowly, seven in all, concluding with the smiling mug of Deputy Headstone.

'Who's the geek?' asked the geeky constable from behind. Frankenstein and Proudfoot gave him a curious look.

'Yeah,' said Frankenstein, 'who is the geek?'

'The gravedigger,' said Proudfoot, 'although you're not allowed to call them that anymore.'

'People Who Dig Large Holes In The Ground For The Purposes Of Burial Of Late Lamented Other Significant People Of Unknown Future Personage?' ventured Corrigan.

They gave him another look, this time Frankenstein stopping himself giving the lad a slap across the head.

'Shut up! That didn't even make any sense. Sergeant, what's the position now? You appear to have left the scene?'

'I've ordered the gravedigger to close the graveyard and to not tamper with anything until we arrive for the full examination.'

Frankenstein nodded and looked around the room. Spare men were thin on the ground, though he was expecting more to arrive the following day, now that they had a new murder on their hands. The thing was getting bigger and bigger as they went on, and a dead chicken at a tombstone wasn't going to help matters. He'd been badgered by the press already that day, and with every new and strange discovery it was only going to get worse.

Police hell.

'Right,' he said, 'I'd better get up there and take a look. Not that I don't trust you Sergeant. You stay here and find something to make yourself useful...'

'A true general...'

'Piss off. Webster and you, whatever your name is, you're coming with me. Bring some of that forensic crap. A whunch for God's sake.'

A quick glance at Proudfoot, Webster and the other guy, Constable Alan Constable, who was always surprised when anyone forgot his name, and then Frankenstein walked quickly outside, pulled the cigarette packet from his pocket and lit up.

They stood in the room watching for a few seconds.

'He's at the fags,' said Proudfoot. 'Things are looking bad. Webster, Constable, you better get a move on, I think he's about to blow.'

A nod and a mock salute, and Constables Webster and Constable got to work.

✂

Barney walked on, right around the island. Past the aquarium and Keppel pier and the lion rock; the wishing well; the marina and the ferry landing slip; the small column at the far end, looking north, where Frankenstein had first encountered Fred and the gang; on round the small bay, back south past the old fish farm, which had once famously been converted into a soccer stadium or something live on BBC tv; the twisty back roads towards the Indian rock, looking out at the tired, grey seas, over to Bute and the hills of Arran; over the small hump and down into Fintry Bay. Mid-November, the café was still open.

A long slow walk, and by the time he reached Fintry, he was ready to sit down. He debated the element of human company that entering would involve, and then walked wearily up the steps and inside.

The place was busy with tourists. He stopped for a second and looked over them all, people wrapped in thick jackets, gloves and scarves and hats discarded. Where have all these people come from? he wondered. He had walked slowly around the island and barely seen anyone.

He walked to the counter, the gloom of the world on his shoulders. Knew the small woman standing behind, frantically rushing around re-supplying the shelves of sandwiches, which had been unexpectedly depleted.

'Busy?' he said.

'Tell me about it, Mr Thomson.' Then she looked conspiratorially around the clientèle and leant forwards, her voice hushed. 'Gloaters and sightseers. Here because that old woman was murdered. Then they come round here because you can look across the water to where the trawler was found. They're just wanting to catch a glimpse of an actual police investigation. The police should sell tickets, I'm telling you, they'd be minted. Really, it's terrible. But then, who's to say, you know, people want what they want. It's like reality tv right on your doorstep. Why sit at home with a cup of tea watching endless adverts on ITV, or the BBC telling you how wonderful they are every thirty seconds, when you can see the real thing in action? But then, we're talking about a woman's life here, aren't we? They should just leave well alone and let the police get on with their work.'

A pause. Barney wondered if she was finished and whether he'd now be able to get his order in.

'You can tell I'm Gemini,' she said. 'Both sides.'

'Thought that was Libra,' said Barney.

'Maybe it was my mum who's Libra.'

107

'Can I order something now?' asked Barney.

'What were you waiting for?'

Barney nodded ruefully and looked into the glass cabinet to see what was on offer. The food was lined up, each item appropriately labelled. Decapitation Doughnuts: £1.75; Murder Muffins: £1.75; Slaughter Scones with Genocide Jam: £1.50; Execution Éclairs: £2.55; Nelly Nosh Soup with Bludgeon Bread: £0.75; Bloodbath Broth: £1.05.

Barney looked up at Meg Braintree.

'Just, you know, giving the public what they want,' she said defensively, arms folded.

'I'll just have a Cappuccino, please,' said Barney.

'Would that be a Carnage Cappuccino or a regular?'

Barney looked deadpan across the counter.

'Regular?' she ventured.

He nodded. She fussed away to make the coffee, Barney turned and looked round at the crowded café. A lot of gloaters and sightseers right enough. As he tuned in to the room, he could hear various conversations, excited chatter about the murder of Nelly Johnson and the mystery of the missing trawler crew. Somewhere in there he even heard mention of The Incredible Captain Death.

The door opened and another couple entered, agitated in discussion, a bustle of coats and scarves and hats and gloves. He was drawn to them, this middle-aged couple over all the others.

'Can you not remember that?' said the woman. 'It was all over the papers.'

'Nope,' said the man. He looked bored. He looked like he needed a cup of Trawler Tea and a Savage Sandwich.

'You're a total eejit. I don't believe you sometimes. Can you remember anything that happened before yesterday?'

They bustled up to the counter and stood next to Barney, perusing the various murder-related foods on offer.

'I can remember the Scotland team that lost 1-0 to Brazil at Hampden in 1973,' said the guy brusquely. 'Went with my dad.'

'Went with your dad,' she said scornfully. 'Like you've never mentioned that before. Where are you when we're

108

sitting watching the television? Do you completely tune out the rest of the planet? Do you completely tune me out?'

'The Cudgel Cake looks tasty,' he said.

'It was all over the papers.'

'Don't remember.'

She glanced at Barney, who was standing next to them, looking at them strangely. Why do people make themselves live with someone else who annoys them as much as this? That was what he was thinking, a thought in itself overwhelmed by the odd feeling he had about them, that somehow this absurd conversational labyrinth referred to him.

'Do you remember it?' she said sharply to Barney, 'or are all you men muppets of equal order?'

'I remember the Muppets!' chipped in the guy from the back.

'Remember what?' said Barney.

'That thing a few years ago. It was in all the papers. The barber. Killed the two lads in the shop, his mother was a serial killer. All that stuff. I cannot believe I'm the only one who remembers that. Everyone thought the bloke had died, but the rumour is that he's down here, in Millport. I just heard someone talking about it. They couldn't remember his name either.'

Barney stared at her, stared through her. He had lived so many years when he hadn't had to think about this, and now, from every angle, it was coming back.

'You're just another glaiket eejit, aren't you?' she said.

Barney looked into her eyes, but he wasn't seeing her. He was seeing Wullie Henderson slide on a puddle on the barber shop floor, he was reaching out to grab him as he fell forward, and he could feel the scissors in his hand accidentally thrust deep into Wullie's chest. Could feel the warmth of the blood which spurted out over his hand and wrist.

'You're the barber here, Mr Thomson, aren't you?' said Meg Braintree, joining the mêlée. 'You'd know if there were any murderers working at the shop. What about that little hunchbacked fellow, he's a bit suspicious looking?'

Barney glanced round at her quickly, sudden annoyance coming with the ugly feeling of the waves of the past.

'Igor's fine,' he said. 'Leave him out of it.'

'Hmph,' she muttered. 'He's short and he can't talk, there's obviously something going on.'

Barney gave her a look which burrowed deep into her head, another sharp glance at the woman who had started off this latest intrusion from the distant past, and then he walked quickly from the café, pushing the door open roughly and almost running down the steps and back down to the road.

The vultures were circling.

The woman who had started this new incursion into Barney's past, watched him go and then rubbed a pensive hand across her hairier-than-acceptable chin.

'Thomson,' she said. 'That name rings a bell.'

Meg Braintree and the husband looked at her expectantly, but eventually she shook her head and the thought that was so close to emerging was once more subsumed in the collective crap of any human mind.

'Think I'll have a Bloodfest Bagel,' said her husband to fill the gap. Then he added, 'And some Ice Pick Tea,' as the opportunity presented itself.

## 4

# A Passing Glance At
# The Dead

Barney walked quickly away from the café, heading back towards town. When he came to the first corner, something made him turn left off the road, through the gate and up the muddy path to the top of the hill, which looked down over the bay and across to Bute and Kilchattan Bay. The ghosts were out to get him, although he still didn't know if those ghosts were real.

He climbed up the short stretch of steep path to the top of the hill and then looked back behind him. The same view that he always had when he stood at this place, the same view that he'd had forty-five years previously when he'd come up here with his mum and his brother for picnics during those endless summer holidays.

He stood for a long time, thoughts suddenly turned back to his childhood. Bike riding, camping, playing in rock pools, ice cream, fish suppers, fresh rolls every morning. The old cinema showing three Carry On movies every week. Crazy golf, rowing boats in the bay, occasional summer donkeys, the boating pond at Kames, the first tentative three iron hit for ten yards at the golf course, Moira MacKay and a pointless teenage infatuation, instant friends and the summer mission, singing songs about Jesus on the beach, playing cricket on a tiny patch of grass.

More ghosts, self-inflicted.

He turned away from the view and started to walk through the field. Haunted, sheathed in melancholy. Lonely.

It is a small island. Hard to move around and not come across someone every few minutes. The cow field met the road at the other side, and as he turned down to his right it was a very short walk past the caravan site and he was passing the graveyard. He glanced in, could see the two police officers hovering over a grave near the back of the cemetery. Black and yellow tape strapped across the entrance, closing the

111

graveyard off to the public. He stopped for a second, wondered what was going on. Did he even want to know?

As he moved on he noticed a guy in a long grey overcoat walking towards him, a cigarette held grudgingly in his fingers. He ducked under the tape and nodded at Barney. They stared at each other for a few seconds, the guy taking an unenthusiastic drag on his cigarette.

'You know what I'm wondering?' he said eventually.

Barney shrugged. 'Why it is that the government persists with PFI when clearly it costs the taxpayer billions of pounds?'

DCI Frankenstein stared at him for a few seconds and then a huge smile broke out temporarily across his face.

'That's funny. The police, we just get shafted by that crap, and consultants. Jesus. Fucking pain in the arse.'

'You're police?' said Barney.

'Can't you tell?'

Barney smiled and nodded. It was written all over the guy.

'So what I was wondering,' said Frankenstein, 'is this. I've been here a few days, and I reckon I've seen you about more than anyone else. You're always mooching round, looking, if you don't mind me being forward, miserable as shite. So my question is this. Who the fuck are you?'

Barney looked him in the eye. Never knew what any police officer was going to think of the revelation of who he was. Perhaps his past would mean nothing to him, perhaps in the past this guy had spent years searching for him. Frankenstein tossed his cigarette to the side and stepped on it. They both looked down at the crushed butt, a minor distraction along the way.

'I'm the barber,' said Barney prosaically. 'I've got the shop next to the incident room. That's why you've seen me so often.'

'I don't think so,' said Frankenstein, 'you're always walking round the town, up and down roads. What is it you're looking for?'

'Is that an interrogative question, or are you just making light-hearted, middle-aged male bonding conversation?'

112

Frankenstein smiled again, shook his head and looked back over his shoulder at the work going on behind him. To his right, he could see Headstone Harmison keeping an eye on his officers, unhappy perhaps that someone else was interfering with his graveyard.

'What's your name?' asked Frankenstein, turning back.

'Barney Thomson.'

'Barney Thomson? The barber?'

Barney nodded.

Frankenstein rummaged about in his pockets and produced another cigarette. Stared at Barney throughout. Lit up, took a deep lungful, slipped the lighter back into his pocket.

'Thought you were dead?' he said eventually.

Barney held his hands out to his side. 'Still here.'

'I remember a time when you were a thing. Had your fifteen minutes. Big serial killer on the run. We had fifty guys a week claiming to be you, handing themselves in.'

'I know,' said Barney. 'I tried to hand myself in once and they turned me away because they thought I was just another faker.'

'Really?' Frankenstein laughed. 'Now that, Alanis Morrissette, is irony.'

Another draw on the smoke, another casual look up and down the road. Barney was getting cold. The shivers of the past creeping beneath his skin.

'So how come you're not dead?' he asked.

Barney shrugged. 'I really don't know. But here I am.'

'How do I know you're not one of these insane guys who was trying to hand themselves in nine years ago, and you never got out of your delusion?'

'You don't.'

Another pause. Barney wondered if Frankenstein just smoked to fill the significant silences.

'And why is it that people start getting murdered the second you turn up anywhere? Could it just be that Barney Thomson isn't the innocent fool, continually caught up in extraordinary circumstances, that everyone started thinking he was? That under the serial killer mask, lurks another serial killer?'

Barney was not going to be fazed by the flick of the detective's switch, jokey light-hearted conversation to serious accusation.

'Is that you doing a schizophrenic good cop/bad cop routine yourself?'

'Yeah, it's a great technique, don't you think?'

'If only you had the right guy.'

'Every guy's the right guy,' said Frankenstein, keeping up the snappy, West Wing-type quick-witted one-liners. 'You just have to figure out what it is they're guilty of.'

Having allowed his gaze to drift away, down past the farm and out to sea and the island, the same longing path that Proudfoot had followed an hour or two earlier, Barney now turned back to Frankenstein.

'And what if they're not guilty of anything?'

'We're all guilty of something, Mr Thomson, even if it's just hanging on to our rented DVD's for a few days too long.'

Nothing else to say, and not of a mind to exchange the kind of banter that it would take a team of twenty-two American scriptwriters a couple of brainstorming sessions to arrive at, Barney lifted a subdued hand and then started walking slowly away in the direction of his forlorn gaze. Back down the hill, time to return to the shop.

'Maybe I'll come and speak to you later,' said Frankenstein. 'A more formal chat. Don't be going anywhere until that happens.'

'Spoke to your sergeant already,' Barney threw over his shoulder without turning.

Frankenstein watched him go, letting him walk off back down the road. Another long draw on the cigarette, and then this time he tossed it into the grass and pressed it down with his foot before it was halfway done.

'Crap,' he muttered to himself.

# 5

## A Row Of Disease

Barney arrived back at the shop to find a queue seven long. He hadn't seen a queue like this since his days back in Partick, when people would queue for hours to get their hair cut by anyone but him. There was a guy under the scissors of Keanu MacPherson, while Igor vigorously swept the floor, something he did accompanied by frequent suspicious glances thrown the way of the packed bench.

As Barney entered and took a swift look along the queue, he realised that three of the men had already obviously had their hair cut, and that none of them were islanders. These people weren't here to be on the receiving end of any barbering services, yet they weren't policemen. It was worse.

Journalists.

'Barney Thomson?' said four of the men at the same time.

Barney glanced at Keanu, who shrugged apologetically.

'Thought they were genuine customers,' he said.

'It's no problem,' said Barney.

Then Keanu approached, holding his scissors at a non-combative angle, and whispered to Barney, 'I'm making them all get a haircut and charging them double.'

Barney clapped him on the shoulder and indicated for him to return to the cut, then he nodded at Igor, who was looking very concerned about the whole thing. Finally he turned and looked at the journalists, wondering as he did so what the collective noun actually was. A pack? A herd? A horde? A scrotum?

'Clearly you're not all here for haircuts,' said Barney.

There was a brief hiatus, as the pack waited to pounce, before finally one of them failed to hold in the full force of his ejaculate.

'You are Barney Thomson, the mysterious and sinister Glasgow barber surgeon from a few years back?' cried one man.

115

Barney looked into the man's eyes, then slowly lowered himself into the barber's chair opposite the ferment. And with that, the first shot being fired, suddenly the scrotum took full voice, every line intersected and overlapping another, a tumult of raw tabloid journalistic over-enthusiasm.

'My paper will give you twenty thousand for exclusive rights.'

'Thirty thousand!'

'Thirty-five!'

'Did you kill the old woman?'

'What have you done with the two missing fishermen?'

'Does death follow you around, or are you the harbinger of death, or are you the executioner himself?'

'Exclusive interview, on your terms, I'm authorised to offer you seventy-five g's.'

'What does it feel like to plunge a knife into someone's eyeball?'

'Do you prefer murder or sex?'

'Have you ever slept with anyone famous?'

'Or snorted cocaine off women's breasts?'

'Talk to us and we'll take you to a secret hideaway, free food and booze for a week, women too if you want, plus one hundred grand, conditional on you spilling all the celeb hairdressing dirt. Have you ever done Justin Timberlake?'

The questions continued, a great morass of journalistic mince, all munged together. Finally, when he heard through the quagmire of absurdity the question, 'What's with the mute, deaf hunchback? He must be guilty of something, just look at him!' Barney finally snapped, stood up and clapped his hands.

The torrent stopped. Everyone stared at him, poised, wondering which gargantuan offer he was going to take.

'I'll tell you what we'll do,' he said, thinking of something on the spot, which was bound to fail. 'No money, no exclusives. You've got the wrong guy for that. You get one question each. No follow-up. I'll choose the order, use your question wisely. If we're in agreement, let's start. If we're not in agreement, then it hardly matters. We cool? Good. You, first from the left.'

116

The guy appeared a little taken aback at being asked, then he regained his composure, re-asserted his id, and said, 'How many deaths have you been directly responsible for in your life?'

Barney looked through the guy, right through his head, right through the wall, through the haberdashers next door, and on and on. The gaze never ended, never came to rest on anything.

How many deaths had he been responsible for? Three was the answer. None of them murders, as such, but three all the same. It was a long time since he had felt the blood of any of them on his hands. Now, however, he felt as if he was drowning in the blood. Even in that of the infamous Brother Steven, who had killed over thirty monks before Barney had put an end to his reign of terror as they'd struggled over a gun in a snowy, far north wilderness. The man had been an insane, psychotic, delusional executioner, but as Barney sat looking at the row of journalists before him, he could see the face of Brother Steven in amongst them, smiling and relaxed, in that nonchalant, Jungian way of his. If Jung had been nonchalant.

'Be cool, Barn,' he could hear Brother Steven say, 'we are all one egg, remember?'

'None,' said Barney firmly. 'No murders,' he added, just to give some element of truth to the answer.

The pack hurriedly jotted down their notes, most of which were comments on how obviously Barney was lying, each writer making a guess at what they thought was the true answer. Barney pointed at random to a guy at the end of the line, barely in his twenties, absurd facial hair that was still some years away from manly cultivation.

'Is it true your mother was a serial killer who ate her victims? And is it true that she wrote a cookbook around her human recipes, substituting chicken for human flesh, and that she became quite well known in Scotland as a celebrity chef before the discovery of her true homicidal nature?'

'That was about six questions,' said Barney, the answer to most of which was no. 'Which one is it you want to ask?'

The man with fusty facial fungus hesitated, then said, 'The one about the cookbook.'

'No,' said Barney, 'it's not true.'

He swung round and pointed to the guy getting his haircut. The element of surprise.

'You?'

Right enough, the man hesitated. Didn't really know anything about Barney Thomson, had just followed the crowd.

'Were you involved in the death of Lady Di?'

'Not directly,' said Barney, 'although I did once cut the hair of someone who said he was the MI6 agent responsible for spiking her driver's orange juice with a lethal cocktail of alcohol, drugs and wine gums.'

'You're kidding?'

'That would be a second question,' said Barney.

He spun back round and pointed to another guy.

'The moon landing?' the bloke said, also seemingly caught unawares, 'true or false?'

'The flag was blowing in the wind,' said Barney. 'Next?'

He pointed, curious as to where this was going. With the first two questions had he stumbled across the only two journalists who knew anything about his past? And the second the thought had formulated, he knew it was a thought he was about to rue.

'Regardless of what's true and what isn't,' said a man in the middle, a guy who, like all the best investigative journalists, looked like a policeman, 'isn't it time you stood trial for the various murders of which you've been accused? Isn't it time you had your reckoning?'

Barney stared at him. Something else he hadn't thought about in a long time, not since he'd tried to hand himself over to the police and had been rejected. And he had no answer for it. Sure enough, he was long overdue in facing up to the past, although it seemed like some higher force had decided that now was the time, regardless of the police, regardless of the press.

'I'm not running,' he said eventually. 'The police are next door, they know where to get me.'

'And I thought you were dead?' said the penultimate guy, not waiting to be asked.

118

'And seriously,' said the last guy, 'what's with the deaf mute hunchback? It's like dredging up the most absurd cliché you can think of. Weird serial killer guy. Deaf mute hunchback. What's with you?' he said, pointing at Keanu. 'Deranged, misplaced weirdo? Seriously, really, this place is like some sort of X-Men scenario, all these weirdoes in one place. It's not a barber shop, it's a freak shop.'

Barney had an Ally McBeal moment, imagined picking up Igor's broom, yielding it like Obi Wan with a light saber, and launching a brutal attack on the row of journalists. The pack. The herd. The disease. The disease of tabloid journalists.

Instead he walked slowly to the door and opened it.

'Time's up,' he said. 'Go and write your stories. I'm sure you'll make most of it up anyway.'

'But my hair's not finished,' wailed the guy in the seat.

Barney glanced at him. Right enough, there was a clear discrepancy between the hair around the right and the left ear.

'Go,' he said. 'Go to Wullie in Largs, he'll finish you off. Though you might want to stick with the look, it distracts from the enormity of your nasal passages.'

Cheap. But Barney enjoyed it. And it had the bloke looking in the mirror.

'Out!' barked Barney.

As the pack rose, they could hear footsteps charging along the road towards them, and they all knew that these were footsteps which were not going to go running by. The barber shop was the hottest place in town. Barney turned, just as another man arrived, out of breath, clutching a notebook and a cardboard cup of decaf machiato, with a clip-on lid.

'Tommy Turner,' he said to Barney, 'the *Express*. Is this the weirdo freak shop with the psychotic slaughter-junky barbers and the vampire wolfman cleaner?'

# 6

## The Parting Of
## The Waves

Later that afternoon, once darkness had fallen, Barney and Igor ended up sneaking out the back door of the shop. The journalists had left the premises, but had not gone far. They had waited outside and nearby, as had a growing collection of the public. Word had got around about all the bizarre characters who worked in the freakshop.

While being concerned for his friends, Keanu was actually quite enjoying it, his main worry being that there was nothing terribly interesting about him that would allow him to live up to the others. He felt too normal. I need, he was thinking, to develop some sort of fake characteristic to keep the punters amused. There's nothing worse than being the normal one. You might as well change your name to Zeppo Marx and retire. Or invent that thing that Zeppo Marx invented, and make lots of money.

Keanu opened the shop door and stood on the step, looking out at the massed collective, creating the diversion that Barney and Igor needed in order to escape the flaming torch mob. He had no idea what he was going to say. Back of the mind thinking about Zeppo and what it was that he'd invented which had earned him his millions.

'Where's the serial killer and his deranged, deformed sidekick?' bellowed a voice from the throng, as they began to close in.

Keanu breathed deeply. This was it. His fifteen minutes. He'd tried the blog and not many people were reading. He'd applied for Big Brother and not got close. He'd auditioned for Pop Idol and been embarrassed. He'd written his screenplay and been ignored by Scottish Screen and quickly rejected by the BBC. But what really mattered more than anything else, more than talent or ability or confidence or balls, was luck. Here he was, in front of the nation's media, a curious public beside them, and it bore no relation to anything that he himself had achieved. A mysterious trawler, a brutal murder.

Luck.

'They'll be out in a minute,' he said. Which was true. If they weren't already out. Just not out front. 'They're prepping,' he added.

'And who are you?' came a voice from the back.

'Like, my name is Keanu MacPherson,' said Keanu, holding the palm of his hand up in the classic alien spaceman greeting. 'Agent MacPherson,' he added suddenly, having just thought of something cool.

The questions quickly rose to a great clamour. Agent? Agent of what? Death? FBI? God? MI5? Serious Crime Squad? Avon?

Keanu spent some time trying to quieten the crowd, as if he was refusing to answer until he was given some space. In fact, he had no idea what to say next. Agent?

The door next to the barbershop opened and DCI Frankenstein appeared, flanked by a couple of officers. A quick glance amongst the throng and he spotted the television cameras. Couldn't be too heavy-handed then. Keep it simple.

He had a commanding presence. Quickly the noise settled down, the tumult was extinguished, as they waited for the leading investigating officer to make a statement. The cars which were backed along the road, due to the fact that the crowd were spilled all over it, stopped beeping their horns. An uneasy silence descended.

Frankenstein suddenly felt very powerful. Maybe I don't have to say anything, he thought. Might be best, given that what comes out will inevitably be expletive-laced, which doesn't make anyone look good on tv. So he lifted his arms and signalled the opposite pavement, in a slow but dramatic movement. He repeated the gesture, and then, as the crowd started to file back he waved to the queue of cars to start moving along the road, which hurried the exodus to the other side of the street. The crowd spread out along the promenade and the public element of it at least, took the hint that the police were here and that nothing much else was going to happen, and started to disperse. It was dark and none of the day trippers really wanted to spend the night in Millport. It was time to get the boat back to the mainland.

The journalists hovered with intent, but they were getting to the stage of needing to write their stories up, and for all the silencing aspect of the police presence, there was still a great story that required little embellishment. Not that embellishment would be a stranger to the following morning's papers.

Frankenstein stood with his arms folded, watching as slowly even the reporters started to drift away, already scribbling in their notebooks. Proudfoot had come to the door to stand at his shoulder. She leant on the doorframe and watched the last of the swarm buzz quietly away into the night. And so, in a matter of a couple of minutes, the pavement across the road was as good as deserted.

'That was very impressive,' she said.

'Thank you.'

'I mean, that was like Moses or something. I don't want to give you a big head or anything, but that was just about the coolest thing I've ever seen.'

'You're taking the piss now.'

'No really, if that was in a movie, you'd be played by Paul Newman.'

'Fuck off, Sergeant.'

'I mean, usually, you're more of a Paul Giamatti.'

'I said fuck off.'

She smiled, took a last look at the dispersing multitude, and then turned back inside. Frankenstein looked along the road, feeling a strange sense of satisfaction, then he caught the eye of Keanu, still standing at the door.

'What the fuck are you looking at?' he said.

'That was my fifteen minutes,' said Keanu. 'We only get the one chance, and that was mine.'

'And I just pished all over it.'

'Like, yeah, you did.'

Frankenstein, feeling unusually empathetic, shrugged.

'They'll be back. You'll get another chance. And this time,' he said, 'you'll have time to come up with a better story than being Agent MacPherson.'

MacPherson looked a little sheepish and tried his best to hold Frankenstein's gaze.

'You heard that?'

Frankenstein looked at him for a while, shook his head, and turned back inside the incident room, muttering *agent* as he went. The two police constables who had flanked Frankenstein throughout, checked once more along the road, making sure that there were no journalists or members of the public going to attempt a pincer movement of some sort, then they followed the boss back inside.

Keanu MacPherson stared out to sea. The Marman clamp. A heavy duty, round metal clamp. That was Zeppo's gold at the end of his rainbow. The Marx Brothers never made any movies about that.

## 7

## Himalayan Refuge

Barney didn't head home. Knew enough about this kind of thing to realise that no end of the journalistic throng would have found out where he lived and would more than likely move on from the shop, at some point in the evening, to lingering outside his house. The wolves were gathering.

He headed west, although that wasn't quite as dramatic a statement as it can be if you live in New York or Shanghai. On Cumbrae, there just weren't too many places to go, and although an obvious destination for him would have been the boat back to the mainland, he had no urge whatsoever to leave the island. He wasn't exactly sinking into some eastern philosophical way of thinking, that everything was happening for a reason, and that it would all soon be explained. Nevertheless, his past was not so much catching up with him, it had left him behind and was waiting to ambush him around every corner. He had no desire to run and nowhere to go.

He walked out along West Bay Road. Reached the old Stewart Hotel, the first of the hotels out that way, and turned quickly into the driveway. He hadn't stayed here before, no need, but he was a regular for fish and chips and a pint of cider. That was what he needed now, although he realised that sitting in the dining room would attract someone's attention.

He walked into the hotel, stopped for a second to listen to the sound of the bar and the restaurant. A quiet night, but he had seen enough people through the window to know that he'd rather avoid having to go in. Andrew, the owner, portly, blond, balding, affable, appeared from the kitchen carrying three plates of beef and ale pie.

'Mr Thomson!' he said. 'Had a feeling we'd see you. Don't know why.'

'Have you got a room?' asked Barney quietly.

Andrew stopped for a second, nodded, and then walked quickly through to the restaurant. 'I'll be thirty seconds,' he threw over his shoulder.

Barney relaxed slightly and turned away. Stood idly, looking at the pictures on the lobby walls. The pose of many a man made to wait in a hotel. Millport Bay on a summer's day. A hare. A photograph of Millport from 1905, looking not entirely dissimilar to Millport 21$^{st}$ century.

Andrew appeared, Barney got sucked from his indistinct ruminations.

'Right, Mr Thomson, just let me get a couple of things. If you want to go upstairs, in case any more people come in. I'll get the key. You want a toothbrush, toothpaste?'

Barney nodded, feeling very grateful, then he turned and walked slowly up the stairs. A little surprised that there was still a room available, given the number of the press and police who had descended. Where were they all staying?

It was the largest hotel on the island, two old Victorian residences joined together. Upstairs there was a small landing, four doors off, a short corridor leading to a few more rooms, another flight of stairs to more rooms in the converted attic. Carpet of deep red, pictures of the sea on the walls.

Andrew appeared, clutching a key, a small bag and a newspaper under his arm. Barney's eyes went straight to the paper.

He stood back while the man opened the door to one of the large front rooms, big windows and a wonderful view out over the sea to Little Cumbrae. And the nuclear power station.

They walked into the room, Andrew closed the door behind them without turning on the light. The room was dark, shadows and orange light from the street lights outside.

'Why didn't you just leave the island?' said Andrew.

Barney walked to the window and looked across the road and the grass, out to sea.

'Ghosts,' he said. 'All sorts of ghosts. It doesn't matter where you are. They don't care if you're in Millport, in Scotland, on a plane, on a boat. What's the point of moving?'

Andrew didn't say anything. Barney stared out the window. Half expected to turn round and find that Andrew had vanished into the night. That would be in keeping with the rest of what was happening to him.

'How did you know I'd be coming?' he asked.

'Just had a feeling,' said Andrew, his voice low in the dark. 'And then I saw this, and I knew for certain.'

The bedside light clicked on behind him and Barney turned. A small lamp, he didn't need to squint into the light. Andrew was holding forward a copy of a newspaper. The Largs & Millport Chronicle, "Special Murder Edition." There were only two paragraphs of writing on the front page, as the bulk of it was made up with the banner, sensationalist headline. *Death Comes To Millport: Barbershop Murder-Junky Walks Amongst Us!*

Barney looked at the headline for a full minute. He'd had headlines like this before, but most of them had washed over him. He'd been on the run, he'd been hiding, he hadn't needed to care. Now he'd finally made a life for himself in a small town, and everyone was going to know about it.

'There are sixteen pages,' said Andrew.

'All adverts as usual, I hope,' said Barney.

'No adverts, just large print.'

Barney smiled ruefully. Andrew realised that he was still holding the newspaper up, as if there were people in the audience who hadn't seen the cover, so he folded it up, laid it down on the bed and walked to the door.

'I presume you don't want to eat in the restaurant?'

Barney shook his head.

'I'll bring up fish & chips and a drink for you.'

It was a statement rather than an offer, and he immediately opened the door, walked out and closed it softly behind him. Barney stood for a second and then turned off the small bedside light, pulled up a comfy chair and sat at the window to look out at the early evening.

✂

Later, as he sat at the small table eating his dinner, Barney looked through the newspaper. William Deco had done a thorough research job, working against a frantic deadline, to get his story out there before all the dailies the following morning. Barney might almost have been impressed, if it hadn't been for the fact that there was a sixteen page newspaper special devoted just to him.

*Barney Rising: How It All Started, And The Genesis Of A Perfect Executioner; Blame It On The Parent; The Massacre Of The Monks; Death Becomes Him; Bloodfest Barber And The Trail Of Annihilation; Dead No More! The Undead Zombie Barber Walks Again!; Cabinet Carnage, Who Was Really To Blame?; If You See This Man, Don't Let Him Near You With A Pair Of Scissors; Barbershop Murder Addict Signs Mad Hungarian Hunchback To Death Squad.*

Barney started reading a couple of the articles as he ate his dinner. However, for all of the man's thorough research, very little of what he read even remotely approximated to the truth, and he quickly tired of it. And so, not long after he'd finished eating, and even though it was not late, he laid the newspaper down, turned off the light, slouched down in the window chair, and allowed the tiredness, which had built up through the stress of the day, to wash over him and cover him in a deep, deep sleep.

## 8

## The Worst Of Ghosts

Bernard and the Dog With No Name waited by the makeshift trawler out by Farland Point, eating snacks and hoping that the killer would arrive. They talked lightly of food they had eaten, sandwiches they had made, restaurants they had demolished and snacks they had invented, such as the peanut butter and onion jelly brioche. They looked at the sea and felt cold and glad that they'd been able to get the fire going. And they waited for the killer, part of them hoping that he would turn up, so that they could get on with solving the case, part of them hoping that there would be no Trawler Fiend and no Incredible Captain Death, because the concept of a Trawler Fiend or an Incredible Captain Death who chopped old lady's heads off was not a comforting one.

They waited and they waited. But they waited in vain.

Meanwhile Fred, Selma and Deirdre were back at the small apartment they had appropriated for the duration of their investigation, having outrageously wild three-in-a-bed sex.

✂

Detective Chief Inspector Frank Frankenstein stood at the window of the police incident room, looking out at the dark of night, across the white promenade wall, to the lights on the mainland. Glanced over his shoulder, took in the fact that the room had mostly been cleared. The bulk of the extra police squad had returned to the mainland, only a couple of constables were left, the guys who would man the cell for the night. Proudfoot was also still there, sitting in a corner, trawling through old Barney Thomson files. She still hadn't discussed him with Frankenstein, and remained unaware that the two had had a chat by the graveyard.

'Walk with me, Sergeant,' said Frankenstein suddenly.

Proudfoot looked up from the PC, took a moment, sensed that there was something coming in this chat, and shut the computer down.

Jackets on, the two of them walked out into the night. Frankenstein turned to the right, to the pub Proudfoot presumed, and she fell in beside him. He fiddled a cigarette from his pocket and lit up. They walked in silence for a while, along the front and on into Crichton Street. The pub had been bypassed, and she realised that this was a general mooch about town discussing the facts. For some reason she began to feel uncomfortable with the silence.

'That's really gross, you know,' she said.

He glanced at her. Blew smoke out the corner of his mouth.

'Selfish,' she added. 'If you want to smell repugnant and kill yourself, it's your shout, but to do it to everyone else.'

'Are you all right?' he said.

'My uncle used to compare it to a vote in an election,' she went on. Babbling. 'Does it make any difference if some guy blows smoke in your face? Not really. But enough people blow smoke in your face, you'll get lung cancer. You know, if one person votes...'

'What happened to your uncle?' said Frankenstein, cutting her off. 'Died of lung cancer?'

'Moved to Canada, runs a chain of Vietnamese restaurants in Vancouver,' she replied.

Frankenstein looked at her strangely, confused. Never understood women. Had a soft spot for Proudfoot, so was more likely to put up with her crap than anyone else's.

'You want me to put this out?' he said.

'Sure,' she replied, surprised.

He dropped the cigarette in front of him and stood on it as he walked.

'Now maybe we can talk about Barney Thomson,' he said.

She nodded, thrust her hands deeper into her pockets.

'The sensationalist mince of the press notwithstanding,' said Frankenstein, who had cast a hurried eye over the murder edition special of the Largs & Millport Chronicle, 'we do need to consider his presence on the island when there's all this bad shit happening.'

She still didn't say anything. Like others before her, her husband the ex-DCI Mulholland included, Proudfoot thought Barney incapable of murder, and would be marked down as

129

last suspect on the list of every investigation. All coincidences aside. And there had been a lot of coincidences.

'So, did you have a nice chat with him today?' asked Frankenstein.

'How d'you know we talked?'

'I'm a police officer. I know things. It's my job.'

Round the bay, they passed the police station. Could see Gainsborough inside, looking at some papers. Vaguely wondered what he was doing, but the local policeman had been mostly removed from the investigation and allowed to content himself with whatever it was that local policemen did on these islands in the long, bleak winter months.

'Barney's got nothing to do with it,' she said. 'He's harmless. Kind of different from how I remember him, but he's not a killer.'

'Why different?'

They passed the bay, headed along the road out of town, the road that would take them past the Stewart Hotel, where Barney already slept.

'Seems more self-assured. He used to be bumbling, incompetent, wretchedly lacking in confidence. Dour. Nothing attractive about him whatsoever. Now, there's more of the Sean Connery about him. He's been around, I guess. Come through it all, come out the other side, sanity intact.'

'What makes you, or him, think that he's on the other side?'

'Fair point. And then there's the possibility that he's not Barney Thomson at all. Barney Thomson died at the foot of a cliff, so how come I was sitting having a coffee with him this morning?'

'Different guy would explain the different personality. So maybe he is someone claiming to be Barney Thomson, when in fact he's just some former spotty bore who didn't have a life of his own, so he took on someone else's.'

'I don't think it's that. I'm guessing that he thinks he's Barney Thomson, and doesn't think he's ever been anyone else in the past.'

'So?'

'Haven't a clue,' she said. 'But I don't think it's anything that we're going to get an answer to. I guess we could talk to him again, might as well take the time to establish his movements the past few days. Even then, I'm not sure what we'll do if we get suspicious.'

'You read that stupid newspaper tonight?'

'Yeah.'

'There'll be more of that tomorrow. We might have to bring him in just to save him from the crowd.'

'So where are we going?'

'To be honest, Sergeant, I'm not entirely sure. The investigation is quickly sinking into a quagmire of bloody confusion.'

'I meant, now, where are we going right now?'

'Ah. To see Stan Koppen.'

They were passing the Millerston, the second of the hotels out that way. They glanced in, could see a few people in the bar, could smell the food. He checked his watch.

'Maybe we'll stop in there on the way back,' he muttered, although he doubted they would have the time.

'I've been wondering why we hadn't gone to see him yet,' said Proudfoot.'

'Thought I'd let him stew. Let his defences drop. To be honest, he may be prime suspect material, but I don't think he'd be that stupid. So, I really don't think the guy is going to have gone anywhere. As soon as he heard about the old bird, his defensive wall would have shot up, but now he's had a day to relax again. Probably thinks he's clear for today, and when we get round there he'll be slumped on the sofa, watching porn and pulling his pudding.'

They walked on in silence, just another couple of hundred yards along the road. As they turned the corner, the wind drilled into them with greater force, and they both pulled their coats in more tightly. The hills of Arran were clear of cloud for once, etched against the dark sky.

They could hear music from the Westbourne as they walked by. The blinds were drawn, they couldn't see inside. Avril Lavigne's *Happy Ending*. Reminded Proudfoot of a walking holiday she and Mulholland had taken in Switzerland. A genuine happy ending, unlike poor young Avril and her tale of Shakespearean betrayal.

They reached the small semi-circle of cabins. No lights on in any of them. He glanced at her, wondering if his instinct was going to prove to be inaccurate. Should it be the case that Stan Koppen had fled the island, taken the forty minute trip up the road to the airport, and was already somewhere in middle America on the run, he was going to feel very stupid. He was a confident man, full of hubris and brusque poise, but there's no one, not even the most self-assured, who does not have moments, however fleeting, of testicle crushing fear and doubt.

'Probably watching some sicko-pervo-porn with the lights off,' said Proudfoot, feeling the same fear as Frankenstein.

They came to the door, Frankenstein knocked loudly.

'Sicko-pervo-porn?' he said. 'Is that an actual genre?'

His mind running through the possibilities. Telling the chief superintendent. Telling the press. Waiting for the full details to get out. They had interviewed him the night before because of a tip-off. The person who had made the tip-off was brutally murdered. They then took another twelve hours to go to interview him again, before finding out he was gone and issuing the nationwide alert. It was a job-endingly cataclysmic scenario. Suddenly the assurance he'd had about toying with Koppen, leaving it rest for the day, seemed unbelievably foolish. Five minutes earlier he had explained himself to Proudfoot and it had sounded sensible as it had crossed his lips. And now, now his stomach curled as he contemplated the end of his career.

He knocked again, harder, some of the desperation in him finding its way into the pounding of his fist.

'Kick the door in,' said Proudfoot. 'He's...' and she let the sentence drift off. No point in stating the obvious.

Leg up, heel out, Frankenstein booted hard at the handle and the slight wooden door flew open. Hand in first to the light switch, and they walked quickly into the small main room of the cabin.

Frankenstein's jaw set in stone. Proudfoot would later tell her husband that she had felt a palpable weakening of the knees, a reaction out of a book or a film. She leant against the

132

door and quickly turned away, after her eyes had absorbed the full horror of the scene before them.

✂

'Kingly conclaves stern and cold, where blood with guilt is bought and sold...'

Barney Thomson stirred. Still slumped in his seat by the window, finally being roused from a deep sleep. The voice seemed to be part of a dream, but a dream which woke him up.

'You can never escape guilt, my old friend, it's always there.'

He sat up in his chair, looking out of the window. Saw the reflection in the glass and turned. The monk was sitting on the bed. Barney felt no fear, no awareness of the supernatural. Still dreaming. A waking dream, perhaps, but a dream.

'I'm dreaming,' he said.

The monk smiled and leant forward, holding out his hand. Barney stared it at suspiciously, and then finally leant forward and shook it. A firm grip.

'Feel real enough?' said the monk, smiling, and he clasped his left hand on top of Barney's right, to make the handshake even warmer. 'Good to see you again, old buddy.'

Barney detached himself from the conviviality of the impossible handshake and leant back. Only a vague feeling of uneasiness. More curiosity.

'I killed you,' said Barney. 'On the snow near Durness. I saw you dead. Brother Steven.'

'You died too, buddy,' said Steven. 'Bottom of a cliff. Everyone says so. Yet you're sitting here in front of me as clear as I'm sitting in front of you.'

Barney made a small movement of his hand. Couldn't explain that either.

'So, if we're both dead...?'

'Nobody's saying that anyone's dead, my friend. The finality of death is over-estimated.'

Steven smiled, then he stood up and walked to the window. And now that he was standing up straight, his robes unfurled, Barney could see the red marks in the area of the stomach, and in the back. The marks where the bullet had entered and travelled through his body and out the other side.

'Good view of the power station,' said Steven. 'Doesn't matter where you are in this town, you can see it. It's kind of ominous, don't you think? Got that whole, portending doom bag, like you're just waiting for it to go up. Waiting for the rumble, the accident, and then the whole of the west of Scotland is blanketed in deforming radioactive gloom for decades and centuries.'

He looked down at Barney, noticed that he was staring at the gunshot wounds.

'Some say that everything portends, everything foreshadows. You can watch cherry blossom slowly emerge on a spring morning, and from that draw a prophesy for the world.'

Barney was still trying to extract something from this bizarre encounter. This wasn't guilt. He had no guilt about his part in the death of Brother Steven. It had been an out and out accident, and came only after Brother Steven had gone on a deranged murder spree and was in the process of trying to kill Barney. No guilt.

'This is not just about guilt, my friend,' said Steven. 'There's worse than that in the ultimate reckoning we must all face before God.'

Barney looked up into his face. There was a knock at the door. He turned, the knock seeming to have been against his skull. A dull thud.

'Come in,' he said.

The door opened, and Andrew poked his head round the door.

'Everything ok, Mr Thomson? Just up to collect your plate.'

Barney stared at him, then turned back to the window. Brother Steven was gone.

Of course Brother Steven was gone. Brother Steven was dead. Brother Steven had never been there.

'Aye, it was great, thanks. Sorry, I should have put the plate out on the landing.'

'Ach, don't bother yourself, Mr Thomson.'

As Andrew came fully into the room to lift the plate and the glass, Barney rubbed the palm of his hand, where he could still feel the firm grasp of Brother Steven.

## 9

# Scenes Of Crime Fantastic
# Five (SOCFF)

The wolves had gathered. The police had been mobilised, and another boatload had been brought back across from the mainland, dragged from comfortable evenings in front of the television or down the pub.

Frankenstein's strongest emotion, on discovering the decapitated head of Stan Koppen, had been relief. He would still face questions on why he had not visited this house earlier in the day, but at least it wasn't as bad as the man having done an OJ Simpson, and Frankenstein being hung out to dry.

The body of Koppen had been left sitting upright on the sofa. His head had been severed with a very sharp instrument and left sitting on top of the television. The blood which had run down the television screen had long since hardened, and the sicko-pervo-porn which had been running on a continuous loop, had been playing behind a screen of drip-dried red. The colour of sun-roasted tomatoes.

The pathologist, Dr Trio Semester, had come down from Glasgow, himself sucked from watching an episode of Midsomer Murders, a show he clung to out of loyalty to Bergerac. He had made his initial examination, and was on the point of allowing the head and body to be bagged up. Frankenstein was waiting for a chat, Proudfoot was outside, sitting on the steps of one of the other cabins, looking out over the cruel, black sea.

Semester removed his rubber gloves with a satisfying smack, placed them in the makeshift forensic bin, closed his bag, and wandered over to stand beside Frankenstein, who had watched over him for the previous forty minutes. The two men stared at each other, Semester shrugged.

'He's definitely dead,' he said.

Frankenstein laughed. Semester turned and looked over the crime scene.

'Too early to say the cause of death.'

Frankenstein laughed again.

'You're a sick bastard.'

'Thanks. Died a while ago. At least fourteen hours, maybe twenty. I'll let you know. Either way, it's probably too late to stick the head back on. I mean, they can do amazing things these days, but this...'

Frankenstein was still laughing. Clapped his hand on Semester's shoulder.

'Anything, apart from the obvious, that we should know about? Murder weapon?'

'Well,' said Semester, taking his time, because he rarely said anything without thinking carefully about it, even if it was a sick gag, 'I'd say we're looking for a guy with a sword. Or a very, very big axe. Same as your other headless wonder along the road.'

Frankenstein folded his arms and looked into Koppen's dead eyes.

'You think we're in Highlander territory?' he said seriously. 'Immortals, there can be only one, all that kind of thing?'

'Yeah. I mean, not actual immortals, just someone who watched the movie twenty years after everyone else, and has decided to have a go at it himself.'

Semester nodded at the possibility then patted Frankenstein on the shoulder. 'There's weirder shit than that in the world,' he said.

He walked past Frankenstein to the door, stopped at the step.

'I'll get on with it now, if you can get the body up to the lab as quickly as possible. I'll get what I have to you first thing in the morning. Anything to save having to go home.'

Semester saluted and walked off into the night. Across the short driveway, Proudfoot watched him go, watched the bustle of activity, and then caught Frankenstein's eye. They looked at each other for a while, Frankenstein wondering with the look if he was going to have to get a new sergeant for the job. Everyone knew the delicate balance that was the mind of Detective Sergeant Erin Proudfoot, and this was no longer an investigation into the mysterious disappearance of a couple of guys from a trawler. Suddenly, and unexpectedly, they had a serial killer on their hands. Twenty-four hours earlier they had been in an episode of Scooby Doo. Now they were in a Hannibal Lectar movie. In some ways, for him, that seemed more manageable. Which was not the case for Proudfoot.

A small van pulled to a stop at the bottom of the driveway. A couple of police constables on duty walked quickly over to it, as four people and a dog leapt out.

'Hey,' said the blond man at the head of the gang. 'MI6,' he quipped, flashing a card.

The policeman studied it with curiosity, and then looked round at Frankenstein. Frankenstein, while not exactly ecstatic at the arrival of the security services, waved them through. Fred, Bernard, Selma, Deidre and the Dog With No Name came quickly up the driveway and bounded up the steps to the small cabin.

'The Incredible Captain Death?' said Fred with enthusiasm.

'What?' said Frankenstein looking incredulous, although he invariably looked incredulous at most things.

'The Incredible Captain Death has struck again?' said Fred. 'Another murder!'

'I, em...' he began, but was for once more or less speechless. So, instead of telling Fred to fuck right off, which he was disposed to do, he stood back and ushered the gang into the small front room of the cabin.

The four-people-and-a-dog collective walked in and stood hunched together in the middle of the room.

'Jeepers!' said Deirdre.

'Like, wow, man,' said Bernard, 'this guy's got no head!'

The Dog With No Name barked.

'Let's look for clues,' said Fred. 'There might be something here to point to the killer's true identity.'

He caught Frankenstein's eye, couldn't help but notice the continuing look of scepticism and wonder.

'It's all right, friend,' said Fred, 'there's always someone behind the mask.'

Frankenstein shook his head and turned away. Minced across the driveway and sat down on the step next to Proudfoot. She shuffled over, repositioning her forearms on her knees.

They looked out over the sea. They were spending a lot of time looking out over the sea, but nothing attracts the gaze of even the most hardened heart like a large body of water. They sat for a long time, various police officers came and went. Forensics. Looking for clues. Like Fred and the gang.

'I'd be smoking by now,' said Frankenstein, 'but I'm not, so that I don't kill you. Or your uncle......I just wanted you to know.'

She smiled weakly, pulled her coat more closely to her. She was cold, sitting here so long in still silence.

Soon be Christmas, she thought. Six weeks. She and Mulholland were going to spend a couple of nights on Skye. Was she going to be in any mood for it now? This would take longer than six weeks to recover from.

'Who are those guys?' she asked. 'The ones with the dog. I wasn't listening.'

'MI6.'

'You're kidding?'

'MI6. I checked them out. Not that any cunt will tell me why they're here, sticking their noses into our investigation, but what the hell. If they help solve the crime so that we can get back to Glasgow, I'll take anything.'

'You must be desperate.'

'Sergeant, I'm getting that way. That was a sick weird guy who did that in there, as sick as the other one he did last night. Assuming we're only dealing with one guy, and it's too scary to think that there might be more than one of them in a wee place like this. I hate this. It's a shitty crime to be investigating. I hate it, I want off it, but I'm not so stupid as to want to be pulled. Which I might well have been had Koppen done a runner, rather than had his head lopped off. As it is, I'll still have some explaining to do when the Chief gets the full story.'

She had nothing to say. It was a horrible investigation, for all sorts of reasons. Sitting here staring out at the sea wasn't really helping anyone, but there had to be some amount of reflection in any case. Thoughts never became coherent if you didn't take the time to let them fall into place.

'They think there's a masked killer called The Incredible Captain Death,' said Frankenstein, and then he started to laugh.

'What? Who?'

'Four guys and a dog over there. They're calling the killer The Incredible Captain Death.'

'MI6? And they're calling the killer The Incredible Captain Death?'

Frankenstein was laughing harder. He nodded, started coughing. It was infectious, Proudfoot leant forward, hand running through her hair, a curious smile giving way to laughter. Cathartic laughter.

In the bushes across the road, the freelance photographer, who sold every photograph he took to Getty Images, was lurking in the bushes. He got a couple of good shots of the two principle investigating officers in the dark and sinister case of The Incredible Captain Death, besides themselves laughing. After taking the pictures, he stood up, still obscured by shrubbery and darkness, surveyed the crime scene, and decided that it was time to upload everything that he'd just done.

'That's a wrap,' he said to himself.

## 10

## The Millport Dawn

A sunny day, Barney woken by the light, the sun cutting across the room. He lay still for a long time, trying to piece everything together. Truth and imagination. Where he was and why he was lying in a strange bed. He remembered Brother Steven.

He finally sat up and looked out the window. The familiar view, the world was unchanging.

He noticed the pile of newspapers sitting on the table just inside the door and, draped over the armchair, a clean set of clothes. It was like he'd been unconscious in a Bond movie. Checked his watch. 7:45am. Hadn't missed much. Still forty-five minutes before he had to open the shop. If he was going to open the shop.

He slid out of bed and walked over to the newspapers. There was a small note placed on top from Andrew: *Thought you might like to see these*. Barney scrunched the note up and threw it into the bin, then looked at the front page of the Scotsman. *Barber Surgeon Back With A Killer Bang*. He started to read the report, but then moved the paper to the side and leafed quickly through the headlines in the other papers.

The Mail: *He's A Killer All Right, But Is He Also An Illegal Immigrant?*; The Herald: *Hairdressing Fiend In LibDem Leadership Bid*; The Sun: *Amazing Sex Secrets of Barbershop Death Junky*; The Express: *MI6 Insider Claims Diana Still Dead!*; The Mirror: *Bloody Killer Mauls Next Victim, Trawler Heroes Feared Slain*; The Times: *"I Did It!" Bastard Killer Confesses All To The Times*; The Star: *Police Laugh-a-thon As Death Toll Soars*; The Independent: *Mass Millport Slaughter Fails to Stem Planet Population Growth, World Running Out of Water*; The Guardian: *Guardian Re-Re-Launch Unaffected By Killer's Return*; The Daily Record: *Killer Barber In Incredible Captain Death Head Slash Thriller*; The Telegraph: *Unlucky Barber Once More Caught Up In Death Frenzy, Likely To Be Unfairly Persecuted*.

Barney piled them up, turned away and walked to the window. The road outside was quiet. A few cars parked, none driving by. No pedestrians. A woman and a dog in amongst the long grass on the other side of the football field. A couple of kids on the charge across the grass, a smaller dog running wild between their legs.

After newspaper headlines like that you might expect to see a horde of expectant rumour desperadoes on the doorstep, Barney playing the part of Graham Chapman in *The Life of Brian*, standing naked at the window to find a crowd of hundreds at his feet. But there was no one. And that wouldn't be because there was no interest or there were no rumourmongers. Andrew had been as good as his word. Hadn't told a soul. Discretion was something rare, to be prized in this age.

Barney turned away from the window and went into the bathroom, removed his t-shirt and boxer shorts and stepped into a steaming hot shower.

✂

Fifteen minutes later, as he got to the bottom of the stairs, Andrew appeared from the bar, as if on cue. The two men looked at each other for a second, Barney shrugged.

'I was just about to bring your breakfast up,' said Andrew. 'Thought you might need a full Scottish.'

'I appreciate it,' said Barney. 'When the ghosts are coming into your room at night, might as well get out there and face whatever tune is playing. Which way for breakfast?'

'Just into your left,' said Andrew, then he took a step closer and lowered his voice. 'A word of warning. There are three journalists in there, and someone else, I don't have a clue who it is. Watch him. The guy in the gorilla mask.'

Barney smiled curiously, patted Andrew appreciatively on the shoulder and walked through to the small breakfast room. It was the room directly below Barney's, and the sun was streaming straight in, making it bright and warm.

There were three people sitting at the table by the window, talking in low voices, although the room was small enough that everything was clear. Their topic of discussion appeared to be whether or not the legendary outlaw Barney Thomson

142

was also The Incredible Captain Death. Or the Trawler Fiend. Three tables were empty. There was one other table, occupied by a lone figure, currently eating scrambled egg, bacon, mushrooms, two types of sausage and black pudding, with a full rack of toast and a teapot overflowing with abundance.

He glanced at Barney as he entered. He was wearing a grey jersey, light blue jeans. It was clearly a man, but his face was obscured by a full-head gorilla mask. The holes for the eyes and mouth were pronounced enough to allow good vision and space into which a full fried breakfast could easily be fitted.

Barney nodded at the guy in the mask, the masked head nodded back with, if Barney wasn't mistaken, a certain amount of panache.

'Barney,' it said.

Barney couldn't stop himself staring at it. He had become, he liked to think, a fairly cool guy over the years. Maybe not Sean Connery, as some claimed, maybe not Clint Eastwood, but reasonably cool. Val Kilmer in Tombstone, at the very least. However, the past few days, the visitations, the remembrances of his past, they had dented that cool. He was on edge, he no longer had the air of a man that women would be automatically drawn to. And he had become the kind of guy apt to stare at men in masks. Particularly when he was sure that he recognised the voice, even if he couldn't place it straight away.

'You look worried, Barney,' it said. 'Tired. You should get more sleep at night. Or maybe you can't. Can you sleep at night, Barney? After all that you've done and all you've got away with? Can you sleep at night, never having faced your reckoning?'

Barney tried to look through the mask, tried to place the voice, but there wasn't a single clear thought to be had in his head.

'We'll all be judged, Barney,' said the gorilla. 'You can't escape.'

'Who by?' said Barney, finally finding a voice. 'The courts? God? History?'

The gorilla carefully bit off the end of a long, round sausage. Barney could see the teeth behind the mask. Sharp points, like a pike or a barracuda. Felt the shiver of unease, a shiver that he was feeling more and more each day, as the incidence of ghosts escalated.

He forced himself to turn away and sit down at a small table. Looked down the room, caught the eye of one of the reporters sitting at the window table. The guy showed no sign of recognition and looked back at his coffee and toast.

'Humanity, Barney,' said the gorilla from behind the mask. 'The same as judges everything. Humanity. And we're a vindictive collection of bastards, aren't we? Not one of us quick to forgive. Not me, not Chris.'

Barney turned quickly, unable to stop himself. Wullie Henderson. But the gorilla was gone, the table at which he'd been sitting, completely deserted. Not a plate, not a sausage, not an egg, not a cup of coffee.

Barney's head twitched, he felt the shiver, he looked away. His eyes drifted past the window table, noticed that all three of them were looking at him, quickly averting their eyes when he turned in their direction.

Barney stared at them for a few seconds. Footsteps padded into the room. Barney turned again and caught Andrew's eye. Andrew was looking baffled.

'What happened to the guy in the gorilla mask?' he asked.

One of the journalists looked at him with curiosity, the other two ignored him.

'You saw him,' said Barney, a statement of fact. 'One of mine.'

'One of your ghosts?' said Andrew.

Barney nodded. Andrew laid the teapot on the table beside Barney, and placed the rack filled with three warm slices of toast in front of him. The table was already equipped with butter and marmalade, all that Barney would need.

'Aye,' said Barney. 'An old one. The one who started it all.'

He stared past the collective, out at the day. Lost in thought. Things didn't happen without reason.

'Can I get you a hot breakfast?' asked Andrew, slightly unnerved by the disappearing guy in the mask – he'd thought it had been the Daily Express journalist from room number six

144

– but didn't like to display any sign of anxiety to the customer.

Somehow the question found a way in.

'Two fried eggs, bacon,' said Barney.

Andrew nodded. He glanced at the other table to ascertain whether more toast was required, and then turned quietly away and out of the breakfast room.

Barney sat in silence, the three journalists had fallen into tranquillity. A soporific calm, born of the morning and the food and the warmth of the sun. A melancholic calm. A car drove past, but somehow even that seemed muted and lethargic, a fleeting nod in the direction of a life outside the walls of the room.

Barney buttered a piece of toast, the sound of the crunching knife filling the room. One of the reporters heard the crunch, reached for some toast, and discovered a minute after Andrew had gone that more was required.

He caught the eye of one of the others at the table, then the three of them shared a look. But they weren't thinking about toast.

Sometimes they work in packs, sometimes as individuals against the rest. This was a tailor-made pack situation.

'You're not Barney Thomson, are you?' said the guy sitting nearest to Barney.

Barney looked up, having had his head down, immersed in thought and food and a cup of tea.

'Who are you?' he asked brusquely. Already defensive, even though he told himself that defensive was not going to help him in this situation. If anything, it would make matters much worse.

'Evan Blikla,' he said. 'Daily Telegraph. I mean, I'm freelance now, but you know how it is. They laid me off, now they pay me per article, and of course it costs them much more and I earn a lot more. Suits me. These other guys are more or less the same. It's how it works these days.'

'Why did you feel the need to tell me all of that?' asked Barney.

'Background information,' said Evan Blikla. 'Seriously, you're Barney Thomson, the serial killer?'

'I'm Barney Thomson, the bloke,' said Barney. 'I've never killed a cereal in my life.'

'Have you been questioned by the police in relation to the two murders on the island?'

'Two murders?' said Barney. 'Does that include the dead crew member of the trawler?'

There was a moment's hesitation from the three, and then one of them pointed his pen at Barney, a pen which he had produced from nowhere, along with a notebook. In order to write down one word in every three, before rearranging those words into an order of his choosing.

'Smooth, Barney,' he said. 'Almost as if you're not responsible.'

'Were you abused as a child?'

'Do you see yourself as some sort of avenging angel of God?'

'What's your favourite part? The look on their face just before they realise you're going to strike them down, or the first scream of agony, torture and despair, and the realisation of inevitable death?'

'When you disappear for years at a time, do you go to Darfur and the Congo and that kind of place, where you can kill at will, and you just blend in with everyone else?'

'I've been authorised by my newspaper to offer you eighty-five thousand dollars for exclusive rights to your story.'

'Don't even think about it, we can go to ninety-five.'

'Name your price,' said the third.

Footsteps in the doorway. Andrew was there, armed with a rack of toast and a fresh pot of tea. He looked sternly at the window table. The three members of the press corps looked sheepish, little kids standing in front of the headmaster.

'Are they bothering you, Mr Thomson?' he asked, without taking his eyes off them.

'Aye,' said Barney, 'but I can take it.'

Andrew looked harshly at each of the members of the journalist's ring.

'I'll not give you your toast,' he said.

'Sorry,' said one of them in a small voice.

'Yeah, me too.'

146

The third one had been well versed by a succession of editors in never apologising. He nodded his head and stared at the floor. Andrew walked forward and placed the toast and tea on the table, then turned slowly, raising his eyebrows in a gesture of solidarity with Barney. Barney shrugged and smiled his appreciation.

Andrew left, but a word from a strong man was all that had been needed. Barney ate the rest of his breakfast in peace. However, once they had demolished the fresh toast, which didn't take long, the journalists dispersed and scurried away in search of electronic notebooks and laptops and a quiet place to take to their cell phones.

## 11

## Raindrops Keep Falling
## On My Head

Barney took to the hills behind the Stewart Hotel and cut along to his right, up amongst the gorse bushes, out of sight of the road below. Wearing a coat, the collar pulled up high, and a hat pulled low over his ears. A cold morning, but no harm in at least marginally disguising himself.

In no rush to get to the shop, but he had no intention of not going. It was time to face up to his next fifteen minutes in the sun. Get it over with and let them move on to the next poor sod. He came out up the farm road, just opposite the bowling green, intent on going down along Howard, right down the hill at Church, turn right at the bottom to the shop. A quick route. Knew that he was going to have to talk to the police this morning, and that in fact it might be better just to go straight there and get it over with, but he wanted to go to the shop first. Force his way through the crowds, if he could, speak to Keanu and Igor, sort out a few things, and then hand himself over to the police next door and see what became of him. Assuming the police would take him. Frankenstein did not seem the knee-jerk, jump to conclusions type.

He turned the corner onto Stuart Street, striding confidently. Wondering how many people would be waiting outside the shop, and determined to confront his fate head-on.

No one. Stuart Street was as busy, or as deserted, as it usually was at this time on any other morning in November. Barney felt the force of the wind and quickened his stride. He was trying to be cool, trying to be George Clooney, unsurprised by anything, but he seemed to be failing, literally at every turn.

He got to the shop some twenty minutes after opening time. He opened the door to find Igor sweeping up and Keanu cutting the hair of one of the town's old regulars, Ginger Rogers. Another of them, miserable old James McGuire, was waiting on the bench.

Barney closed the door behind him and looked curiously around the assembled company.

'You're here at last,' grumbled McGuire, not one to be short of a complaint. 'You don't think it's murder on my acute vertebrae scolorium to be sitting on this bench. If you can call it a bench. It's more like two bits of wood stuck together with broken glass.'

'I'll be right with you, James,' said Barney, taking off his coat and hat. 'Quieter than I expected,' he said to Igor and Keanu.

'Arf!' exclaimed Igor, obviously surprised but pleased to see Barney.

'Spent the night at the Stewart, getting my head together. Not that I even remotely achieved my objective.'

'I got here just before eight,' said Keanu. 'Thought I'd open up before there was too much bedlam. I was too late of course. It was like nineteen eighty-five Madonna fever, you know. It was like the Beatles arriving in America. Except of course, I wasn't the Beatles, I was Gerry and the Pacemakers, and America didn't want to see me. So I got in here, a couple of folk came in feigning interest in getting their hair cut, but you know, mostly folk waited outside. Then, about fifteen minutes ago, word got around that there'd been another murder, and like, you know, like wham, they were gone, man. Totally gone.'

'I heard about that at the hotel,' said Barney. 'Old man Koppen. I don't know, wasn't like her...'

'No!' said Ginger Rogers, bursting with information. Barney stopped what he'd started, which was gathering his tools together to cut the hair of McGuire.

'Oh, there you go,' said McGuire, 'give the man pause why don't you? As if I haven't been waiting long enough to get my hair cut. At this rate I'll be looking like Alice Cooper before I get anywhere near the barber's chair, and God knows what all that extra weight on my head will do to my neck muscles.'

'Who is it this time?' asked Barney, unconsciously reacting to McGuire by sorting out the comb and scissors and getting the cape ready.

'Ward Bracken,' said Keanu. 'Been dead a couple of days they say. Killed during the storm. Old Thomas Peterson just found the body this morning when he went round to borrow his tv. And you know what Peterson's like. That's him screwed for the rest of his puff.'

Barney let out a long sigh. Ward Bracken. Another of the ancient collective that made up the town, and now another one of them who was dead.

'Come on,' he said to McGuire, 'you're up.'

'I heard Bracken had had his head chopped off and put on top of the tv while he was watching porn,' said Ginger Rogers, with some relish.

'That was Koppen, you eejit!' exclaimed McGuire, as he took his place at the big chair. 'Bracken had had a small explosive device placed inside his ear that literally blew his head off.'

'Come on, fellas,' said Keanu, 'stop making stuff up.'

'Arf!'

'It's bad enough as it is,' said Keanu. 'Three dead, each with a beautiful clean cut of an axe.'

He hesitated and then decided not to say anything else. A gruesome moment, when he realised he was matter-of-factly discussing the grotesque, as if talking about the previous night's television. This was real, it was horrible and it was people they knew.

'Arf,' said Igor quietly, and he went back to sweeping the floor at the rear of the shop, his hunch seeming to drive him a little bit lower than he already was.

Barney started to cut the thin hair on the top of McGuire's head, the gentle click of the scissors now loud in a shop suddenly brought to silence. Barney had seen and heard too much of this in his life. Ginger Rogers felt slightly abashed, even though he had endless stories from the Ardennes in '44 which seemed to him to have some correlation with the horrific events now taking place in Millport. Keanu had sunk into sullen silence, recalling the fact that he had cut the hair of both of the male victims. This kind of strange event held no end of ghosts for Igor.

McGuire, however, was not so perturbed.

'Make sure you do a good job up there now. If you get sent off to prison, this is going to have to last me a long while.'

Barney caught his eye in the mirror. The door opened. He turned slowly, somehow having forgotten his mauling in that morning's press, expecting it to be just another old geezer wanting a Josh Lucas or a Leonardo.

Detective Sergeant Proudfoot closed the door behind her against the cold November wind. She looked at Barney and nodded sympathetically.

'It's time,' she said.

Barney stood back from his cut. Probably for the best, he thought, although he didn't think for a second that it was going to take him away from the weirdness which was now enveloping his every day.

'Typical,' said McGuire. 'Here I am, getting the best haircut I've probably ever had in my life, and along come the polis to completely mess it up. I'm shocked. I don't think I've ever been this amazed. Really, I'm stunned. I cannot believe that I'm sitting here and something bad has happened to me.'

Barney caught his eye in the mirror and silenced the sarcasm.

'Have I got time to finish cutting the miserable remnants of this gentleman's hair?' asked Barney.

McGuire gave him a look, but it was more dumb acceptance and acknowledgement of the remark, than insult.

'Your young friend there can finish him off,' she said. 'You'd better come now.'

Barney hesitated, scissors poised above the crusty old napper of James McGuire, and then he turned and laid down his implements and smiled at Keanu.

'He's all yours, son,' he said.

Barney washed his hands, dried them slowly, and put on his coat. He turned to look at his friends in the shop, realised that they were all watching him. Igor, Keanu, McGuire and Ginger Rogers. Watching him. Viewing the last acts of the condemned man. They had all read the papers that morning, mostly with a large bout of scepticism, but equally aware that a man cannot have that kind of public pillory heaped upon him without the police being seen to be doing something.

And as he got ready to go, not one of them in the shop felt for a second that Barney would ever be back.

Igor approached him, stood before him for a second. Wanted to hug the man, his friend. He had been grudgingly accepted in this town before, but Barney had been the first person to truly treat him as an equal. Not knowing what to do in this unfamiliar, emotional situation, Igor held out his hand. Barney shook it and smiled, and then pulled Igor towards him and embraced him.

'I'll be back soon enough, my friend,' he said. 'I haven't done anything wrong.'

He patted Igor on the back then disengaged. Could sense that there were tears in Igor and didn't want to put the man through that. He walked quickly to Keanu, shook his hand.

'You'll stay on until I get back?' he said.

'Of course.'

'Good. Igor's in charge, though, ok? I want no power struggle in my absence.'

He smiled at the joke, Keanu couldn't raise the smile to join him.

'Of course,' he said again.

Barney clapped him on the shoulder and moved away. He embraced the two customers with a quick look. Ginger Rogers was already thinking of the story he could tell around town, of the day they came to get Barney Thomson, a tale that was quickly becoming more Butch and Sundance than the mundane reality of this non-confrontation.

'See you guys,' he said. 'You're in good hands.'

'Take care,' said Ginger Rogers.

'Aye,' said McGuire. 'And watch you don't get shagged up the arse in prison. And watch they polis, bastards the lot of them.'

Barney clapped the old guy on the shoulder as he walked past him, then held out his hands in a gesture of capitulation to Proudfoot.

'Here,' said McGuire from behind him, determined that sentiment would not intrude into any part of his life, 'watch my collar bone, you know how much gyp it gives me.'

'Right,' said Barney, not hearing the last of the old man's complaints, 'I'm all yours.'

She stepped away from the door, opened it and ushered Barney out into the cold. He turned, looked once more around the small audience to his capture, nodded finally at Igor, a nod of reassurance, of determination that he would be back and that Igor should not be overly concerned, and then he stepped out the door, out onto the cold street and the bitter wind. She followed him, quickly closing the door behind.

He was expecting to be directed straight into the incident room next door, instead she ushered him towards a police van which was parked immediately outside the room. A constable leapt from the van and opened the rear door for Proudfoot, who ushered Barney inside and then followed him.

The door slammed shut behind them, and Barney Thomson was, for the first time in his life, in police custody.

# Part III

# 1

## He Went Like One
## That Hath Been Stunned

Back inside, the shop was empty. There were still four people in there, two customers, a barber and a deaf, mute hunchbacked sweeper-upper, but the spirit of the shop was gone, in a way that it hadn't been that morning before Barney had arrived. Now there was no expectation that he was about to turn up, no expectation in fact that he would ever be back. Something had died, and there were none of the four in the shop who did not feel it.

Igor leant on his brush and stood at the window, looking out across the white promenade wall, to the sea and the inscrutability of the waves. Keanu had returned to cutting the hair of Ginger Rogers in sullen silence, somehow feeling that his talents as a barber were strangely diminished, now that Barney was no longer there. Ginger Rogers looked at himself in the mirror, imagining the gun battle which had led to Barney's eventual arrest.

Old McGuire sat and stared at his reflection, trying to decide if the small mole on his chin was cancerous. He was, however, unnerved by the silence. He needed noise, even if it was just the sound of his own voice complaining about something.

'Think I might have early onset Alzheimer's,' he said, to break the melancholic tranquillity.

A pause. Igor did not turn. He had felt the vibrations, but did not need the conversation.

'Early onset?' said Ginger Rogers suddenly. 'You're ninety-one!'

'And the way my muscles are going I think I've got motor neurone coming on. And did you see that shite on the tele last night?'

✂

154

DCI Frankenstein and Dr Trio Semester were attending the latest crime scene. Ward Bracken, relatively recent arrival to the town – at least in comparison with all the old fellas who'd been there since being sent home from Gallipoli with shell shock – and his decapitated head.

Frankenstein was standing at the window, looking out over the town and the sea. Had spent so much of the previous few days doing just this. Wondered if that was all the town's people did. If that was all anyone who lived by the sea did. You looked at it long enough, and eventually you felt like you had to go out on it. And then you became beholden to it and then you died. Did anyone live happily by the sea? Did it not always lead you on to wanting something you couldn't truly have?

'That you getting sucked in by the grey mass of moving water?' said Semester, approaching and following his gaze out past Little Cumbrae. 'You're not going to get all nautical on us and start quoting Coleridge, are you?'

'How does anyone ever get anything done here?' he said. 'It's like watching Armageddon.'

Semester glanced at him, curiously.

'You think the end of the world is going to be an ever-changing, yet ever constant landscape, the same year after year after year?'

'I meant the movie with Bruce Willis and Ben Affleck.'

'Ah… Then I still don't get you.'

'You know, you've seen it ten times before. It's an ok movie, not the best, but ok. You're flicking through the channels, searching for something to watch for ten minutes before you go to bed, boom, you come across Armageddon with Bruce Willis and Ben Affleck. You think, this'll do for my ten minutes, and then you see Steve Buscemi and he makes you laugh, and you think, shit, I'd forgotten he was in it, he's pretty funny, and then wham, the next thing you know, it's an hour and a half later and you're still sitting there. Is the film any different from the previous fifty occasions you've seen it? No. But can you stop yourself looking? Not a chance.'

Semester smiled. He had picked up on the allusion after the first sentence, but had been quite happy to listen to Frankenstein unnecessarily explain himself in full.

'Aye,' he said eventually, 'I see what you mean. Like Casablanca.'

'Totally different,' said Frankenstein. 'Casablanca is acknowledged as one of the greatest films of all time. Of course you get sucked in by it when you stumble across it on the tv. But Armageddon. No one's putting that on their all-time list. If someone says to you, what's your favourite all-time movie, you don't even think about it. And yet, can you put it off? No way.'

Semester looked at a small cargo vessel, far out in the Clyde, the other side of Little Cumbrae, heading north and about to be obscured by the island.

'You want to hear about our headless friend here?' asked Semester, thinking that he might as well drag things back to the present, aware perhaps that he too could be sucked in to endlessly looking at the sea.

'Tell me about Stan Koppen first,' said Frankenstein.

He knew that Semester had worked through the night, and that he had already been on his way back down to the island when the news had come through of the discovery of a yet another two day old corpse.

'Well, to be honest, it would be telling you the same thing. A clean cut, both times. The woman as well. Same weapon each time, cut by the same hand. It wasn't a completely straight blade, so we're looking at a large axe head.'

'Definitely an axe?'

'Well, it wasn't a cucumber.'

Frankenstein snorted. 'How large an axe? Will you be able to pin it down? A brand?'

'What can I say? It wasn't small, not the type your Mr Average might have in his shed because he bought it once when it was on offer in B&Q. Something bigger.'

'Prints, identifying marks of any sort?'

'He entered by whatever means your guys will have established, he wore gloves, he chopped their heads off, he

156

left. From what I hear, it doesn't look like he even had any blood on his shoes.'

'And this guy was definitely first of the three murders on the island?' said Frankenstein.

Semester nodded, walked over and gently kicked the leg.

'Feel that,' he said glibly. 'Stiff as a board. If I could get erections that stiff these days the wife would be a lot happier.'

'Nice,' said Frankenstein.

'This guy,' said Semester, 'during the storm some time. I'll try to pin that down a bit further, but don't get too excited waiting. Then Nelly Johnson the following night and Stan Koppen not long after. Could be the killer left old Nelly's house and went straight round to Stan's.'

Frankenstein walked past him, heading for the door. Time to get on with establishing some sort of mundane line of inquiry, time to get away from the decapitated heads.

'Let me know if you get anything else,' he threw over his shoulder.

'Sure,' said Semester, 'you let me know if there's anyone left alive on the island by the weekend.'

Frankenstein hesitated, smiled and then walked quickly out of the small house. As soon as he had stepped onto the short path he saw them, charging in through the front gate with unbridled enthusiasm.

'Jeepers, Detective Frankenstein,' said Selma, 'we heard there'd been another beheading.'

'Like, totally,' said Bernard. 'It's the Trawler Fiend again!'

'The Incredible Captain Death!' ejaculated Fred, pushing for his favourite serial killer appellation of the moment.

The gang of four and the dog stopped. Frankenstein looked around them all, not in the mood for their youthful enthusiasm. Not that he would have been able to imagine a time when he would ever have been in a mood for it.

'Just like the security services,' he said. 'Turn up after everyone else has done all the work.'

'We were looking for clues down at the boatyard,' said Fred.

'It was creepy!' said Bernard.

'Why do you people have to shout everything you say?' asked Frankenstein. 'Jesus, on you go. The pathologist is still

157

in there. You'll like him, he performs his work to a laugh track.'

'Gee, thanks, Chief Inspector,' said Deirdre.

'You sure were a help,' said Fred, 'we're just going to go into the house and look for clues!'

Frankenstein waved a desultory hand as he opened the gate. Maybe, he was thinking, it was time to check with MI6 again, just to make sure.

# 2

## On A Pale Afternoon

Barney sat in a small room, on a chair at a desk, looking at a blank wall. There was a police constable standing by the door. A clock on the wall, the second hand ticking silently round. Occasionally he would turn and look at it, but only because it was there. He wasn't interested in the time.

He wasn't thinking about the future. No thoughts of where this might take him, the prison in which he might end up. He had wandered long and restlessly, and had never really known what it would take to allow him to settle. Now, maybe, this was it. His reckoning. Face up to the past, answer the questions, and then finally he might be able to find peace. Albeit, peace from inside a prison cell.

His list of crimes:

1. Manslaughter. Accidentally stabbing his boss Wullie Henderson in the chest with a pair of scissors.

2. Failing to report the crime. Rather than calling the police and confessing all, he'd bundled the body into the back of his car and taken it round to his mum's.

3. Failing to report his mother's crimes. On discovering that his mother had been a rabid serial killer, with a freezer stacked full of butchered bodies, he'd taken them all to a rubbish dump, rather than call the police. Or Channel 4. Such a pity that it had all happened before the current trend for reality tv.

4. More manslaughter. Accidentally killed his work colleague Chris by knocking him over with a broom. Probably more seriously, he had then set up Chris's flat to make it look like he had been the serial killer, rather than Barney's mum. As part of this nefarious plan, he had turfed Chris's body into a loch.

5. Another touch of manslaughter. While wrestling with Brother Steven – the Monastery Murderer – he had inadvertently shot the guy in the stomach. The fact that there had been two police officers in attendance who had witnessed

159

this and then sent him on his way notwithstanding, it was still a charge that he would need to answer in court.

And that was more or less that. There had been other adventures, he had had the misfortune to stumble across murderers, weirdoes, crackpots and deranged psychopaths at every turn, but that had been his fate. Of the events that he could control or really would have to answer for, the list was short and several years in the past.

Crimes, however, always stuck around for a long time. And there was the possibility of him having to answer to no end of deeds for which he was not responsible.

Everything in life has a momentum. Sport, romance, relationships, family, business, travel, politics. Things stagnate, things build up speed, life goes on. Once something has a certain impetus behind it, then sometimes there can be no stopping it.

The door opened, footsteps. Barney looked up as the two chairs were pulled away from the desk opposite him. Frankenstein and Proudfoot. They sat down, they looked across at Barney.

Everyone stared at everyone else. The clock turned silently. Barney found himself looking up at it. Just because it was there.

'Constable,' said Frankenstein, 'you can leave us now. Note it down that I asked you to.'

The constable at the door, PC Harrington – who had been staring at the floor, bored and disinterested, thinking about Scarlett Johansson, working on the principle that since anything in life is possible, anything, there must be some way for him to meet her, and in a situation where she wasn't going to think that he was weird – snapped out of his torpor and looked at Frankenstein. He'd heard his voice, but the words hadn't gone in. Frankenstein wasn't familiar with Constable Harrington, therefore there was a little confusion.

'You want to stick to your post, Constable?' he said.

'What? Sir? Yes, I should stick to my post.'

'I'd like you to leave.'

'You want me to leave?'

160

'Jesus Christ, how hard is this? Constable, get out. Go and arrest someone.'

Constable Harrington finally got the hint, opened the door and stepped out into corridor, not entirely sure what had just happened. And no nearer to meeting Scarlett Johansson.

The door closed. Frankenstein watched it for a second, then turned to Barney.

'The way I see it,' he said, 'we've got you on manslaughter, perverting the course of justice and obstruction. Probably a lot more besides, and that's just based on the things that we know are true. Then there are all the rumours and your possible involvement with no end of other murders. The fact that everywhere you go, people get killed. It's piling up.'

He paused. Stared across at Barney. Barney met his eye, Proudfoot looked at the table.

'How do you see it stacking up for you so far?' said Frankenstein.

Barney raised an eyebrow. Glanced at Proudfoot, looked back at the DCI.

'You think I'm going to confess to everything, with no lawyer contact and after you've sent the constable out?' said Barney. 'Is this where you leap up, grab my head and bang it off the table?'

Proudfoot smiled.

'Piss off,' said Frankenstein. 'You've been watching too much tv.'

Barney shrugged. Felt a little stupid about the remark. Frankenstein shook his head.

'I had you down for more intelligence than that,' he said.

'Well what do you want me to think so far?' said Barney. 'No phone call, no lawyer, no real reason to arrest me right now at this minute other than the fact that the press are all over me, and yet you bring me in.'

'I haven't arrested you,' said Frankenstein.

'So I can go?'

Frankenstein looked at Proudfoot, turned back to Barney. Held his hands out in a conciliatory gesture.

'Sure,' he said. 'If that's what you want to do.'

Barney stared ahead. His eyes met Frankenstein's, but they weren't looking at him. They were staring into dead space. Not even calculating the odds. Barney wasn't going anywhere and it seemed that everyone in the room knew it.

'But you don't, do you?' said Frankenstein, confirming Barney's thought. 'You've been on the run long enough. There's not many people happy who constantly wander. It's human nature to have somewhere to call home, even if it seems dull. We need dull in our lives, we need that monotonous constant, somewhere to go back to. To slow down or to pick back up, depending what the rest of our lives bring. But you, you don't have it, do you? You wander from place to place and you never find peace. Because that's what home is. Peace. And you don't have any.'

Proudfoot quickly glanced sideways at her boss. He liked to come across as thick-skinned, brusque. But he didn't just know Scooby Doo.

'I thought maybe it was Millport,' said Barney, aware that Frankenstein's one minute appreciation of the human spirit was luring him into conversation. Proudfoot may have had increasing regard for her DCI, but to Barney it was all a game. Given, however, that he had every intention of owning up to any genuine charges which were thrown his way, and that he didn't actually care whether or not that was done in front of a lawyer, it didn't seem to matter.

'What happened?'

Barney made a small gesture with his hands.

'The crew of a trawler went missing, an old woman got her head sliced off...'

'And so your ever decreasing circle went on...'

'So it seems.'

'Why Millport?' he asked quickly.

Barney wondered if Frankenstein thought that he was playing his prisoner, if he was going to walk out of there and say to his sergeant, 'That guy was putty. Putty!' However, he wasn't bothered by it, wasn't amused by it either. Things would pan out the way they were going to and at some point he would come out the other side. The only question was where that was going to be.

162

'Holidays forty years ago. Happy days. Saw the barbershop for sale in a Glasgow paper, came back to look, it felt like home.'

'Peace.'

'Peace.'

Frankenstein placed his hands on the table in a sudden gesture of finality. He leant forward, a panther poised to leap on his prey, although in this case it was a panther poised to walk out and leave his prey to it.

'Mr Thomson, I'll be honest. I haven't the faintest idea what to make of you. Or your weird life. Or the fact that you used to be dead, yet here you are and you appear to be who you say you are. And do I think you're responsible for the spate of deaths on the little island over there? Not for a second. You might be, I'm not ruling anything out, but if I was to put money on it, it wouldn't be you. Of course, the sad fact of this investigation so far is that I wouldn't even know where to begin placing my money. No real clues, no suspects. Apart from you. Which is why you're here. The press are all over you, they'd be all over me until I brought you in, as was my Superintendent this morning, demanding to know why you were still at large. So, that's why you're here. To protect you from yourself, or more accurately, to protect you from your reputation, deserved or otherwise. You've not been arrested, I'm not about to charge you with anything. I sense, however, that you might want to have a chat about your past. So, I'm going to leave you to talk to my sergeant, who I believe you know from your previous days of actual crime. She's going to tell me everything you tell her. We'll hold you here for a day or two, in the hope that...well, God knows. That we find the killer in the meantime? That the media forget about you? This is sticking plaster police work, I admit it. Seat of my pants. And I know, I know, I'm monologuing. I'm leaving, you two have a chat. I can't promise you that we won't charge you in connection with any of the previous stuff you did, and I can't promise you that we'll ever find you your peace that you've been searching for.'

He stood up, his words having been delivered at machine gun pace. He looked down at Proudfoot.

'Sergeant,' he said, and then he was gone, the door closed firmly behind him.

Barney looked across the desk at Proudfoot, who produced a notepad from her pocket and laid it on the desk.

'Where are we exactly?' asked Barney.

'Saltcoats,' said Proudfoot.

Barney smiled and nodded. Had never been to Saltcoats in all his years of holidays on the Clyde. Passed through it on the train, had looked out at the people and the cold beaches.

'No tape recorder?' he said.

'Really, Barney,' she said, 'this is so informal it's not happening. We don't want to get into charging you with all that crap from before if we can help it. You were dead, it's a shame we can't just leave it at that. So, no tape recorder. We'd get hung if we did that. Just a chat, a few notes, you tell me what you feel like telling me.'

Barney sat back, let out a sigh. Time to tell his story, to a sympathetic audience. Trusted her completely, wasn't even too bothered if it turned out that he was wrong to do that. Looked round behind him to check if he'd missed the large two-way mirror that you always get in the movies.

'This is Saltcoats,' said Proudfoot, reading his mind.

He smiled. Looked into her eyes, read the genuine smile that was returned there. Old friends, it seemed, however odd that might have been.

'I worked in a shop,' he said suddenly, the story finally getting the chance to burst forth, 'me and two young guys. I was Jack Nicholson in *About Schmidt*, they were Bill and Ted...'

# 3

## Bladestone

Frankenstein sighed heavily. Turned away from the sea, the view that was beginning to bewitch him. He didn't like getting bewitched by anything. Usually it was women. Occasionally a tv series. But the sea? He needed to get back up to Glasgow, where maybe he could content himself with occasional glances at the river.

He was back on the island, back in Millport. Always going somewhere he'd already been. The place was so small, so few people, it didn't seem credible that so much carnage would happen and no one knew anything about it. And this was no horror movie small town, where all the villagers were sinister and obviously hiding a dark secret. They had small town sensibilities, sure enough, but there was nothing sinister about them. They were making their presumptions that there was a reason each of the people had been murdered, and if they themselves did not feel that they were in the firing line, then it didn't affect them and it didn't cause them any fear. Just curiosity. Something to talk about, which was unexpected in this place in late autumn.

And so Frankenstein was baffled. And he no more liked being baffled than he liked being bewitched.

He was walking past the football pitch. Glanced round at the Stewart Hotel, could see a couple of journalists sitting in the bar. Unconsciously pulled up the collar of his coat and hoped they wouldn't notice him. They'd be along for the ride in a shot, reality tv on their doorstep.

Walked on, turned left off the main road and down the short track to the boat yard. Creaked open the gate and walked inside, past the main building and into the centre of the yard, in amongst the few yachts and small vessels which still came here for the winter.

There was no one around, no one working on any of the boats, even though most of them were under some kind of repair, and all of them had been battered around by the severity of the recent storm. He turned full circle, counting. Seventeen boats in all, that was it. Not much of a yard. Nothing substantial, nothing even as large as the trawler the *Bitter Wind*. Presumably the individual boat owners hadn't had time yet to come down and check. Maybe they wouldn't until the spring now. Maybe that was why they paid to be in a boat yard, so that the yard master could take care of all that kind of thing. Frankenstein stood there realising that he knew nothing about boats, or the yards, or the people who went out in the boats.

There were a couple of thirty-five foot yachts, a few smaller yachts. A number of small motor boats of various types, wooden and plastic. Frankenstein had no feel for this kind of thing at all. Decided, immediately, that he would have to find someone from amongst the police investigation team with more than basic knowledge of this stuff, and then come back here with him.

He shook his head at the thought of the *Bitter Wind*. He had almost forgotten about the *Bitter Wind* and the missing trawlermen. So much more recent death and bloody murder, that he had lost sight of working out how to find the two men who could possibly still be alive. Not that he thought for a second that they were.

'Who the fuck are you?'

The voice barked at him from behind.

Frankenstein turned, confronted by a middle-aged man wiping his dirty hands in a rag, walking towards him, all Wellington boots and hole-filled woollen jumper.

Oh my god, thought Frankenstein, a walking cliché. He whipped his badge from his pocket.

'DCI Frankenstein,' he said. 'Just taking a look around. You're Mr Cudge Bladestone, I take it? You fit the bill.'

'I've had enough of you people,' said Bladestone. 'Two lots of incompetent constables round asking the same questions, and then that bunch of meddling kids this morning. Wish you'd all just fuck off and let me get on with my job. What do you want? Frankenstein for fuck's sake. You made that up.'

Frankenstein smiled. It was so much easier to deal with people who were this upfront. Artifice and sophistry were for

166

other police officers to handle. Much better to deal with plain thuggery, rudeness or stupidity.

'I can't account for the meddling kids...' he began.

'MI6 they said they were,' said Bladestone, 'but they were just a bunch of spotty little shitheads if you ask me.'

'Oh, they're MI6 all right, but I can't argue with you about their meddling. Any chance you'd tell me what kind of questions they were asking?'

Bladestone barked out a laugh.

'Cheeky cunt!' he erupted. 'No. Now piss off!'

Frankenstein turned away abruptly and started walking around the boats, looking them up and down, trying to get a feel for them. A feel for the sea, a feel for the people who took to it. Although these boats weren't the boats of people who took to the sea every day, the sort of people whose skin he needed to get under.

'There can't be many people left on the island currently involved in the fishing business. Or who were involved in it in the past,' he said, running his hand down the side of an old wooden yacht, paint crumbling beneath his fingers. Rapped his knuckles against the wood.

No reply. He turned and looked at Bladestone, who was watching him from under dark eyebrows, gravely stitched together in the middle.

Bladestone was well aware of the relationship between those who had been murdered, as well as their connection with the *Bitter Wind*. He now lived in fear, haunted by the darkness of night, every noise making him glance over his shoulder. He imagined honour amongst thieves however, thinking that the darkness came from outwith the small collective which had been meeting once a month in the room above the Incidental Mermaid on Cardiff Street.

'You ever work on a trawler?' asked Frankenstein.

Bladestone growled and turned away. Walked over to another boat, a plastic twenty-foot yacht, and started straightening out the tarpaulin which covered the deck. Frankenstein continued his inspection of the wooden hull, tapping every now and again, wondering at the sounds, the differing qualities of the wood.

167

'It seems to me,' he went on, 'that anyone on this island who ever worked in the fishing business, might be a wee bit worried about this flurry of gruesome murders.'

'I've got nothing to concern me,' said Bladestone resolutely. 'I've never done anything other than a hard day's work, I've never double-crossed anyone, never done anyone any harm.'

'Very honourable.'

Bladestone growled. Tugged harder at the tarpaulin, as he moved around the boat. Water splashed off the top.

'So, if this killer comes calling, you'll offer him a cup of tea and establish that you mean him no harm?'

'Aye, well, let's just say that I don't think any killer will be paying me a call.'

'How can you be so sure?'

Bladestone pulled at the last ripple of canvas, then turned to face Frankenstein.

'Believe me,' he said, 'I don't doubt there's a killer out there, not for one minute. The evidence is mounting up. But it's just some guy in a mask, and there's nobody in a mask got any business with Cudge Bladestone.'

'Aye, and why would he put a mask on?' said Frankenstein. 'No one's ever seen him. He turns up at someone's house, he takes the head off, he vanishes. Doesn't seem to matter if the person who he's killing gets to see his face.'

'And how d'you know that no one's seen him? Have you asked?'

Bladestone moved over to the next boat in line and began to check the bindings on the tarpaulin. Frankenstein watched him, thinking that he was fighting a battle that he was never going to win. Not with Cudge Bladestone. Not yet, at any rate.

'Who repairs all the storm damage to the boats?' he asked.

'Up to the owners,' Bladestone barked in reply. 'Course, if they want me to do it, and most of them do, they have to pay me.'

'The storm was good for business then?' quipped Frankenstein. Bladestone turned quickly.

'You accusing me of starting the storm now? You think I'm a fucking X-Man?'

'Whatever,' said Frankenstein, and he waved his hand. The pleasure of his rude bluntness was wearing off. Frankenstein moved on to a plastic boat, tapped the hull, heard the difference in sound and quality.

I'd have a wooden boat, he thought to himself. A thought quickly followed by self-loathing that he had even considered the notion, however slightly, of having a boat at all.

'Anything in the yard, any shipping tool, that could be used to cut someone's head off, you know, with one clean swipe. Not a saw or anything. Any piece of equipment that could be used like a scythe?'

Bladestone hesitated, rested his hands on the side of the boat. Turned slowly, eyes staring straight at Frankenstein.

'Yes,' he said, 'as a matter of fact there is. Would you like me to demonstrate it for you?'

'As a matter of fact,' said Frankenstein, 'no, I wouldn't. None of your crap. Just show me.'

Bladestone walked forward, staring at the ground now, shaking his head, annoyed that he had made the gallus demonstration offer, when he was now going to have to look stupid.

'Can't,' he said harshly. 'Come here.'

He beckoned Frankenstein onwards and the policeman fell in behind. They came into a small, dark workshop. Every inch of space, on the worktops and the floor and the walls, was filled with stuff. Pieces of boat, pieces of wood, tools, nails, screws, instruments, hammers, paint pots. Frankenstein had to watch where he put his feet.

'I had an axe,' he said, 'kept it hanging there.' He pointed at the place on the wall, and sure enough there was a clean mark where the axe had hung, unused, for year after year. A huge axe. 'Nothing fancy, but big. You can see the mark. Didn't really need it, but I got it one year on offer in B&Q.'

'What happened to it?' said Frankenstein, easily managing to keep the smile off his face.

'Went missing about a week ago,' said Bladestone. 'Total bastard. Been a while since I was that pissed off.'

'Did you report it?'

'Who to? Gainsborough? Chocolate teapot material if ever there was.'

'Did you tell anyone?'

Bladestone looked dismissively at Frankenstein.

'Are you about to ask me what I was doing between the hours of seven and nine on the twenty-fifth?' he said mockingly.

'Christ, you're funny. Did you tell anyone about the axe being taken?'

'No,' said Bladestone, 'I didn't.'

'So, if it turns out that any of these people have been killed by your axe, or an axe like it, you expect me to believe you and to pin the blame on someone other than you?'

'I expect nothing from you people, although it would be nice to be left alone.'

'Was anything else stolen?'

Bladestone breathed deeply, leaning back against the worktop. His backside bumped a can of oil, which toppled over. There was nothing in it to spill.

'A couple of tarpaulins, some rope. A winch. The axe, that was about it. But then, does it look like I keep an inventory? They probably took some other stuff, who knows?'

'And you didn't report this because, what?...'

'Because,' said Bladestone, straightening up and making himself more forceful before Frankenstein, 'the police on this island are useless, that's why. I wouldn't waste my time, that's all. Nothing sinister, nothing suspicious. You can read something interesting into it if you want, but that's your shout and your time you'll be wasting. Suit yourself. Now, would you please, pretty please with sugar on it, just fuck off out of my boatyard and let me get on with some work. There's a lot of damage still to be repaired after that magical storm I whipped up out of thin air.'

A hard stare across the workshop, then Bladestone walked back outside, storming past Frankenstein, finally deciding that he didn't care what the policeman did.

Frankenstein followed him outside, stopped, took a last look around the yard. Another small building, a shady green door.

'What's in there?' he said to Bladestone's back.

Bladestone turned and followed Frankenstein's gaze.

'None of your fucking business,' he said. 'You can have a look if you've got a warrant, but I presume you don't, so once more, if you'd finally like to pay attention to me, just fuck off.'

He turned away again, Frankenstein looked at the door, one last look around the yard. He would be back, warrant or not.

'One last thing,' he said, 'before you selflessly go and attend to other peoples' problems.'

Bladestone stopped. Didn't turn this time. Frankenstein realised that what he was about to ask was incredibly childish, but he had to know. Even if the chances of Bladestone answering him were virtually nil.

'Did you tell the MI6 guys about the axe theft?'

## 4

## Deputy Dawg

Fred and the gang were down by the rocks at West Bay. Looking out over the sea to Little Cumbrae, Arran and Bute. Could see Kilchattan Bay. Mid-afternoon, they were eating a sandwich and chewing the fat. They had plundered the stocks of the Ritz Café, and were now tossing the pigskin of investigation around and seeing if they could catch anything in the endzone. Fred, Selma and Deirdre were eating a fairly plain cheese, ham, lettuce and tomato on brown bread. Bernard and the Dog With No Name were sharing a sixteen-decker, ham, bacon, fried banana, peanut butter, chocolate chip, papaya, guava, blue cheese and Mars Bar deep fried sandwich. With extra mayo.

'Like, man,' said Bernard, through a mouthful of food, 'this is the spookiest case I've ever been on.'

'It sure is,' said Fred. 'We came here to investigate a diamond smuggling ring running out of Ireland and instead we end up with this creepy Incredible Captain Death mystery.'

'But I don't think there's any doubt they're connected,' said Selma. 'I'll bet three pigs to the dozen that sooner or later the killer will lead us to those missing diamonds.'

'If only we could catch sight of him,' said Fred. 'It feels like we're always one step behind him, arriving just after he's chopped someone's head off.'

'Like I don't think I'm bothered about that, eh, Dog With No Name?' said Bernard.

The Dog With No Name barked in agreement.

'Maybe it's time we pulled forces with the local law enforcement,' suggested Selma, dabbing at the corners of her mouth with a napkin.

'I'm not so sure,' said Fred. 'If ever there was a suspicious character, then DCI Frankenstein fits the bill.'

'He sure does have a weird name,' said Deirdre.

'Exactly,' said Fred. 'I've kind of got a feeling that when we find these diamonds and this killer, and it comes time to pull the mask off some bad guy's head, I wouldn't be completely surprised if it wasn't DCI Frankenstein under the latex.'

'What we need are clues,' said Selma.

'Exactly,' said Fred. 'And I think I might just have a plan.'

'Uh-oh,' said Bernard, cramming the last of the sandwich into his mouth, 'I don't like the sound of that.'

The Dog With No Name barked. Fred stood up and looked out to sea, wondering if everyone who looked across the grey and mysterious waves found them as bewitching as he did.

✂

Barney and Proudfoot were round the corner of the mainland, further south, but still looking out across the sea to Arran. Sitting on a bench beside the beach, watching a couple of small children playing in the sand. The kids were both in shorts, their jackets long since tossed to the side, running around in very thin jumpers. Barney and Proudfoot were drinking coffee, jackets pulled tightly around them, both bitterly feeling the cold.

'Why didn't you just run when all this started?' she asked. They had been sitting in silence, in the cold, for almost fifteen minutes. She had needed the air after three hours of listening to Barney's story. She had known some of it already of course, having played her part, but there was plenty that needed filling in.

A life on the run. Would anyone have done anything different? Everywhere he had turned he had found death. This time, it seemed, death had come looking for him. He had even told her of the ghosts that had arrived in the previous few days. The actual Proudfoot, sitting there in front of him, seemed no less of a ghost than Brother Steven, or the old man who had walked into his shop five days earlier.

'Kids are amazing, aren't they?' he said, as her question had an obvious answer. She knew it already. Where was it he could go to escape judgement? 'If you made them go for a walk in this weather they'd bleat at you like you were killing them. But give them some sand, it could be high summer. They don't care.'

They watched the kids, glad to be free of the small interview room and the claustrophobic tale of endless murder, death and atrocity that had been Barney's life.

'Pain in the arse, of course,' he said, smiling. Proudfoot laughed. Barney thought of asking the question about her intentions regarding children, but knew better. Never ask a woman about children. Let her volunteer the information.

'You're wanting to ask me about children,' she said, reading his mind again.

'You should be in the police force,' he said.

'I'd be wasted there,' she said. 'Had two miscarriages. Keep trying. One day we'll get there.'

'I'm sorry.'

She made a small gesture with her hands.

'Just something else,' she said. 'Course, it's a shit world to bring a kid into. Global warming.'

'Population explosion.'

'Terror, government terror, death, illegal diamonds, child soldiers, famine, genocide, bird flu, nuclear arsenals, disastrous weather, earthquakes...'

She finally depressed herself so much she stopped.

'Celebrity Big Brother,' said Barney.

She laughed again. Footsteps behind them. They didn't turn, although it occurred independently to both of them that this could be a member of the press, having picked up on Barney's presence in Saltcoats.

'You two look like you're enjoying yourselves far too much,' said Frankenstein.

Proudfoot straightened up but did not stand.

'Did you get me one of those, Sergeant?'

Proudfoot shrugged.

'Thought I'd be gone longer,' said Frankenstein.

He sat down at one end of the bench, pushing Proudfoot closer to Barney. Barney budged up. The three of them sat and looked out over the cold sands and the cold sea, watching the children arguing over a small red spade. Having been playing nicely for the entire time that Barney had been sitting there, the kids were now acting like mortal enemies.

'You can see how wars start,' said Barney, glibly.

174

'Little bastards,' said Frankenstein. 'Can't stand them myself. Glad you're resisting the urge to pollute the planet with any more kids, Sergeant.'

Proudfoot hid her face behind her coffee cup. Barney glanced over at her.

'This thing,' said Frankenstein, 'it's moving on, don't you think? Maybe it's passed us by already. It's four days since the trawler was found, a day and a half since the most recent murder. Maybe it's over. A tempest. It blew up, wreaked havoc, and now it's gone.' He snapped his fingers. 'We needed to grab it as it passed. Maybe it's too late.' He stared morosely out to sea. Waves chopped and danced, played endlessly, stretching for miles away from him.

'No,' said Barney suddenly. 'It's not over yet.'

'How can you be so sure?' he asked.

'Been here before,' said Barney. 'These things don't just blow over. Not this.'

The children had suddenly patched up their differences, without the intervention of the UN, and had started working together to build a damn across a small stream which was trickling down to the water. Barney was watching them, letting his mind drift. He had spent three hours dredging up more ghosts and memories than he would have liked, now he just wanted to switch off. The ingenuous fun of two young children was perfect to distract him. Proudfoot wasn't so easily distracted, her own demons and nightmares having been reawakened by her three hours with Barney. Frankenstein was looking at the waves. Bewitched.

'I'm going to make you an offer, Mr Thomson,' said Frankenstein. 'Might seem a bit odd, but there's always something stranger just around the corner.'

Barney tipped his head to the side and looked across Proudfoot. Proudfoot also turned, wondering what her boss was going to suggest. A one-way ticket to Buenos Aries and three hundred thousand in cash if Barney promised never to darken Scotland's doors again?

'I'm going to make you a deputy,' said Frankenstein.

He let the statement slip out into the cold November afternoon and get carried away by the wind.

'Can you do that?' asked Proudfoot.

Barney smiled.

'I was being melodramatic,' said Frankenstein. 'Obviously, for official purposes we'll have to couch it in more modern terms. We'll hire you as a consultant on the case. Day-by-day basis, until we have our murderer, the case is solved, or we give up. It'll be a fairly free-flowing, ad hoc arrangement.'

Proudfoot looked at Frankenstein, very impressed. Unusual for anyone in public service to be that sensible or proactive.

'What if I turn out to be the killer?' asked Barney.

'Then I'm going to look very stupid.'

Barney thought about that for a while, thought about the risk he was taking for him.

'And what if the press find out? If you record it officially, it's bound to get out. You'll get crucified, won't you?'

'I won't record it officially,' said Frankenstein. Had thought it through on the short drive to Saltcoats from the Largs ferry. 'At least, not in your name. The contract will be noted down in a false name, for a false consultancy firm. When the whole thing's over and done with, I'll need to do some juggling of the books. Won't be easy, but I know a couple of people in finance. I have an idea or two on how to get it all cleared up.'

Barney looked out across the grim sea, the sky darkening behind them, the sun beginning to sink unseen away to the west behind thick banks of cloud. In the distance, emerging from behind Little Cumbrae, he could see a nuclear submarine on its way out from Faslane, off for a few months lying in deep waters. The cold wind bit harder, and Barney Thomson, barber, accepted that this would be his fate. For now, at any rate. This would not help in his final judgement, but if it brought it a little bit closer, then he might as well.

'Sure,' he said, 'why not?'

Proudfoot shook her head. She smiled. After hearing the full Barney Thomson story, this didn't seem any more bizarre than so much of what had gone before in his life.

'Don't think you're getting a badge,' said Frankenstein.

## 5

# The Barbershop
# Must Go On

The shop had returned to its previous state of calm. The word had got round that Barney Thomson had been taken into police custody and would be held there for at least seventy-two hours. All that was left of the freak show of the Millport barber shop was Igor, the deaf mute hunchback, and Keanu, the surfer dude barber. Neither was enough to drag anyone onto the boat across to Millport, and the town residents already knew everything there was to know about the two of them. The shop had returned to its normal November state of two or three customers a day.

And so it was a bit of a surprise for both Igor and Keanu when two men entered. Fred and Bernard.

As the door opened, Keanu had been trying to balance a tea spoon on his nose, Igor had been watching him, full of melancholy, thinking that Barney had never tried to balance a tea spoon on his nose. Not in public, at any rate.

'Like, hi!' said Bernard. 'Any chance of a haircut from you fellas?'

Keanu took the spoon from his nose and looked at the two newcomers. Had seen them around the island, had heard talk of them. Knew that they were here because of the murders, although had heard it said that they'd been on the island even before the tragedy of the *Bitter Wind* had taken place. Immediately suspicious.

'Sure,' said Keanu. 'Who's first?'

'I'll go first,' said Fred, 'although I don't want a cut. Just a bit of a quaff.'

Keanu was even more suspicious. He invited Fred up to the chair and wrapped the cloak around his neck. Bernard sat down on the bench, eyeing up Igor as he did so.

'Hey, pal,' he said, 'Any chance of some food while I wait? Maybe a sandwich or some biscuits?'

Igor could pick up speech from merely paying attention to the vibrations. But then again, sometimes he elected to be completely deaf in all capacities. He continued to sweep up.

'Say, what's the thing with your wee friend the sweeper-upper guy?' asked Fred. 'Seems like a bit of a freak?'

'He's cool,' said Keanu. 'Sure, he's a deaf, mute hunchback, but that just means he can't hear, he can't speak and he has trouble getting a suit to fit.'

'Was he in Bavaria in 1876?' asked Fred.

Keanu stood back and eyed Fred in the mirror. Fred had the decency to look a little sheepish, before smiling and trying to make out that the question had been a joke.

'What exactly do you mean by quaff?' said Keanu.

Fred had a thick mat of blonde hair which looked like it had already undergone a fair amount of personal quaffing that morning.

'Just, you know, kind of bouffed up a bit.'

'Like, yeah,' said Bernard from behind, 'Fred's into that whole metrosexual thing. He takes like eight hours in the bathroom every morning.'

It was at about this time that Igor decided to take himself out of the loop and into the back room. Time to make a roll 'n sausage for himself and Keanu, something which wouldn't be produced until Bernard had gone.

'And where's Barney?' asked Fred. 'Barney Thomson,' he added, just in case Keanu had thought he meant Barney Rubble, Barney Miller, or Barney the big pink homosexual dinosaur.

'He got taken into police custody this morning,' said Keanu, reluctant to discuss Barney, but hoping that confirmation of his absence might lead them to leave sooner than they were intending. 'To bouff your hair to the extent that you're requesting, I should probably wash it first,' he added.

'I don't think so,' said Fred. 'Maybe just some mousse.'

'Did somebody say mousse?'

'I should have told you, friend, that we're from MI6. We're meant to say that as soon as we start talking to people.'

Keanu stared awkwardly at him in the mirror. He'd already heard the MI6 rumour of course, but hadn't believed it. Still didn't believe it.

'What's MI6 doing working the UK?' he asked.

'We were here on a team building exercise. Then when this mystery started, the police asked us to help out.'

Keanu sprayed some of the cheapest product he had lying around into Fred's hair and started to bouff it up a little.

'So that grumpy old police guy who's in charge of the investigation, asked you four kids and your dog to help him.'

'Like, sure, why not?' came the voice from the bench.

'You don't believe us?' said Fred.

Keanu worked his hands through Fred's hair, hating the artifice of it all, knowing that at the end his hair was going to look exactly the same as it did when he first walked in. He was suddenly caught up in some stupid game that he didn't want to be part of.

'MI6,' said Keanu. 'I know it's not all James Bond and beautiful women and car chases. Mundane stuff working in embassies, meeting people in cafés, paperwork.'

'Man, you've got some inside information,' said Fred. 'Who have you been pumping?'

'The thing is, it's still all based in deception. In your working environment, you can't just say that you are who you are. You're all trained to lie, to deceive. You work in misinformation. So can anyone ever believe anything that any of you say? Is the fact that you say you work for MI6 not a contradiction in itself? Does not the fact of saying that's what you do, mean in itself that you don't? The statement, I work for MI6 is of itself a complete paradox. Maybe you're CIA, maybe you're MI5, maybe you're from Blue Peter, maybe you're KGB.'

'Very twenty years ago, friend,' said Bernard from the back.

'Whatever. There's still KGB in Belarus,' said Keanu.

'Aha!' said Fred. 'You sound like you might be from the intelligence community yourself!'

Keanu ran his hands through Fred's hair so that it was sticking straight up in the air. Then, while Fred was distracted by the whole intelligence community debate, he grabbed a can

179

of P&G's Instant Cast-Iron Styling Spray, covering the label with his hands so Fred wouldn't notice, and drenched his hair with it.

'I read the newspapers,' said Keanu. 'Now, gentlemen, we're pretty busy this afternoon, so I'm going to have to ask you to leave.'

Bernard looked around the empty shop. Fred looked at his hair in the mirror. He looked like he'd just seen a Trawler Fiend. He lifted his hand to try and run it through his hair, but couldn't get it in. His hair was rock solid, standing to attention.

'It should wear off in a few weeks,' said Keanu.

'Funny, friend,' said Fred.

'It's a good look for you,' said Keanu. 'It's about time you tried something new.'

'Like, how do *you* know he's looked the same for forty years now?' said Bernard.

'That'll be £45 please,' said Keanu, stepping back and ushering Fred from the chair.

Fred looked up at the price list on the wall, which started with Short Back & Sides: £4.25 and ended with A Bit Of A Bouff: £7.50.

'It was a special,' said Keanu. 'Small island sensibilities, London prices. Wanted to make you MI6 fellas feel at home.'

Fred took his coat down from the rack, searching around in the pockets for some money.

'I can call in an air strike, you know,' he muttered. 'Or have you sent to Laos.'

He handed the money over to Keanu, who turned and put it in the till.

'Now,' said Keanu, turning back, arms folded, 'you can fuck off.'

'Arf!' barked the voice from the back, Igor having appeared to stand in the doorway, armed with a broom.

With the door open the smell of grilling sausages wafted out into the shop.

'Like, oh my gosh!' said Bernard. 'Is that sausages I can smell? I love sausages.'

Keanu walked to the door of the shop and opened it to the dying of the day.

'This gentlemen,' he said, 'is the door.'

Fred looked at Bernard, and ruffled his hair.

'He's showing us the door, Bernard,' he said. 'And you never even got your haircut.'

'Like, I never get my haircut anyway. Wow, man, I'll need to go in search of sausages.'

And with that, the two nefarious agents of MI6 walked out into the cold late afternoon and Keanu closed the door over behind them. As they walked off along the road, headed for the Ritz Café and all the rolls 'n sausage they could eat, Keanu looked out to sea. Igor came up and stood next to him, leaning on the broom, following his gaze out across the water. The afternoon was getting hazier as it was getting dark. Some of the lights on the mainland which were usually visible were obscured. Another fog was closing in on the island. A fog just like the one which had fallen on the night when the *Bitter Wind* had lost its crew.

'Looks nasty out there,' said Keanu. 'Time for a late afternoon sausage sandwich.'

'Arf!' said Igor.

## 6

## Nardini

By the time Barney Thomson, DS Proudfoot and DCI Frankenstein had returned to Largs to catch the ferry across to Cumbrae, evening had fallen and the fog had completely descended.

Frankenstein slowly drove down the short stretch of road along which the cars queued for the ferry. Got to the end and parked behind the only other two cars in the queue. They could see the ferry parked up at the pier, there didn't seem to be anyone sitting in the cars at the front of the queue.

'God's sake,' muttered Frankenstein. 'It's a bloody ghost town.'

He stepped out the car and looked angrily up the pier, being the type of person to be quick to irritation. The fog was so thick that he could barely make out the end of the pier, even though the pier at Largs is not long. He turned, looked all around him, had that briefly helpless feeling of having no one to shout at, then walked quickly towards the ticket office in the small building at the head of the quay.

In the car, Proudfoot turned to Barney, who was sitting in the back seat, staring out at nothing. Wondering what he would have to do to earn his consultancy money. Write a large report using phrases such as *knife and forked it*, *blue envelope* and *cubicle monkey* and then charge them forty thousand pounds for every day's work.

'I should go and make sure he doesn't fall into the water,' said Proudfoot.

'I'll stay here and guard the warmth,' said Barney.

Proudfoot smiled and stepped out into the fog. Closed the car door, pulled her coat tightly against her. The mist was thick and freezing so that it felt like you were swallowing it every time you took a breath. She shivered. Could see Frankenstein disappear off into the mist ahead and walked quickly after him.

The fog masked all sounds. It was only just after six o'clock on a weekday evening and yet the place seemed deserted. She couldn't hear any cars, couldn't see any people. Somewhere, only a few unseen yards off the shore, she could hear a metal chain clank mournfully against metal on a small boat, moved by the slight swell. The sea, what she could see of it as it washed peacefully onto the shore, had the eerie calm that comes with dense fog. She shivered again, began to get affected by the silence. Could feel the hand of the fog creeping up her back.

She stopped. Looked around her. Back at Barney, sitting in the car, elbow on the door, head leaning on his hand. Relaxed. Had he seen so much, was he immune to this feeling? Turned, wondered what had happened to Frankenstein. Looked at the café opposite the car queue, Nardini's. There wasn't a kid on the west coast of Scotland who hadn't eaten ice cream from that shop. The lights were on, she could see people inside. She relaxed a little. A sign of life.

The hand touched her shoulder.

She jumped, half screamed, whirled round, stepping back, hands up, automatic reflex, breath wheezing dramatically.

'Jesus!' said Frankenstein. 'What's with you?'

She breathed deeply, hand to her chest. Instant hot flush to go with the cold sweat.

'Heebee geebees?' said Frankenstein, and in her mixed up state, Proudfoot let out a bark of a laugh at the sound of the childish expression coming from Frankenstein, all gruff and angry irritation.

'Yeah,' she said, 'heebee geebees.'

Frankenstein stamped his feet, the harsh sound, even so close, dulled by the thick mist.

'Not a bastard around,' he said. 'The ferry's parked up, the ticket office is shut.'

'Thick fog,' said Proudfoot.

'Piece of crap,' said Frankenstein. 'If these bastards want to continue to get government subsidies, they better bloody run regardless of the weather. Piece of crap.'

Proudfoot looked out to sea, indicated with her hand that you could barely see twenty yards.

'We'll need to get onto someone back at the station, get them to speak to some bastard at CalMac. Bastards will probably be closed for the night.'

In angrily looking around him, he noticed the lights and the people in the café across the road. They could hear a car driving slowly, fifty yards away, round the curve of the main road through Largs.

'Come on,' he said, 'we'll check in here first, probably find the crew of the ship with their feet up, drinking latté.'

He walked quickly across the road, Proudfoot behind. Now that she had her brusque boss for company and she no longer had the fog and her imagination to lead her astray, the fear had gone. She could stand back and watch Frankenstein get mad at someone, which was always, at the very least, entertaining.

✂

Barney was watching the sea mist drift past the car. So thick that he wondered if he'd be able to touch it if he rolled down the window and stuck his hand out. The car was cooling down already, and as he sat and watched Frankenstein and Proudfoot, saw her comical jump as Frankenstein had walked up to her from behind, he contemplated the move into the café. Coffee. Ice cream.

How many ice creams had he had in that place over the years of waiting for ferries at the start of summer holidays? Sometimes they would come down by train and their mum would always hustle them straight onto the boat. But on the times when they would come by car, he would hope there was a huge queue for the ferry, and she would always acquiesce and take them into the shop for ice cream. A hundred flavours, he had always had vanilla. Two scoops.

His mother. The serial killer.

The front passenger door opened and closed quickly, Barney felt the sudden draft of cold air. He turned. It wasn't Proudfoot. It wasn't Frankenstein.

'Hello, Barney,' said the voice, each word creaking out like the groaning of an old barn door.

Barney Thomson, barber, could feel the blood drain from his face.

Frankenstein opened the door of the café, held it briefly for Proudfoot and walked inside. Proudfoot followed, immediately unzipping her jacket against the wonderful warmth of the shop.

There were three occupied tables. Two, seemingly, the passengers from the two cars which were parked outside, waiting forlornly in the mist for a boat that was unlikely to sail that night. A middle-aged couple, who were tucking into rolls 'n bacon and cups of tea. A man on his own, who had taken out a laptop and was writing frantically at the table. Frankenstein straight away pegged him as a journalist.

At the third table were the people he had come in here to see. Three men in the thick dark blue sweaters of Caledonian MacBrayne, the shipping company. The captain amongst them was evident by the fact that he was older and possessed a carefully quaffed Captain Birdseye white beard.

'Evening,' said the man behind the counter. 'Not many people out tonight.'

Frankenstein looked around the shop, aware that everyone except the speed-writing journalist, was eyeing him suspiciously.

'Why is that?' asked Frankenstein. 'Must normally be busier than this at this time?'

'Well,' said the guy, 'it's the fog. Thick as soup, that's what they're saying. Thick as the fog the other night, when the crew of that trawler vanished, that's what they're thinking. There's a lot of people scared around here. Scared.'

There was a noise from the kitchen. The quick-fingered tap-tap from the computer. Some strange piece of kitchenware gurgled and rumbled somewhere out back. One of the crewmen slurped noisily at a still too-hot cup of tea. The woman smacked her lips noisily over her bacon sandwich.

'Watch yer falsers, Mabel,' said the man, self-consciously.

'It's just a fog,' said Frankenstein.

'Aye, it's a fog all right!' said the captain, suddenly from the table. 'And there's a killer out there waiting to get anyone stupid enough to go out in it. The Incredible Captain Death, the Trawler Fiend, call him what you will.'

Frankenstein stared deadpan through the café. Deadpan. Inside he was completely gobsmacked, but generally he didn't do gobsmacked. He did deadpan. He was Bob Newhart, not Jim Carrey.

'You think there's a Trawler Fiend out there?' he said, because he couldn't think of anything else to say. There was a rustle to his right and the counter guy produced a copy of that day's Evening Times and laid it out for Frankenstein and Proudfoot to see.

Beside the gargantuan headline, written in small print to squeeze it all in, *Trawler Fiend: First Pictures! Evil Green Monster Of The Deep in Cahoots With Barber Surgeon! Exclusive!* was a picture of a giant lizard/dinosaur type of thing, about eight feet tall, walking on its hind legs, through a foggy, seaweedy sea shore.

Frankenstein was still gobsmacked, although he remained resolutely in Bob Newhart mode. He glanced round at Proudfoot who was staring at the picture. She caught his eye and shrugged.

'That's the stupidest thing I've ever seen in my life,' said Frankenstein.

'You may think it's stupid,' said Captain Birdseye, 'but that thing there chopped a man's head clean off with its bare claws.'

'And chopped another man's head off with an axe,' said one of the crewmen.

'And chopped a woman's head off with an axe 'n all,' said the third.

'And,' chipped in the woman from behind her bacon roll, 'Mrs Clafferty says she reckoned it stole her underwear off her washing line last Tuesday.'

There was general murmuring of agreement around the café. The Trawler Fiend was capturing the imagination of the public, in an even more dramatic way than Barney Thomson had ever managed. These were dark days. The nation was slipping into hysteria.

'I know that these murders have been committed,' said Frankenstein, 'I've seen the bodies, I'm not denying anything. But this, this picture,' and he held it up so that they could

186

better see it, noticing as he did so that everyone else in the café – except the hardworking journalist, who hadn't even noticed that Frankenstein was in the room – recoiled at the sight of the evil beast, 'is a man in a suit. What lizard walks on its hind legs like that?'

'It's not a lizard,' said the guy behind the counter. 'It's a Trawler Fiend. It's its own species, there are no rules. That's what it says in the article inside by an actual scientist.'

Frankenstein stared at him, still flabbergasted. Looked round at Proudfoot, who was at least finding the whole thing pretty funny. She took the smile off her face to nod seriously at him.

'Don't you start,' he muttered.

He turned, walked quickly up to the table with the three crewmen.

'Right you, I'm ordering you to start operating that ferry. We need to get back over there, right now.'

The captain bit meatily into a hearty sandwich.

'You don't control me,' he said, spitting food onto the table. 'I don't take any orders from the police. You can speak to HQ, if you want, if there's anyone there this time of night, but you know what? Even then, I'm still not taking the ferry out. Not in this fog, not with that…thing, out there. The union'll back me, I know they will. To the hilt. They did it before when the Jetty Monster was at large.'

And there was another low grumble of discontent around the café at the mention of the Jetty Monster.

'Fuck me,' muttered Frankenstein. 'Fuck me.'

He turned, held his hands out in exasperation at Proudfoot.

'Right, Sergeant, can I ask you to put a call through to our HQ. Let's not even waste time trying to sort out this shower of heid the ba's, just get a boat of some description down here as quickly as possible.'

Proudfoot nodded, took her phone from her pocket and turned to go outside to make the call.

'Coffee?' asked Frankenstein.

Proudfoot stopped, surprised.

'Sure,' she said, 'that'd be lovely. Cappuccino would be nice.'

Frankenstein grumped. Suddenly, behind them, the journalist rose in triumph, having written his two thousand words in under fifteen minutes.

'Finished!' he cried. 'Listen to this. *Incompetent Police Stumped As Trawler Fiend/Barber Combo Cut Bloody Swathe Through Children's Holiday Resort.*'

## 7

## The Devil Rides In

Barney looked at the old man who was sitting in the front passenger seat. The captain of the old trawler, *Albatross*. He had pulled down the visor and was inspecting his hair in the small mirror, flicking casually at the sides.

'Nice job,' he said. 'Been a while since I had a cut this good. Might have a chance with the ladies now, what d'you think?'

He winked at Barney in the mirror. Barney was pale, trying to be cool. How many ghosts did he have to encounter before he felt comfortable in their presence? If this was a ghost. Just a guy in a mask, he told himself. A guy in a mask. Why did he even have to be wearing a mask? Get a grip, Barney! It was just a guy.

'I still owe you money,' the old man said, then he tapped his pockets and shrugged. 'Sorry. Maybe next time.'

Finally he turned and looked Barney in the eye. The smile remained, but now there was an edge. The harmless, quiet, bordering on genteel buffoonery was gone. It was all in the eyes.

'To crush, to annihilate a man utterly, to inflict on him the most terrible punishment so that the most ferocious murderer would shudder at it beforehand, one need only give him work of an absolutely, completely useless and irrational character.' He paused, the smile never wavered. 'Still cutting hair, Barney?'

Barney shook his head. Trying to retain the cool which had been his for a few years now. Yet he was aware that it had been an accidental nonchalance. Had he strived to achieve it, it would never have happened. You can't force unflappable serenity. And now he was aware that he was turning back into the man who had once dully haunted the window end of the small barbershop in Partick. Unsure of himself, lacking in confidence. Nervous. He wanted the old new Barney back.

The old man reached out to tap Barney on the knee. His hand passed right through Barney's leg. Barney pressed back against the car seat. The old man laughed, a light, airy giggle.

'Only messing with you, Barney,' he said, and this time he tapped Barney's knee firmly with his hand and sat back. 'Life is full of choices. But you don't make them without consequences, that's all. Every junction you come to there's a right and a left. But it doesn't matter which one you choose, you have to live up to your decision. Ain't too often you can go back.'

The old man seemed to eat Barney up with his stare. His eyes didn't just burrow into Barney's head, didn't just read his thoughts. They consumed him, condemned him with every unblinking second. They reached into him and grabbed his soul, dragged it out, screaming, from the pits of his body.

Barney closed his eyes, a long, deep breath escaped from him, his body expelling everything that it could. It was no use, eyes closed, eyes open, the old man's gaze tore into him, ripped him open, laid him bare.

'You made a pact with the Devil, Barney Thomson, and it's time for you to pay your share!'

The car door opened. Barney opened his eyes, the words wrapping around his head like barbed wire.

'Barney, come on,' said Proudfoot. 'I'll get you a coffee.'

Barney stared back at her. Dry mouth, nerves shredded, heart thumping.

Cool? Was there any vestige of cool left within him? The unruffled imperturbability which had come so naturally for the previous few years, which had defined his personality for so long, had now been torn apart, every ounce and inch of it ripped piece by piece and thrown in the gutter.

'You looking terrible, Barney, you all right? Come and get a coffee, come on.'

Barney opened the car door, soul shredded, on auto-pilot. Started walking across the road to the café. She fell in beside him.

'Thought I saw someone in the car beside you,' she said.

He didn't answer. Having heard the story of his last few days, she felt a shiver down her back. She held Barney's arm just before he opened the door to the café.

'Ghosts?' she said.

Barney stared at her feet. He had told her everything up until now, but this? Had he made a pact with the Devil? Was that how he had managed to escape from justice for so long? He'd had genuine evil on his side, a dark angel at his shoulder.

Is that how pacts with the Devil are made? Unconsciously. In your sleep, in your dreams. In your nightmares. He thought back to the time when his life had first made the acquaintance of Hell. Two accidental murders on his hands, a host of brutal, calculated murders on the hands of his mother, which had left him with a freezer full of human flesh. How had he got through all that?

By accident, he'd always thought. By fortune smiling on him at the right time, by stumbling across the occasional cogent thought to help him through awkward moments. But maybe it hadn't been fortune which had smiled upon him. He remembered his dark half, the sensible, switched-on side of his brain, which had appeared from nowhere to ease him through the moments when he would have succumbed to the authorities. Had that been it? By listening to that voice, had that been the end for him? When he first sat back and let his darker half take over, let his darker half wrap Wullie Henderson's body up in black, plastic bin liners, had that been the moment when he had sold his soul to Satan for all eternity?

'Barney,' said Proudfoot, waving her hand in front of him.

He looked at her, the fear still in his eyes. He was being played with, and whoever was doing it, was succeeding magnificently. A life, a soul, sliced into slivers.

'You all right?'

'Not really,' said Barney, finally regaining some sort of capacity to communicate. 'My id has been completely fucked.'

'Your id?'

He nodded.

'You need coffee. Come on.'

## 8

## A Cry In The Fog

The fog was all consuming. Dense, dark, claustrophobic. Total. A brutal fog, nightmarish. The small police launch inched away from the pier at Largs. It had come from Ardrossan, just ten miles along the coast, but it had taken a long time to get there. Long enough that the café had cleared of people and then closed. Long enough for Frankenstein to be frustrated, and then angry, then incandescent with rage, then resigned, then worried that something had happened, worried that the driver of the launch had been taken by the killer. A fear he did not share with the others, as he sat in the car with Barney and Proudfoot, engine running to combat the cold.

When Sergeant Clifford Kratzenburg had knocked on the window of the car, the fog had become so thick that none of them had seen him approach. Stepping out into the mist, they had realised that it had descended with much greater gloom even than when they had last been outside the car, and Frankenstein suddenly doubted the sense in trying to get to the island at this time. However, he now felt, as did Barney, that the fog was all part of this strange circumstance. There would be something happening in Millport that night, and there was little point in them being across the water.

And so now they edged quietly out into the firth of Clyde, inch by inch, the motor barely running. Making the direct run across the firth to the slipway.

Kratzenburg increased speed a little, keeping a close eye on the small radar system in the corner of the cockpit. Frankenstein sat beside him at the front of the boat, Barney Thomson and Proudfoot behind, close together, some solidarity in fear and unease.

They weren't necessarily scared of the actual killer, they weren't scared of being on the open sea in a dense fog. Had they discussed it, perhaps they couldn't have explained why they were so uneasy.

'Can you trust that thing?' asked Frankenstein, pointing at the radar. Felt some comfort himself in conversation.

'You want me to be honest, sir?' said Kratzenburg.

Frankenstein smiled. Who ever answered that question by saying 'no, make some shit up, I don't mind'?

'Yes, Sergeant,' he said, 'you can be honest.'

'It's a piece of crap. The whole boat is a piece of crap. Every bit of equipment in the police service is a piece of crap. But then, every bit of equipment is provided by the lowest bidder, so go figure.'

Frankenstein nodded. Kratzenburg applied a little more speed, although they were still slow. The boat eased through the calm waters, heading into total darkness, a blank wall of fog.

Behind them Barney felt Proudfoot's hand in his. He squeezed tightly.

'You all right,' she said.

'No,' he replied. 'You?'

'Having a horrible feeling of fear, right down to the pit of my stomach.'

'Me too.'

They squeezed hands again.

'Who was in the car, Barney?' she asked. 'I saw someone.'

Barney leant forward, ran his hand through his hair. Took his hand away from her, put his face in his palms. Searching for the other Barney Thomson, the one who had been laconic and indefatigable for the previous three or four years. Where was he? Had the Devil taken him back?

Suddenly there was a noise to the right of the boat. There had been nothing but the grim silence of a dense fog, the gentle purr of the motorboat cutting dully through the mist. Now there was a mutter of another boat, closing quickly, though not yet visible through the fog.

A laugh, a low cackle. Maybe not all that different from the Joker in Batman, but in the tense, claustrophobia of the fog, enough even to get to Frankenstein.

'Gun it, Sergeant!' he shouted, and Kratzenburg leant on the lever, forcing everyone back, as the nose of the small police launch leapt in the air and the boat shot forward into the black of the night.

They looked to their right, the angry sound of the engine now drowning out any other sound.

'Did we lose him?' shouted the sergeant, looking anxiously ahead, believing he was still some way short of the island, but not trusting anything in this grim night.

'I can't tell!' Frankenstein yelled back at him. 'Any sign?' he shouted at Proudfoot and Barney, who both stood holding on to a railing, searching the fog. However, out here, out in the middle of the channel, the fog was just as dense as it had been on shore.

'Impossible to say!' Proudfoot yelled back at him.

'Keep going!' shouted Frankenstein, 'keep this up. No point in slowing yet.'

The boat sped through the mist, now shooting towards the island of Cumbrae at a fantastic pace, across flat calm waters. Kratzenburg looked ahead, the others stared around the boat into the darkness, waiting. Tensed, coiled, full of fear and adrenalin, waiting to react.

'We're getting close, sir!' yelled Kratzenburg shortly. 'We're going to have to slow, can't risk this speed any longer.'

'Ok, ok!' shouted Frankenstein, making the *slow down* gesture with his hands.

Instantly Kratzenburg cut the speed. A slight lurch, and then the boat was easing its way in towards the shore. A shore that they could not yet see.

The fog clawed the boat, enveloped it. They waited for the hull to strike a rock, to suddenly jerk onto the land. They were all poised, standing straight, holding onto the sides and the metal bar which ran across its centre between the two rows of seats.

'We just ran away from the killer, right?' said Proudfoot. Felt the need for conversation, anything to break the silence which was as damningly horrible as the fog.

Frankenstein didn't respond. Searched the mist directly in front of him. The thought came to him that perhaps it had been someone from the press. A stuntman sent by the Sun to

194

make fun of the police. At least, he decided, they wouldn't have been able to get any decent photos of the police on the run.

With a wrenching jolt the small boat thudded into a rock, the hull scraping along it, before coming to a dead stop a second later as it ran hard onto a rocky beach. The engine died. The four on board were all braced for it, but when it came it was with such suddenness that it still caught them by surprise, still threw them all sideways, forwards, onto the floor.

Proudfoot banged her head on the side of the boat, an ugly sound, an instant dull pain. Kratzenburg badly bruised his back, being spun round and hitting the wheel. Barney pitched forward, banging into the back of Frankenstein, who fell awkwardly to the side, thumping rudely onto the floor. A moment of moaning, unpleasant discomfort.

'We all ok?' shouted Frankenstein, although there was no need for the shout. Now that the sound of the engine had gone, they had been pitched into silence, as suddenly as they had been pitched onto the island.

Proudfoot groaned, listlessly leaning against the side of the boat. Barney and Kratzenburg muttered affirmatives, Barney immediately moving to Proudfoot's side, putting his arm round her waist.

'Come on,' he said, 'we should get off.'

Frankenstein leaped over the side of the boat onto the stony beach, Kratzenburg next. Then they helped Proudfoot off, before Barney was last onto the island.

They stood the four of them, still surrounded by mist, at the edge of the sea, listening to the almost imperceptible sound of the gentle waves crawling up onto the stones.

'Are you all right, Sergeant?' asked Frankenstein.

'A good crack of the head,' she said, rubbing her temple, 'but I'm ok.'

'Good. Come on, we should get up onto the road. Shouldn't take us too long to walk into town.'

'I should get back to Ardrossan, sir,' said Kratzenburg.

The others stopped. Frankenstein stared into the depths of the mist.

'You can't go back out in that, Sergeant,' he said. 'And you don't know how badly damaged the boat will be after hitting the rocks. Leave it until morning.'

Kratzenburg hesitated. Wanted to get back to Ardrossan for mostly romantic reasons, the greatest driver of them all. Didn't like the thought of a night in Millport. The murderer that lurked in the midst of the town.

'Are you worried about what we heard out there, sir?' he said.

Frankenstein twitched. Didn't want to say. Now that they were on land, now that they were away from the menace, it seemed absurd that he had yelled Gun it, Sergeant! like they were in some Hollywood action movie. Regardless of what it was that had made that noise, he now felt stupid. He didn't think Proudfoot would later mock him to others for it, but Kratzenburg was someone he didn't know. Why shouldn't he make fun of the DCI back at the station?

'I had a thought about that noise, sir,' said Kratzenburg.

Frankenstein stared at the rocks beneath his feet.

'I know, Sergeant,' he said. 'I had the same thought. Someone out to make fools of the police. More than likely the press.'

Kratzenburg nodded, looked to the others for confirmation.

'How did he find us in the mist?' said Barney.

'They have better equipment than us, Mr Thomson,' said Frankenstein. 'And if we're really unlucky, they'll have had sophisticated camera equipment that can take pictures through a miserable as Hell, dense fog. We...I...am going to look bloody stupid.'

They all turned and looked in the direction of the sea. None of them could feel it, not one amongst the four. The suspicion of imminent danger. The beat in the fog.

'So,' said Frankenstein, 'when the guy suddenly comes running up that beach out of the fog in the next few seconds, we shouldn't run away.'

'We should trip him up and pull his mask off,' said Proudfoot, straight-faced.

'Exactamundo,' said Frankenstein.

They faced the sea and awaited their fate.

'I should just give the boat a quick once-over, Sir, make sure it's ok, then I can head back out.'

'All right,' said Frankenstein, 'come on. Thomson, you make sure the sergeant's ok, and don't drift off anywhere, I don't want to lose the pair of you.'

'We'll look for the guy in the mask,' said Barney glibly.

Frankenstein grunted. He and Kratzenburg moved through the mist to the boat, which was hardly visible, even though they had barely walked five yards up the beach.

And then, despite the jokes, despite the belief that they had been spooked by the press, despite the half-laughing testaments to their intentions towards the guy in the mask, when the low cackle of laughter which had tormented them out on the water, suddenly came again, it took them all by surprise, immersed them all in instant dread. Even the sceptical Kratzenburg felt the leap of the heart, the zing of the skin.

'Right, Sergeant,' Frankenstein said to him, 'no running.'

The two men braced themselves, and Barney Thomson found himself standing firm, ushering Proudfoot behind him.

## 9

# Heads Up!

The town slept early. Barely after nine, but there was a great sense, a collective will, to put the evening to rest, get it behind them. They knew that something ill was afoot, and they wanted to snuggle down under a warm duvet, fall asleep and wake up the following morning with the fog gone, clear blue skies and a light chop to the waves. And hopefully, some climactic event would have occurred and the town would awake to find answers and the police packing up their things to head home.

Igor stood at the bedroom window of the house he now shared with the town lawyer, Garrett Carmichael, and her two children. He stared out into the dense fog, unable to see the other side of the street, never mind the sea. Could sense the feeling of ill-ease and restless evil which had come sweeping across the town with the late afternoon fog, and which now cloaked it in fear and dreadful anticipation.

There was a noise behind him as Carmichael came into the room, pyjamas on, ready for bed. She watched him for a few seconds, concerned. She was beautiful, an attraction to all the men in the town. And she was all Igor's, her heart swept away by the boldness and romanticism that lay hidden behind the bane of his baleful exterior.

'Come to bed, Igor,' she said. 'I know something's happening out there, but it doesn't involve us. We need to sleep it off.'

'Arf,' said Igor darkly.

There would be no sleep for Igor. They both knew it. The town could hide its head all that it wanted to, could hide behind thin bedwear and hope that they would not be the ones selected to be dragged screaming from that bed, but that was not Igor's path. He could not hide from this, not when it involved his friend, Barney Thomson.

She came and stood beside him, her arm on his shoulder. A clichéd scene from a thousand movies, the woman spending the possible last few moments with her man before he goes off to war. She was full of spunk herself, and would have gone too, but for the two children who lay sleeping in the next room. Their father already dead from illness, she would not put herself at such risk. Had already begun to think privately to herself, thoughts she had yet to share with Igor, that maybe it was time they moved away from Millport, if this place was suddenly as cursed as it appeared.

'Arf,' Igor said again.

She nodded. Like Barney, she was completely in tune with Igor's grunts and noises, the only sounds he could make.

She kissed him on the cheek, squeezed him harder, then stepped back. Knew that he had to get on with it and she wasn't about to make things harder by being dramatic.

'Put on a coat,' she heard herself say.

Igor smiled crookedly, pressed her hand and then walked slowly from the bedroom. Down the stairs, put on his jacket, opened the door, stepped out into the cold. Closed the door behind him and stood still on the pavement. Let the fog claw at him, soak into his face and his hands, soak his clothes. A damp, drenching fog. Down here, he could still not see the other side of the road.

No sound. No wind, no cars, no people, no sea. The town was sleeping. Or dead.

Making his decision, Igor turned to his right and walked slowly in the direction of the pier.

✂

They waited, knowing that the killer could see them, even if they couldn't see him. And then, in a rush of fog and a fevered crunch of stones, he appeared from the sea.

No Trawler Fiend this. An old man, dressed all in black, an axe held high above his right shoulder, his left arm bent across his chest. Longish hair down his neck, a long, thin beard.

They may not have been seriously expecting an eight foot lizard, but they weren't expecting some old grandpa either. And in the adrenaline-fuelled rush of it all, in the heart of the thick fog, they could see no mask, just an old man with a weapon.

He stopped his headlong rush a few yards short. He stood poised, axe raised.

'Fuck me!' yelled Frankenstein, astonished. A thousand thoughts pouring through his head in an instant, one fantastic moment of shock-induced clarity.

'Come on then!' he shouted, immediately after his previous exhortation, stepping forward.

Kratzenburg fell in beside him, the two forming a wall, almost as if Barney and Proudfoot were to be protected.

The old man seemed to hesitate, but the gentle laugh which crawled out from the rubber lips displayed an enjoyment of the kill rather than reluctance.

The laugh died, Frankenstein and Kratzenburg seemed to hesitate too, as if it might be wrong to attack an old man, regardless of the axe, regardless of the fact that here was obviously the Millport murderer. Suddenly, from behind, they heard the rapid crunch of footsteps.

Barney had found his mojo.

He burst between the two of them, running straight for the old man, his plan no more than to dodge the swipe of the axe and to grab his legs, bring him down. Barney, alone among them, while not knowing the identity of the man beneath the mask, knew that he was no old soul.

He met him full on, but as he did so, the killer swung his left arm down in a quick and sudden movement, catching Barney full on the chest, a vicious, swift, crunching blow, sending him reeling, flying. He was tossed backwards, spiralling into the air, several feet off the ground, and came to a crunching fall, so far away that he was lost in the mist. He thudded into the ground, dazed and battered, barely able to tell the direction from which the noise was now coming.

Frankenstein, empowered by this show of strength from the enemy, stepped forward. He never even got as close as Barney, as another swing from the arm, a low uppercut, caught Frankenstein in the chest and sent him flying straight backwards, back to where Proudfoot was standing, helpless.

Kratzenburg dithered, given necessary pause by the expeditious way in which Barney Thomson and Frankenstein had been summarily dispatched. His hesitation made no difference however. The old fella had his eye on him.

As he made his first step towards him, Kratzenburg suddenly had a thought of the guys in the red jerseys who you always knew were going to get killed at the start of the old Star Trek, the guys who were sent down to the planet surface with Kirk and Spock entirely so they could die in the first five minutes.

'Shit,' thought Kratzenburg, realising that he was the newcomer to the investigation, the officer who was not really part of it, 'I'm dead.'

And so, rather than blindly throwing himself at the old guy, Kratzenburg made the sensible, but ultimately futile decision to run away. He made the first move to turn, and that was as far as he got. The killer descended on him.

He swung the axe, blade turned away, at his legs, tripping him up and sending him into the stones on his face. Kratzenburg stumbled on the beach, turned his head in fear. Just in time to see the final swing of the executioner's cleaver. His eyes showed shock, the axe descended.

Kratzenburg's head flew to the side in a high arc, almost as if his head had been severed with a nine iron. Somewhere in the mist, out of sight, the others heard it land heavily on the stones.

The killer stood over Proudfoot and Frankenstein, blood dripping from the axe, the weapon still held to the side. Then suddenly he seemed to relax, his body language became dismissive. He didn't need to kill anyone else here. To his right, Barney Thomson crawled into view across the stones, feeling that somehow he should be the one who was there facing this demon.

The killer surveyed the three of them, the eyes gloating behind the mask. He smiled, he winked at Barney.

'Barney,' he said, and then, as suddenly as he had arrived, he ran past them and disappeared back into the thick mist, heading up onto the road.

He was gone.

Silence.

The mist ebbed and flowed around them, swirling in nebulous patterns, sweeping in from the sea, turning this way, sweeping down and up, swallowing them.

Barney crawled over to be beside the others, both of them dazed, horrified.

'You all right?' he said, directing the question at Proudfoot, the only one who had not felt the full force of the killer's wrath.

She nodded. Couldn't speak. It had been a long time since she had witnessed something that horrible. Frankenstein, more used to drunks and thugs and gangs of youths, could not find his mouth either.

For Barney Thomson, however, this felt like his life. This was real, constantly surrounded by bloody death, bloody murder. The old New Barney was back. Stripped of fear, embraced by a charismatic nonchalance that drove women wild. If his continuing life, the horror and the blood, was the work of Satan, well Satan could come and get him. He was ready.

'The old guy seemed to know you?' said Frankenstein, pulling himself up. 'Who was it?'

'I don't know,' said Barney. 'It wasn't an old guy though. The face, the hair, it was a mask. A Dostoevsky mask. Fyodor Dostoevsky,' he added, just in case anyone had thought he'd meant Agnes Dostoevsky.

Frankenstein and Proudfoot looked curiously at Barney.

'What?' she said.

'Where the fuck do you get a Dostoevsky mask?' said Frankenstein dismissively. 'And how the fuck would you even know what he looks like? What the fuck is that? A Dostoevsky mask?'

Barney looked from one to the other. To him it was obvious. Crime and punishment. This, however, did not seem like a good time to get into Russian literature and any correlation with his own life.

'I don't know,' he said. 'Come on, we should get back into town.'

He looked down at the stricken, headless body of Sergeant Kratzenburg.

'The big man's going to have to wait. There's likely worse than this going to happen here tonight. We stick close, all the way round. Close enough that you can see the other two at all times. If you lose one of them, call out the instant it happens. The instant. And we cut across the back road into town. We cool?'

Proudfoot nodded.

'We're cool,' said Frankenstein, curious and a little wary of Barney's sudden determination.

As they started to walk up the beach, Frankenstein put his hand on Barney's shoulder.

'I made you my deputy,' he said, awkward censure in his voice, 'not my fucking boss.'

## 10

## A Soul For A Soul...

Igor had found his way round to the boatyard. He moved more quickly than other men in this dark time of no light and thick fog, his senses more attuned to his outside world. He had walked along the front and investigated the pier. Nothing to be found there, except the creepy and uncomfortable calm of all piers in a thick fog. Then he had come along Crichton Street, past the unoccupied police station, round past the football field, a field which he knew was there but which, the barest of edges aside, he could not see.

He did not pass another single person on his way, at least, none of which he was aware. Perhaps someone had passed him on the other side of the street, out of sight, the sound of footsteps muffled in the fog. But Igor walked on, driven only by curiosity about what was out there. Fearless.

He knew that the three murders which had been committed in the town had all happened in the sanctity of peoples' homes, the inviolable had been breached, and maybe that was what was going to happen again tonight. But the murderer had to get from house to house, had to move around somehow. A car, a bike, padded footsteps dragged through the night.

Even though Millport was small, it wasn't so tiny that he was guaranteed to stumble across anyone who might be out, especially not in this weather. But Igor had a nose for it, a sense that he would inevitably find what he went looking for. And all his senses told him that this strange mystery, which had started with the disappearance of a fishing trawler, would in some way involve the boatyard and the last remnants of seafaring on the island.

He stopped at the entrance to the yard, felt out the door. Listened in the night for any sound from within. So still, so cloaked was the evening, that even the clang of the chains, the constant sound of any boatyard, had been silenced.

Nothing.

He wondered about old Bladestone, a man with whom he had only exchanged grudging acknowledgements in the past, despite him being a regular in the shop from the days long before Barney's arrival.

Igor opened the door slowly, the hinges unavoidably creaking in the night. He cursed slightly under his breath. No sound could he make. Any advantage he had would be lost.

The door opened as little as possible, he squeezed through the gap. Instinctively wanted to close the gate over, the obsessive-compulsive inherent in him, but he fought the urge.

Knowing that the floor of the boatyard was littered with anchors and wooden beams and masts, he edged along the wall until he got to the first shed, and then turned and moved along the shed wall until he got to the end of that. Stopped there to get his bearings, to try and get a feel for the place.

The fog was no less dense inside the yard. He could see the dark outline of a hull a few feet in front of him. Did not know the yard well enough to recognise it.

*Phht!*

A stumble. A dull sound in the night. Followed by a curse and another small trip. Igor's heart raced, he pressed himself back against the wall. Head working. It couldn't be Bladestone, he would know his yard well enough not to trip.

He tensed, arms up, waiting to defend himself against what was coming his way. Could sense two figures before he could see them. Was tempted to shout out, perhaps make them run away. But he knew he had to deal with this now, right here, given that the opportunity was falling into his lap.

The figures approached, Igor inched away from the wall, giving himself more room. He eased himself into a tae-kwon-do position, ready for action, the hump of his hunchback exaggeratedly protruding above his shoulders. Held his breath.

They emerged from the mist, leaning forward, walking faster than they ought to have been given the total lack of visibility. Igor tensed.

Bernard and the Dog With No Name jumped, each one letting out a yelp.

'Arf!' hissed Igor.

Bernard settled down, standing in front of Igor, the Dog With No Name snuggled into his leg.

'Like, Igor, pal, you scared me, man!'

*I'm not your pal*, hissed Igor in reply, although, as ever, all that came out and all that Bernard heard was Arf!

'Like sure, man, but what are you doing here? We're looking for clues, aren't we Dog With No Name, old buddy? But it's so foggy, like, we can't see a thing!'

Igor was torn between believing they were looking for clues, and wondering whether they played a more sinister part in all of this than it seemed on the surface. They were MI6 after all, and Igor had never trusted MI6. Yet, while they may have been acting suspiciously snooping around the boatyard late in the evening on a foggy and dark night, so was he.

'Arf,' he hissed quietly, indicating for them to fall in behind him.

'Like, sure, pal,' said Bernard, and he and the Dog With No Name filed in next to Igor against the wall of the shed and began to inch their way along.

'Like, Igor old buddy,' said Bernard a few seconds later, 'you didn't bring any food with you on this expedition, did you? We're starved!'

✄

Barney, Frankenstein and Proudfoot came into town down the back road, coming onto the road at Kames Bay. Walking quickly, Frankenstein in the front, Proudfoot behind him, Barney at the back. They passed The Deadman's Café, saw the dim lights inside, realised it was still open. Frankenstein stopped, turned to the others.

'Anyone use a coffee?' he said. 'Myself, I need intravenous caffeine.'

Barney didn't wait for Proudfoot's answer, opened the door and ushered the other two inside. They walked quickly in from the cold, closing the door behind them. They stood inside and surveyed the surroundings. Deserted. Lights on, door unlocked, but the heating was off, the premises not much warmer than the cold, dark night outside. No customers, no one behind the counter.

'Alice?' said Barney.

Nothing.

He looked at the other two, their faces both showing the resignation and acknowledgement that here was another potential grim finding. The feeling of doom hung in the air, an air of portentous death that no sixth sense could miss.

'Alice?' Barney called, a little louder this time.

'You still need that coffee?' he said.

Frankenstein exhaled a pent up breath, followed by a low curse.

'Fuck,' he said. 'This is all we need. Alice!' he called more loudly, then added, 'who the fuck is Alice anyway? The owner or the woman who does nights?'

'Both,' said Barney.

Frankenstein placed his hand firmly on the counter top and vaulted over it, landing awkwardly on the other side. Barney, more familiar with the place and now fully possessing the old nonchalance that had so deserted him the previous few days, lifted the counter top to the right and walked behind. Frankenstein gave him a look, then they both pushed through to the back of the shop.

Barney, in front, stopped suddenly, Frankenstein having to step quickly to the side to avoid walking into him. They saw the words written on the kitchen wall in blood, before they saw the decapitated body.

Barney stepped back, two steps, hit the wall, couldn't go any further, although he did not leave the kitchen.

*A soul for a soul, Barney Thomson!*

The words were written in fresh dripping blood, each word beneath the other, *Thomson* written along the wall just above the work surface. Next to it, on the kitchen top beside the chopping board and an opened box of raw chopped onion, was the head of Alice Witherington, perfectly sliced at the neck. Placed so as to be the full stop in the giant exclamation mark

Her body lay on the floor. A pool of blood. Alice Witherington, who had spent so many happy nights in the den of thieves above the Incidental Mermaid, who had spent the last few days living in justifiable fear.

Frankenstein had moved on from his own personal fears. It was time for anger and determination. He walked forward, ran a finger rudely through the blood on the wall. Still fresh, still damp. Rubbed his forefinger and thumb together.

'Recent,' he said. 'The last ten minutes.'

'Should I come in there?' said Proudfoot from the café.

'No,' said Barney quickly. 'We'll be out in a second.'

'Shout out if you see anyone with an axe,' said Frankenstein acerbically, and could hear Proudfoot's exasperated groan from outside.

'So, Barney Thomson,' said Frankenstein, voice low, 'is this all about you? Murder follows you around?'

Barney said nothing. Murder did follow him around, but he didn't want to think for a second that all this blood was on his hands. He couldn't live with that.

Maybe that was the intention.

'Couldn't you go and live in England and have some of that lot murdered?'

Barney laughed, an ugly grunt of a laugh, in keeping with the ugly bloody scene in which they were standing.

'Deputy Thomson, consultant to the police service, this is as if they knew you were coming this way. It's done for your benefit. Where are we heading now? The boatyard maybe? Does that make sense? The whole town is between us and there. Are we going to find a murder in every establishment we pass? What d'you think, Deputy? What is your Dostoevsky up to?'

Barney had no answer. He had heard a rumour of the clandestine Incidental Mermaid club, but had no idea of why it existed and was completely unaware of what connection there might be between it and him.

'The faster we get there, the better,' he said, and turned quickly from the kitchen. Proudfoot was sitting at a table on the other side of the counter, her head in her hand, pale, beautiful, wondering how she had managed to walk into such a situation again. Why her? Why her, every time? Except that she kept on running into Barney Thomson.

Barney walked to the door, opened it once more back out to the mist and the lonely, desolate evening.

'We need to go,' he said to Proudfoot. 'I'm sorry, I know you need a break. We need to, and we can't leave you here.'

She gazed into his eyes, believed him, wanted to believe that he meant her no harm and that none of this was truly his fault.

'Who wants your soul, Barney?' said Frankenstein. 'You make a pact with Satan?'

Barney looked at him, stopped still in the doorway.

'Not that I know,' he said. 'But maybe we all have.'

He walked quickly out into the night, Proudfoot and Frankenstein behind him. Proudfoot at the back, trailing in the others' angry wake. She looked down and saw, in the dim light of the shop, the marks from Frankenstein's shoe, where he had stepped in the trail of blood that had been left from the decapitation of Alice Witherington.

## 11

## Closing Time

Fred, Selma and Deirdre, crack MI6 agents, on the trail of a killer and a gang of international diamond smugglers, left the small seafront apartment which they had rented for the duration of the investigation, having just had another bout of pretty spectacular three-in-a-bed sex. Although, on this occasion it had been three-in-a-bath sex. A lot of water had ended up on the floor.

'That sure was fun, girls,' said Fred, as they stepped out into the cold night.

'It certainly was,' said Deirdre. 'I especially liked what you did with the empty shower gel bottle and that three litres of lighter fluid.'

Selma shivered.

'Jeepers,' she said, trying to switch her mind back on to the investigation, 'it sure is misty out here. I hope Bernard and The Dog With No Name are ok.'

'We said we'd meet them at the boatyard,' said Fred, stating a fact that everyone already knew, which was something which he did on a regular basis, and which the others generally found really annoying. 'It wasn't so misty a while back, but I guess we were in that bath for a lot longer than expected.'

'Like, I'll say,' said Deirdre.

'I think we need to get to the boatyard as quickly as possible,' said Selma, always the first to get back to the business at hand.

They stopped on the street and looked around, assessing the fact that they couldn't see further than a few yards. They were just along from the crocodile rock, the other end of the front stretch from where they wanted to be, only a couple of hundred yards ahead of Barney Thomson, Frankenstein and Proudfoot.

210

'We need to stick close together,' said Fred. 'Girls, stay on either side of me and hold my hand. If you get detached, scream really loudly or something.'

Suddenly they felt it, rather than saw anything. A whooshing in the dense fog, something brushing past them in the night, a few yards away. They tensed, Fred pushing the girls behind him, staring intently into the fog. They could just make it out, the shape of the figure in black, as it seamlessly moved past them along the road, either oblivious to them or ignoring them.

'Like, shit, did you see that?' said Fred. 'That was a man in black. He must be like a bad guy Let's get out of here!'

He turned and started to move off in the opposite direction, but Selma pulled his hand, making sure he wasn't going anywhere.

'That guy is going in the same direction as we want to, which means he might be going to the boatyard! We need to get there before he gets to Bernard and The Dog With No Name.'

Fred hesitated, then reluctantly nodded.

'Ok,' he said, 'here's what we're going to do. We're going to stick together and run to the boatyard as quickly as possible. My guess is that the Man in Black knew we were here and just decided to completely ignore us.'

'But why?'

'I don't know, Deidre. But someone's been misleading us on this case all along. There is no Trawler Fiend or Incredible Captain Death, just an evil guy dressed in black. I don't know who it is, but I mean to find out. Come on!'

And so, Fred, Selma and Deidre headed off into the night, along Glasgow Street, only a few paces ahead of the unseen Barney Thomson and the two police officers for whom Barney was doing, so far, unpaid consultancy work.

✄

There was a reason that the mysterious diamond smuggling cabal had met in a private room above the Incidental Mermaid pub, half way up Cardiff Street. The bar manager and occasional barman, Kent Carrington, was one of the ten. He was not, however, the particular one of the ten who was currently running amok through the town dressed in black and a Fyodor Dostoevsky mask. And so Kent Carrington had been living in fear for the past few days, a fear that would have been even greater had he known that Alice Witherington, his close confidante amongst the group, had recently lost contact with her head.

Dr Trio Semester turned away from the television screen and placed the empty pint glass down on the bar. It had been a long, slow night, watching *Celebrity Get Me To The Toilet In Time!*, *Top 50 Celebrity Nose Job Botch Jobs*, *Most Amazing Celebrity Police Videos 7* and *Celebrity I Hate My Clitoris!* He had come back down to Millport to speak to Frankenstein about the case. He could easily have spoken to Frankenstein over the phone, but something about his wife made him want to spend as much time away from the house as possible, so he had engineered another away trip. That he had since become stranded on the island seemed an added bonus.

However, the town was completely dead, and he had found that everyone wanted to head indoors, put up the barricades and wait for the dawn. Not that he did not sense the danger himself, for he felt it with every fibre, but his way of dealing with it had been to get out and find company.

And so he had sat in the Incidental Mermaid for two hours, hoping that someone else would join him there. No one had come. Two hours with only Kent Carrington for company.

Carrington, filled with dread, had chattered incessantly at first. Semester, however, was not one to put up with incessant chatter for an entire evening. So, after an hour of listening to Carrington burble randomly, badly articulating every single thought he had in his head, Semester had taken a bite out of the social bullet and told Carrington that he was going to have to shut up, because Semester was trying to concentrate on the celebrity rhinoplasties. Which he hadn't been.

The fact that he'd sat there for another hour was testimony really to his own desperation and unhappiness, and testimony perhaps to the even more uncomfortable truth that he was scared to walk back along to the hotel. The Stewart. He should have followed his instinct, ignored his years old edict, and just drunk in the hotel bar.

Carrington had watched the tv, unable to concentrate, just grateful that there was someone else there with him. Believed, wrongly, that there might be some safety in numbers.

Finally, as the theme music to *I'm A Celebrity, Pluck My Nasal Hair!* finally faded into the adverts, Semester glanced round at Carrington, and Carrington waited fearfully to see if his customer was going to add to the three pints and four packets of crisps he'd already consumed, or whether this was him about to leave.

'Think I'll head on back to the hotel,' said Semester. 'Let you get on home.'

'No!' said Carrington, in a strange, high-pitched cry.

Semester looked curiously at him, then lifted his hand in a gesture of closure. And, at that moment, the door to the outside swung open. The men turned, Carrington buoyed at the thought that here was someone he could talk to. Someone to stop him being stuck in this wretched bar alone.

No one. The door swung on its hinges, creaked halfway back, and then stayed there. Open, letting in the cold of the night, the fog. The men stared at each other, then looked back at the door.

'Oh shit,' said Carrington.

Along with the dread cold evening, they could feel the malevolence sweep in, a tangible presence.

'We should close the door,' said Semester.

Neither man moved. They stood where they were, propped against either side of the bar, waiting. Semester found himself nervously drumming his fingers, mind in an instant battle. He saw death every day. Literally every day. Sometimes murder, sometimes heart attack, sometimes accident, but it always came his way. Why should he be afraid of it or anything that might cause it?

'I should go and let you close up,' he forced himself to say.

'Not yet,' said Carrington desperately. 'Just let me lock things up and I'll come with you. It'll be a bit Butch and Sundance. But not in any homoerotic way.'

Semester gave him a glance.

'I'm babbling,' said Carrington.

'Butch and Sundance weren't gay,' said Semester.

The words were barely out of his mouth when the door was suddenly thrown back, crashing into the wall behind.

The two men turned quickly, gaping at the sight of the masked man dressed in black.

'Fuck!' shouted Semester. 'Dostoevsky! That's not normal. Have you got a gun back there?'

Carrington shook his head.

'I've got lots of skooshers,' he said.

'You think we can spray the guy with tonic?'

'You never know what's going to defeat people,' wailed Carrington.

Dostoevsky raised the axe above his head, his left arm across his chest, in the same pose that had heralded the end of Sgt Kratzenburg, then began to walk slowly towards them. From behind the rubber they could hear a low, ominous laugh. Mocking, threatening.

'Give me a bottle!' shouted Semester.

'What of?' said Carrington, nervously.

'Anything, for God's sake, just give me a bottle!'

Carrington lifted the first bottle that came to hand. Fifteen year old Glenlivet. Passed it over. Semester grabbed it from him then smashed it on the side of the bar. Glass and whisky sprayed. Carrington gasped, taking time out of his terror to be shocked at the appalling waste of a decent whisky.

Semester pointed the jagged edge of the broken bottle. He'd never used a bottle in anger before but at least had seen, on many occasions, the devastating effect to which they could be used.

'Come on then, you old Russian bastard,' he said loudly. Dostoevsky came upon him, but he was not here to murder the police pathologist. He had his list of suspects to take care of, Kratzenburg having been an added bit of fun, for the continuing benefit of Barney Thomson. Adrenalin pumping, Semester hoisted himself quickly up onto the bar. Carrington had backed off, nowhere to run, pressed against the glasses and bottles which fell around him.

Semester, suddenly full of brio and derring-do, leapt dramatically at the old man, but he did not even get close. Swinging the axe like a baseball bat, axehead turned down,

Dostoevsky caught Semester full on the side and sent him flying away to his right, off the bar and crumpling into a heap on the floor, head cracking loudly off a heavy wooden table. He lay dazed and battered and bruised on the floor. He tried to lift his head, then the effort proved too great for him, and his face hit the floor once more and he passed into unconsciousness.

The killer looked across the bar at Kent Carrington.

'You must have known I was coming,' said Dostoevsky. 'I'm disappointed you didn't lay on more of a reception.'

'Well, can I get you a drink?' said Carrington. 'On the house?' he added, voice thin and nervous.

'In despair there are the most intense enjoyments,' said Dostoevsky, and he laughed again, malicious and low. Then he lifted the axe once more grandly above his head. Carrington's mouth dropped open. Nothing came at first, but as the axe hovered in the air with the expectation of the final, cutting blow, he cringed and cowered and found the strength to scream, a high, desperate wail.

## 12

## The Temperature Of The Night

They heard it. The six people out in the street, in two groups of three, heading towards the boatyard. This scream, this cry of terror and fear, this wail that told of impending bloody and gory death, had travelled through the town, in every direction, almost as if the fog, rather than muffling the scream, conducted it, propelled it on its way.

And the people of the town of Millport, who had all sensed the terror in this awful night, crawled further under their blankets, and turned out any lights that were still on, and prayed that whoever it was who screamed such a terrible scream, was not someone they knew and loved.

'Come on, girls,' said Fred. 'Sounds like someone's in trouble.'

'It sure does,' said Deirdre.

They started to run faster into the mist, passing store fronts that they barely recognised in the gloomy, misty darkness.

'Stop!' hissed Selma, and she tugged at Fred's hand to slow him.

The three crack MI6 agents stopped dead, just by the closed doors of the amusement arcade.

'What's up, Selma?' said Fred.

'Listen!' she said.

They craned their necks into the mist, and sure enough, now that they had stopped moving, they could all hear it, the sound from behind. Footsteps, coming their way, following them.

'We're being followed!' whispered Fred, insomuch as he could manage a whisper.

'Oh my gosh!' said Deidre, 'do you think it's the Man in Black?'

'I don't think so,' said Fred. 'I think whoever let out that terrified scream has just encountered the Man in Black!'

The footsteps approached, clear now, although the runners were still out of sight in the mist. Fred stepped forward.

'It sure is a misty night,' he said loudly into the fog.

Frankenstein, Proudfoot and Barney Thomson came running into view, unavoidably surprised by the sudden intervention of MI6. They crashed to a halt, out of breath.

'Fuck me,' said Frankenstein. 'That scream?' he added quickly, not wanting to get into any amiable discussion about the weather.

'It came from just up ahead,' said Deirdre.

'I won't ask what you freaks are doing out here,' said Frankenstein. 'Come on.'

He took off, and they charged full-tilt into the mist. Not far and they were at the bottom end of Cardiff Street, just down the road from the bar, although the Incidental Mermaid remained well out of sight.

'Barney?' said Frankenstein.

Barney stared into the mist. Still thick and clawing. Perhaps that was the worst thing on this dreadful evening. He had seen death before, he had seen so much blood, so many dismembered limbs, he had become anaesthetized to it. But this mist, this fog which so enshrouded them, it seemed that even though they were outside, they were encased in a walking coffin. No escape. The only way to be able to see further than a few feet was to go indoors, and when they'd done that there had been blood and death. As there inevitably would be the next place they entered.

'The pub up the road,' said Barney. Gut instinct. 'The Mermaid.'

He looked around the group, waiting for some contradiction perhaps, and then he pushed on into the fog. Up the road fifty, seventy yards, and the dark frontage of the Mermaid appeared out of the gloom in front of them. The door was ajar.

Away to their left Fyodor Dostoevsky ran up the hill, the sound already lost in the fog. Barney turned, made sure the full assembly was behind him, gave Frankenstein a look which said to expect more of what they had seen in Deadman's Café, and then he pushed the door fully open and walked into the chill of the pub, the others piling in behind them.

217

The body of Kent Carrington lay slumped over the bar, his severed head placed on the counter beside him. His eyes were still wide open in fear, his lips drawn back.

'Fuck,' muttered Frankenstein.

Barney walked over to the bar, Proudfoot held her head in her hands, the turmoil boiling in her head. She needed to breathe, she needed space, but she was experiencing the same feeling of complete entrapment, of being incarcerated in a deep, dark cave.

'Jeepers!' said Deirdre.

'It sure looks like he's had a spot of trouble,' said Fred. 'Come on girls, let's look for clues.'

Proudfoot leant her head against the wall, back turned. Barney looked at the blood spattered wall of the bar, red marks in an arc that would have been familiar to him had he seen any of the earlier victims, across the bottles and glasses and peanuts and other savoury snacks. No message written on the wall this time, but perhaps the killer had known how close behind they were. No time.

Frankenstein noticed the prone figure on the floor, walked over quickly. The head still attached, he knew instantly that this person would not be dead.

Turned the head round. Semester.

'Fuck,' he muttered again. Bent over him, listened to the heart beat. He slapped Semester's face a couple of times, a very slight reaction.

'Barney!' he called. 'Whisky, get me some whisky.'

Barney looked down at the prone figure, and then walked hurriedly round the bar, stepping on blood, not caring about this dreadful scene of carnage, and grabbed a bottle of Teachers.

'Chief Inspector,' he said. Frankenstein looked up and Barney under-armed the bottle perfectly into his outstretched hand.

'Good throw!' said Deirdre. 'Have you guys ever played slow pitch softball?'

Frankenstein sat Semester's head on his knee, poured whisky into the cap, then dabbed some around his nose and gently poured a little onto his lips and into his mouth.

'This shite'll wake anybody up,' he muttered.

A second or two, a cough, and then Semester was choking and spluttering, forcing himself to sit up. Frankenstein thumped him on the back, Semester pulled himself away from the detective and dragged himself up onto his knees. He looked at Frankenstein, the horror of his last waking moment still on his face, then down at the bottle of Teachers in Frankenstein's hands.

'Christ, did you have to?' he asked.

'You all right?' said Frankenstein.

'Aye,' said Semester. 'Where's the barman?' And he looked past Frankenstein and Deirdre and saw the slumped, decapitated body of Kent Carrington.

'Aw Jesus. He was a dull man,' said Semester, 'but he didn't deserve that.'

'Come on,' said Frankenstein, 'we need to keep moving.'

He helped Semester to his feet. Proudfoot was still leaning against the wall, but had at last allowed herself to look round, giving her some relief at the sight of Semester still standing. Barney Thomson came round from the other side of the bar. Blood on his shoes. Fred was examining the clean cut-off marks of the severed head of Kent Carrington. Selma was down on the floor, beside the bar, looking for clues.

'Right,' said Frankenstein. 'Let's head out. Stick close together, we head for the boatyard.'

'Aha!' exclaimed Selma from the floor, and she stood up, rubbing her thumb and forefinger together.

Frankenstein looked at her with curious agitation.

'I think I might just have found the clue that solves this mystery!' exclaimed Selma.

The others all stared at her. Fred and Deirdre smiled.

'Well, Miss fucking Marple, are you going to tell us what it is?' said Frankenstein.

'I need one more clue and I'll be sure,' said Selma, 'and I think we might just find it at the boatyard!'

'Super,' said Fred, 'let's go.'

And the three agents from MI6 headed quickly out into the night. Frankenstein hesitated a second, looking at the three left in the bar.

'Didn't I say the boatyard?' he said. 'I said the boatyard, and now fucking Catwoman there, the ace defective, solves the mystery. God, these people are pissing me off.'

## 13

## The Dostoevsky Theory

Igor, Bernard and The Dog With No Name were still creeping around the boatyard in the middle of the night. Igor had become the *de facto* leader, not a position with which he was particularly comfortable, but it made sense given the rest of the crew.

They had stumbled over anchors and masts, bumped into boats, tripped over tarpaulins. Igor was beginning to lose faith. He had sensed the danger and evil inherent in the night, and had thought that the same sixth sense would inevitably lead him to it. Instead, he was stumbling around the boatyard, one of three Stooges, having to accept that he had no real idea of what he was doing.

'Maybe we should go inside one of the sheds,' said Bernard, tapping him on the shoulder. Bernard had continued to talk to him throughout, ignoring the fact that Igor couldn't hear him and was making no effort to understand. This time, however, Bernard pointed at the door which they were passing to make sure he got his point across.

Igor slumped a little beneath his hump. Of course they had to go inside, but for some reason he had been avoiding it. Would inside one of these dark, dank sheds make him feel even more claustrophobic than he did out here?

He held up his hand in acknowledgement, put his hand on the door handle hoping it would be locked. It turned slowly, he pushed the door open. The shed was in total darkness, they couldn't see five inches in front of them, never mind the few feet of visibility they had outside.

'Like, wow, man,' said Bernard, 'this is so creepy. You ok, Dog With No Name?'

The dog let out a low whimper. Igor waved his hand at them to quieten them down, but they couldn't see it. Bernard fumbled around on the wall by the door until he found the light switch.

*Click!*

Igor turned and looked at him, bathing the place in light not being part of his plan. Bernard quickly closed the door behind him, the Dog With No Name shuffling into the cramped space.

'Like, come on, my little hunchbacked buddy, it was like super-creepy with no lights on.'

Igor looked daggers at him, but didn't turn the light off. The damage, if there was to be any, had been done. The three of them turned and looked round the cramped shed. Packed full of tools and boating equipment, the same shed in which Frankenstein had talked to Bladestone earlier in the day. Inevitably the three pairs of eyes were drawn to the mark on the wall where, until a few days previously, the axe had hung, its outline still clear on the wall.

'Like, oh my gosh!' said Bernard. 'It's even creepier with the lights on!'

The Dog With No Name buried into his leg, its head lowered. Igor glanced quickly around the rest of the shed. Through the jumble of all kinds of everything that filled the place, there were two doors at either end of the room. One directly in front of them, somewhere that was obviously frequently used, a clear passageway leading through the stramash of equipment. The path to the door at the back was littered with junk.

'Arf,' muttered Igor, indicating with his hand.

Walking past the axe-mark on the way, he led them to the first door. Pushed it open, the small room flooded with dull light from the rest of the shed. Big shadows and dark corners. A sink, a table top, a small fridge. Igor looked around, this insignificant kitchen itself packed with all sorts of spare parts and other assorted workshop paraphernalia.

Bernard poked his head over Igor's hump, the Dog With No Name looked between Igor's legs.

'Like, wow, man,' said Bernard, 'there's a fridge!'

Igor backed off, as the other two raced round either side of him to examine the contents of the fridge. They flung the door open, and tried not to allow themselves to be too disappointed with the results.

Milk and cheese, a bit of margarine.

'It's all dairy, man,' said Bernard, and then, just to bring a little more brightness into his room, he noticed the small loaf sitting in amongst a selection of socket wrenches on the worktop.

'Like, wow!' he said, 'looks like we might be having a sandwich after all, Dog With No Name, old buddy.'

The Dog With No Name barked. Igor left them to it, walked through the shed and started picking his way across the quagmire of equipment and tools and general workshop mayhem which littered the floor between him and the door at the rear of the room. Stumbled a couple of times, went over on his ankle. The single bare light bulb which hung in the entrance to the shed cast long shadows here, a lot of the smaller items which littered the floor were obscured. Igor tread carefully, reached the door.

Tried the handle, it turned but the door would not open. He pushed harder, finally planted his feet and put his shoulder against it. Suddenly, with a loud creak and a scraping along the floor, the door flew back and Igor tumbled into the small dark room at the back of the shed.

He stood for a second, staring into the darkness, waiting for his eyes to adjust to the light. Could make out the flat surface of a table, not much else.

Beneath the table, something scraped along the ground. Igor, heart in mouth, ready for action, fumbled for the light switch.

✂

They walked quickly, knowing the killer was ahead of them, convinced that they were moving in the same direction. None of them really wanted to meet the killer head on, none of them had the faintest idea what they would do once confronted with the swinging axe of death. Except Fred, who was full of plans and schemes, although most of them consisted of somehow tripping the fiend up, pulling his mask off, handing the villain over to the proper authorities, and then heading for the nearest café for a celebratory milk shake and muffin.

'Why that bar?' said Frankenstein, walking quickly beside Barney, Proudfoot tucked in just behind them. 'Why that café?'

'I don't know,' said Barney. 'It's a sleepy town, but there's always weird shit going on in any place. There were rumours that some little secret society used it as a meeting place, but we all assumed it was just small town trivial business. We've had that kind of thing here before.'

'Aha! That might just be the other clue we've been needing!' said Selma, with some finality.

'You think?' said Barney. 'Fantastic.'

'Wonderful,' said Frankenstein, brusquely, 'Who was in this society?'

'Can't help you,' said Barney. 'Don't know what they did, don't know who was in it. Like I said, we've had this sort of business here before, and that kind of thing never, *never* repays curiosity.'

Frankenstein grunted.

'I suppose you're about to tell us who the man in the mask is?' he snarled at Selma.

'It's not a man in a mask,' she said with triumph. 'It's an actual old gentleman with the strength of a man a quarter of his age.'

'Gee, Selma, you think?' said Fred. Fred was convinced it was a man in a mask.

Frankenstein shook his head and walked on. Wishing that he had armed himself, or that there were at least armed officers on the island, so that they could just blast the killer first, then worry about who exactly he was when he was lying flat on his back, twitching.

They walked on, passing the football field, only a couple of hundred yards or so from the boatyard. Tension palpable.

'I reckon,' said Deirdre, 'that this time we might just be dealing with a genuine one hundred and fifty year-old Russian novelist, and if we're looking to apportion blame, we need look no further than the nuclear power station right across the water. The papers are right, there's something weird out there and the government's to blame.'

They all turned and looked in the direction of Hunterston B nuclear reactor, although of course they couldn't see five yards of the mile and a half that separated them.

'Usually people theorise about two-headed fish and giant amphibians,' said Frankenstein caustically.

'Well that may be,' said Deirdre, 'but how can any of us say? We all know that the beaches and the sea within twenty miles of all Britain's nuclear power stations are completely ruined. The government's been covering it up for decades. That's what they do. Could any of us be surprised if suddenly an aberrant mutant pre-Communist era author was accidentally created by these forces we can't possibly even seek to understand?'

Fred and Selma nodded seriously.

'You're insane,' said Frankenstein.

'There's weirder shit than that, my friend,' said Fred. 'I've seen the files.'

Frankenstein grumbled, the MI6 collective walked on, shoulders back, ready for anything, and so they all descended into silence and strode towards the boatyard, determined to meet whatever fate lay in store.

## 14

## Ship Of Fools

The noise came again, Igor fumbled around on the wall, his movements becoming more frantic. A back room, maybe there was no light switch. Another twitch of a foot, or something, a claw or a hand. He stepped to the wall, ran both of his hands over it, coming up against cobwebs, disturbing huge spiders which had lain there unruffled for a long time.

A large black spider scuttled onto his hand and he brushed it away. He found a power point, moved his hand along the small ledge of wood. Another noise behind him, the foot scraped back and forth, back and forth, a frantic movement. One of Barney's ghosts?

He found the light switch, clicked it, another spider on the cuff of his jacket, looked under the table.

There were two men under there, bound together, back to back, arms strapped to their sides and strapped round two table legs. Their feet had been bound, large strips of grey tape had been strapped around their mouths.

Igor noticed the smell of urine and faeces, which had for some reason been hidden in the darkness. This back room was a prison, and these men had been here for some time.

He bent down and struggled with the tape around their mouths. Made a small gesture to them, returned to the workshop, lifted the first sharp implement that he could find, then returned to the back room and quickly slit the gags. And although it hadn't stopped either of them from breathing, they both immediately started panting, desperate for air in their mouths, to inhale large quantities at once.

Igor recognised them both. Colin Waites and Craig Brown, the two missing trawlermen. They must have been bound and gagged here for several days now. They would have trouble walking.

He cut the ropes on their feet and then the straps binding them to the table. The two men moved apart, crawling along the floor, legs and arms numb. Igor stood over them, and then thought of Bernard and the Dog With No Name in the other room, making sandwiches. He held up his finger to indicate that he would just be a minute.

The gate at the front of the yard creaked. Igor tensed, Waites and Brown started trying to drag themselves to their feet. Within seconds Bernard and the Dog With No Name were in the back room, sandwiches abandoned.

'Like, did you hear...,' began Bernard, and then he saw the two guys struggling to their knees and breathed in the stench of the room.

'Like, wow! I'm guessing you two are the guys from the trawler!' said Bernard.

'Who are you?' said Waites.

'Bernard! My name's Bernard,' said Bernard. 'We're MI6.'

'Arf,' muttered Igor darkly.

'Fucking government,' said Waites.

Igor put his finger to his lips and indicated outside. Waites nodded. Bernard glanced out the door, then looked into the small, spider-ridden, malodorous room that was their only other option. Neither called to him as much as running away as fast as he could in any direction.

Igor glanced round the door and looked across the ten yards of cluttered workshop floor to the light switch, then he pointed at Bernard and pointed at the switch.

'Me? I don't think so,' said Bernard. 'Dog With No Name, will you do it for some Unnamed Snacks?'

The Dog With No Name shook its head.

'If you're worried about the guy in the mask,' said Craig Brown, from underneath his matt of shaggy hair, 'it hardly matters, he can see in the dark.'

'You've seen The Incredible Captain Death?' exclaimed Bernard.

Igor poked him and put his fingers to his lips.

'The Incredible Captain Death?' said the other two in unison.

Igor looked around them all, making the *quiet!* sign. There weren't many times in his life that Igor wished he could speak. He enjoyed his existence, hiding behind deafness and his hump and an inability to communicate like most of the rest of

227

humanity. And now that his life was filled with Barney Thomson and Garrett Carmichael, two people who understood everything he tried to say but couldn't articulate, it didn't seem to matter. However, every now and again there came moments when he wished, to the bottom of his very soul, that he had the capability to shout at people, explain everything in thirty seconds and, more than anything else, tell them to shut up.

Not that shouting at anyone to tell them to shut up because you want them to be quiet as there's potentially a masked murderer in the yard actually makes any sense. It would have been nice to have the option, however.

The others in this dim little back room all nodded and looked slightly sheepish. People always assumed that Igor would be a follower rather than a leader. He gave them another harsh look and then edged round the corner of the door.

'Igor?' whispered Craig Brown from behind. Igor turned, a look of annoyance on his face. A look that suddenly died. 'What happened to Ally?'

Igor's face changed. He couldn't speak, but wouldn't have had to say anything in this situation in any case.

'Shit,' muttered Waites.

'I'm sorry,' Igor silently mouthed.

He dropped his eyes and turned back to the door. There would be time for regret and sadness later, but for the moment he sensed the inherent danger.

He looked across the cluttered main room of the shed. Were they going to hide in this dim muddle all night? Looked at his watch. It wasn't even ten o'clock. The fog had made it seem like it had been evening forever, and yet it had only been a few hours. There were still another ten before dawn, and what then? What if this clawing fog was still in place?

He stared at the door, the door which led back out into the gloom. That was really their only option. Get out of here, and get across the road to one of the hotels. See if there was a free room where Waites and Brown could clean up. Hope there was some police presence there. Notify the families of the missing fishermen. At last, some light in the darkness of this horrible few days.

He turned, finger to his lips again and beckoned them all to follow him. Exaggeratedly mouthed *be careful!* as he indicated the floor. Another pause to see that they were actually going to follow him, as he was not used to leading, and then he turned and started edging his way through the minefield towards the door.

Immediately Bernard banged his knee off a small wooden cabinet, a dull thud, and he hopped comically on one leg while the others looked daggers at him.

'Like, sorry, man!' he whispered.

And then, as they all turned away and started to pick their slow and meandering path through the debris, came another sound from outside. The same as before. The slow, agonising creak of the front gate, as it was pushed painfully open. Hearts skipped beats. Everyone looked at Igor, eyes full of fear.

Hesitation, then another sign from Igor, and they started once more to mince slowly across the floor. Seconds passed, nerves held. The two fisherman feeling lost and confused, facing up to the death of their friend, uncomfortable, legs cramped and stiff. Bernard and The Dog With No Name, hungry and scared, and wishing they were back in London, working in an office chasing down distant drug rings and unseen terrorists. Igor, trying to be sure of himself, trying to have a belief in his own abilities to lead this sorry gang of fools out of this place. How could they believe in him if he didn't believe in himself?

They collected at the door. Igor looked them over, and then started indicating with sweeping hand manoeuvres that he intended switching off the light, opening the door and heading out of the boatyard.

'Cool, charades!' said Bernard. 'Light, light. The Unbearable Lightness of Being?'

The Dog With No Name nudged him.

'Switch?' said Bernard. 'You think it's switch? The Switches of Eastwick?'

Igor started cutting his hand across his throat, amazed as most other people were when they met Bernard and discovered his chosen occupation. To give him some due, however, he could keep a secret.

'Beheading…beheading…The Texas Chainsaw Massacre?'

Colin Waites clamped his hand on Bernard's shoulder.

'Shut up,' he said, with great deliberation. 'You're an MI6 muppet. The man is trying to say that he will turn the light out, we will go outside and leave this place. Fucking *capiche*?'

Bernard nodded.

'Did you just say *capiche*?' said Craig Brown.

Igor once more drew a dramatic hand across his neck to silence everyone. They all acknowledged the leader, then Igor quickly put one hand on the door handle and turned off the light. He waited a second, could hear the whimper of the Dog With No Name in the darkness behind him, and then slowly began to lower the handle.

Just outside the door, something scraped along the ground. Another muffled sound. Igor froze.

## 15

## The Breaking Of The Guard

Despite the thick fog, the killer moved easily between the boats, knowing every anchor, every mast, every misplaced nautical item left sitting around the yard. He had a small bag, and every so often he would bend down, turn something over or empty out a small metal tube and place it inside. The bag was slowly filling up.

Beneath his Dostoevsky mask, which he had specially ordered through www.noveltydeadrussiannovelistmasks.com some weeks previously, when his demonic plans had first come to him in the form of a strange and powerfully dark dream, the killer was working his way towards his goal. The operation was at an end, he would clear up on the profits, there would be none of the other ten to share in the bounty or talk to the police. Only dear old Cudge and the two fishermen bound and gagged beneath the table to be taken care of. He had so far been unable to bring himself to dispose of the youthful Brown and Waites, but the time was getting close.

Having worked his way down the line of boats, he came to the small building at the end of the row and stood outside the door. He clutched the small bag in one hand and reached out for the door handle with the other.

✂

Igor looked at the others, but now, with the light off, he could no longer see them, even though they stood only a few feet away, such was the intensity of the darkness inside the shed.

He steeled himself. He had had to put up with much in life, the deaf, mute hunchback's lot. Whatever demon waited for him outside, whatever man in a mask stood on the threshold of this door, regardless of what that man might have done to anyone else in this town, Igor could handle it.

Looking through the darkness, imagining the frightened faces of his small, ragtag army, Igor said with vigour, verve and panache, 'I see you stand like greyhounds in the slips, straining upon the start. The game's afoot! Follow your spirit and, upon this charge cry, 'God for Igor! Scotland and St Andrew!''

Sadly this bold, if highly derivative, rallying call came out only as 'Arf!'

Igor faced the door, handle still depressed, could hear further movement outside, and, heart in mouth, stomach churning, pulled the door open.

Detective Chief Inspector Frankenstein would later admit that he damned near died of fright. He hadn't actually noticed Igor the deaf, mute hunchback on the island before and creeping around a boatyard in thick fog with a deranged lunatic killer on the loose wasn't the best time to get his initial introduction.

He staggered more than stepped back into Barney Thomson, directly behind him. Igor stared at him. The Dog With No Name bravely poked its head out of the door, followed by Bernard and the two fishermen.

'Fuck,' said Frankenstein loudly, a sharp crack of the word, not even swallowed up by the density of the fog. 'Who the fuck are you?'

'Arf!' said Igor.

'Igor,' said Barney, 'my assistant. Jesus, Colin and Craig! You guys ok?'

'Jesus?' said Bernard. 'Jesus is here?'

Craig Brown nodded.

'Physically, I suppose,' said Colin Waites, 'but mentally we're screwed. Probably need post-traumatic stress counselling for decades. And we smell like shit.'

Barney smiled. That was the Colin Waites he knew.

'We should get you across the road to one of the hotels, get you cleaned up, call your families.'

'Hi guys!' said Fred, appearing behind.

The Dog With No Name barked.

'Freddie!' said Bernard, relieved that his own people had arrived.

The gang, now suddenly grown to eleven in number, twelve including the Dog With No Name, gathered in a circle outside the door of the workshop.

'So, you're Waites and Brown,' said Frankenstein, looking between the two fishermen. 'I know you want to get away from here, but this guy has murdered at least three people tonight. You need to tell me everything you can that might possibly help us. Everything.'

Craig Brown's head twitched, he looked blankly to the side of Frankenstein's head. He wasn't saying anything about the mask of Fyodor Dostoevsky. Waites squeezed his arm. Barney and Proudfoot recognised the look on their faces, wanted to intervene to save them from this at this time, but they knew they couldn't. The guy was still out there and Frankenstein had to push them for everything they could think of.

The MI6 gang waited excitedly for anything that might be a new clue.

'There were three of you on the boat,' said Frankenstein. Aware that they couldn't stand there forever but knowing he had to gently ease one of them in to talking about their ordeal.

Waites stared at the ground.

'There were four,' he said.

Frankenstein and Proudfoot looked surprised. The MI6 gang perked up.

'I knew it!' said Selma.

Frankenstein glanced round sharply at her. His face demanded an explanation, but she was too busy making notes in a small book. No time for getting into an argument with the security services. He turned back quickly to Waites.

'Who was the fourth?'

Waites looked uncomfortably at his fellow fisherman, but Brown was staring randomly off into the mist. There was no way back for him, at least not this evening.

'An Irish guy,' he said. 'Crichton, Gram Crichton.'

'What happened to him?' said Frankenstein.

Waites swallowed. Dry mouth. Stared at the floor.

'He got him. The guy in the mask. It was a thick fog out, thick as this. We were coming through the Kyles, puttering. So slow. Then a boat came alongside. Right in beside us. Touching us. But there didn't seem to be anyone on board. Gram says he'll go over and take a look. Just as he steps on board, we're all watching, this guy leaps up out of nowhere, axe held above his head…'

He swallowed again, reliving the moment, the scene, for the thousandth time in the past five days, although this was the first time he'd been in a position to put it into words.

'Swipes the guy's head off?' said Frankenstein.

Waites nodded.

'Clean…' he began, and his voice drifted off.

'And what happened to Deuchar?' said Frankenstein quickly, worried that if he lost Waites for five seconds, it could be forever.

'The guy came on deck,' he said, each word forced out, each strand of the memory dragged from some place in his head where he had tried to hide it away. 'We were all scared. He just stood there, it was like a fucking horror movie. Fucking creepy. Then he steps forward, turns the axe head round and whacked me and Craig on the napper. Hardly had time to move. We woke up back there, tied together, in the pitch black. I didn't even know where we were until we saw Igor.'

'Deuchar?' repeated Frankenstein.

Waites shook his head.

'Just before I got whacked, I saw him collapse. I didn't know what it was. Fainted. Heart attack. I don't know.'

His head dropped, Frankenstein gave him a second. All the time he could feel it though. The menace was out there and, more probably, in here. In the boatyard, possibly only yards away through the mist.

'Who was Gram Crichton?' said Frankenstein.

Waites stared at the ground. The others were becoming restless. They could sense it too. The lurking menace, the foreboding evil. Frankenstein took a step forward, held Waites' arms.

'Who was Gram Crichton?'

'We picked him up in Ireland,' said Waites, his voice beginning to break. It didn't matter who Gram Crichton was or why they had picked him up. All he could see was the look on Crichton's face as his head spiralled through the air.

Craig Brown stared into the fog.

'We were smuggling diamonds,' said Waites eventually.

Frankenstein stared at him, mouth open. Beside him Selma gave a little squeal of excitement. Frankenstein turned sharply.

'You bastards knew about this all along?'

'We're MI6, my friend,' said Fred. 'We know everything.'

Frankenstein stepped closer, away from Waites, getting into Fred's face.

'And you couldn't share that information, you bastard?'

'You were investigating the murders,' said Fred. 'We left you to it. We did our part, you did yours, and now the two investigations have come together. We can share clues!'

Frankenstein felt his blood pressure shooting, the anger pinballing around inside his head far outweighing any feelings of trepidation and impending death. He stabbed his finger into Fred's chest.

'Stick your fucking clues up your stupid arse,' he said, teeth bared.

Fred nodded, mind already working. Memo to Vauxhall Bridge: add DCI Frankenstein to the list.

Igor felt it first. He turned quickly, the others noticed the movement. Eyes, heads followed the look, a frightened stare towards the row of boats, albeit boats which were still obscured by the fog.

Brown looked up for the first time since coming into the assembled group, his face engulfed by terror. He was back.

No time to move. None of them.

The killer was upon them, axe held high above his head, charging into their midst, brutality in mind. The group split asunder, the killer headed straight for Fred of MI6.

'You don't frighten me!' said Fred boldly, standing tall, braced to tackle his masked assailant head on.

The killer swung the axe, a beautiful parabolic swipe, cutting through the mist and then cutting through Fred's neck with ease and grace and panache. Fred's body collapsed instantly, his head toppling off with some force, a few feet from his body.

'Like, wow, Fred!' yelped Bernard. 'Are you all right, buddy?'

Selma and Deirdre took one look at Fred's scuppered body and turned and legged it into the mist. Which is what the others had already done, Barney Thomson included. Fred was gone, there was nothing to be done to help him now.

The killer stood over Bernard. It bent forward, the contempt on his face evident despite the latex.

'Fucking MI6,' he muttered, and then he himself turned and ran headlong into the mist.

The small gathering had completely dispersed. All that remained of the circle outside the door of the boatyard workshop was the crumpled and decapitated body of Fred of MI6, blood spilling out into a pool on the ground. Bernard stood over him, the Dog With No Name nuzzled in beside his leg.

## 16

## The Four Corners

Colin Waites grabbed Craig Brown by the arm and pulled him away. No idea where they were heading, they stumbled across the gate at the exit of the boatyard, out into the small lane leading on to the main road round the island. Confused, frightened, disorientated and hurting. But away from the boatyard, and safe.

Selma and Deirdre ran around wildly, not knowing where they were going, scared and bewildered. It just wasn't like Fred to get his head cut off like that. It would not be long, after a few frantic seconds of bumping into boats and tripping over masts, before they would have gone a full short circle, and would be back beside Bernard and the Dog With No Name and Fred, in his state of bloody woe.

The police contingent, Dr Trio Semester and Igor in tow, rushed to the side in convoy, running into a brick wall, and staying pressed up against it, breathing hard, listening for any further commotion in the fog.

Barney Thomson dashed out of the way, no idea in which direction he'd run. Tripped over something metal, fell against the side of a wooden boat, straightened himself up. Looked around into the heart of the mist. Heart thumping, but the composure was still there. Tense but not afraid. He could hear stumbling, no voices. A flight through the mist, someone moving swiftly between the boats. A few frantic seconds, and then everything had died down.

Silence.

He became aware of the sound of his breathing and made the conscious effort to slow it down, to take slow deep breaths. Clenched and unclenched his fists. Channelled the tension, let the cold sweat pass.

The message on the wall of the café had been there for a reason. This whole thing, whatever it was, seemed to be as much about him. The killer was out there for him, to toy with him. Maybe he and the killer were entwined in a way that he had yet to work out. His ghosts had not been arriving over a long period, building to this conclusion. Whatever unsettled feelings he might have had before this past week, there had been no dark mirrors of the soul into which he could gloomily stare, until precisely the evening, perhaps even precisely the time, that the crew of the trawler *Bitter Wind* had been laid waste.

And so, with his mind working to some sort of inevitable conclusion, he was neither surprised nor frightened when a tall figure began to appear through the mist, although he still found himself pressing back against the wooden hull of the *Golden Cavalier III*, as if he might be able to merge into the boat and make himself invisible.

The man in black emerged fully from the mist and stood before Barney. Two feet between them, the rubber Dostoevsky mask curled into a smile.

Barney considered his options. The classic fight or flight? But that wasn't why the two of them were standing here. There would be no fight, and flight was clearly pointless. It would be the third option in the adrenaline-fuelled, testosterone-laden situation. Dialogue.

'Not running, Barney?' said Dostoevsky.

Recognised the voice. The same as the old man who had come in for a haircut and sat in the front of the DCI's car. An older version, he now realised, of the young guy who had come in looking for a Bruce Willis.

'Nowhere to go,' said Barney.

Dostoevsky laughed.

'At last you've woken up to the ultimately bloody consequences of your fate.'

Barney glanced to the side. Briefly wondered what had happened to the rest of them. At least while this monster was here, the others would be safe. Did he keep him talking until the fog cleared and the morning came?

'You don't think I brought the fog?' said Dostoevsky, still smiling.

Despite himself, despite the previous inner calm which had not seemed forced, Barney Thomson felt the first surge of fear, rising from his stomach like a tornado through his insides.

'Oh, how sweet,' said Dostoevsky, 'you've finally realised you should be afraid.'

The eyes burrowed into Barney as they had back in the car, and this time Barney knew there was no point in closing his eyes. There was no way to escape the gaze. He just had to straighten up, face what was coming, deal with it as he could.

The smile dropped, the mask twisted into a sneer.

'You think you can beat me, Barney Thomson?'

Barney tried to close his mind to positive and negative thoughts alike. An empty mind.

'I don't have to,' he said. 'I can just walk away.'

Dostoevsky snarled, then struck quickly, a swift blow with the right fist. Barney ducked, but the fist whistled straight through his head. He staggered back upright, disconcerted by the feeling of having had a hand pass through his brain. Dostoevsky laughed harshly, maniacally, deliriously. Barney rested his head back against the wooden hull.

Again a fist flew at him, this time thumping him harshly on the nose, trapping his head against the wood, a brutal blow. His nose broken. His knees buckled, then he straightened up quickly. Stopped himself lifting his hand to his nose.

'Very brave.' The smile, the sneer vanished. The eyes once more engulfed Barney, so that the searing pain in his nose seemed to vanish. Then slowly Dostoevsky lifted his right hand, pressed it against Barney's neck, a solid grasp of the fingers, and pinned Barney back against the hull of the boat.

'It's time, Barney Thomson. Time to give up your soul.'

'I don't owe you anything,' said Barney sternly. Bravely.

Another laugh. The clenched hand stayed in place around Barney's throat, but again there was a switch in tone.

'You were lost Barney. You needed help. You were alone in a shop with a dead body, a body that you had murdered. You, no one else. You didn't even need me for that. And I came to your rescue.'

'My mother helped me,' said Barney, gritting his teeth. The grip on his throat beginning to tighten. 'My mother, no one else.'

'Your mother? Your mother with six bodies in her freezer?' The tone turned harsh once more, the fingers squeezed. 'And who do you think was inside your mother? Who is in all evil? I didn't invent this stupid, pathetic little diamond smuggling operation, I didn't decide that one member of this worthless gang of thieves was going to kill all the others, but I am inherent in it all. I am in all evil. I *am* evil, Barney. You came to me for help and now it's time to pay back. For every crime, there is punishment.'

Barney stiffened his back, his shoulders, the look in his eye.

'No I fucking didn't,' he said slowly.

'Give in to it, Barney, a wondrous eternity awaits you. In Hell.'

Barney squeezed his eyes shut, tried to dredge something from the pits of his memory. He could never win this with strength.

His nose throbbed, his arms hung limply by his sides, he could barely breathe, the grip was tightening. He was being toyed with to the end.

'I have followed you around, Barney Thomson. You have reacted so well in the face of the grim realities of this awful life. I even brought you back when you were taken from me too soon. All those questions about your life to which you cannot find the answers, I am the answer, Barney.'

'Why now?' said Barney. Did he care, or was he just saying something, anything, to extend the agony?

'It's been ten years, Barney. Quite long enough, don't you think? The Bank of Hell doesn't like to wait too long before cashing in on its promises.'

Barney looked into the dark, bottomless eyes of Fyodor Dostoevsky. What was behind the mask? Maybe there was no mask.

'Too high a price is asked for evil,' said Barney, his voice a barely audible croak, battling against the tightening fist, 'it's beyond our means to pay so much to enter. And so I hasten to give back my entrance ticket...'

Barney took a sharp breath as the firm grasp relaxed a fraction. The masked head lay slightly to the side. Fyodor Dostoevsky stared at Barney with a vague look of curiosity.

240

Then suddenly the grip of the fingers relaxed completely, the hand fell, and the latex face of the Russian novelist disintegrated into laughter. And yet, the eyes stayed on Barney the whole time, they kept their grip.

Barney, still pressed against the hull of the *Golden Cavalier III*, stared at him. Not knowing which way to think, knowing that there was still nowhere to go and that he remained at his whim.

The laughter switched off as quickly as it had started, replaced by a look, a strange mixture of suspicion and enthralment.

'You paraphrase?' he said coldly.

Barney nodded. All those years pointlessly studying the 19th century Germans and Russians hadn't necessarily been for nothing.

'Of course, I know you know that stuff,' said Dostoevsky, and he flicked his hand airily in the mist. 'Perhaps you have qualities that I never suspected in the beginning. Maybe I can wait a little longer. Delay the execution. Have a little more......fun.'

Barney looked at him, a look of contempt that he couldn't keep from his face. He didn't want a stay of anything. He wanted his absurd life resolved.

'Exactly,' said Dostoevsky, smiling. 'Why would I possibly give you what you want?'

The eyes flashed, he took a step back, away from Barney.

'And while we stood, so bold and energised, but five seconds have passed,' he said, and he snapped his fingers. 'Time to get back to work. Bilbo's the word, and slaughter will ensue!'

'That's not Dostoevsky,' said Barney.

The man in black put his hand to his own neck this time, the shoulders hunched lower, he seemed to shrink in stature.

'Who the fuck said I was Dostoevsky?'

He whipped the mask off and, for the briefest of seconds, a quick flash of horror in the fog, Barney Thomson was looking into the eyes and into the laughing face of his own, dead mother.

And in the blinking of an eye, she was gone, swallowed up by the mist.

✂

The police collective pressed against the brick wall, breathing sharply, trying to control the fear.

'Bastards,' said Frankenstein eventually. 'They knew the subtext of this thing. We've been going up our own backsides for days trying to work it out, and they knew all along there'd been a fourth person on that boat. Diamond smuggling for fuck's sake.'

He was angry, angry at everyone, angry at the situation, angry that his life had been taken over by this preposterous killer on the rampage.

'We need to find this guy in the next two minutes,' he said, then he turned and looked along the line of unwilling lieutenants. 'I remember from this morning another door along here. Maybe an office or something.'

'Arf,' nodded Igor in agreement.

'Right. We go inside, get a light on, see if anything's doing, regroup.' He breathed deeply. Had no real gut feeling for what they should do, but had to do something. Another pause, a moment's hesitation, hoping perhaps that someone, anyone, was going to suggest something more constructive. 'Right, come on.'

He began to inch along the wall, Igor, Proudfoot and Semester in tow.

'I'm too old for this shit,' said Semester from the back, and then he started to giggle. Frankenstein glanced over his shoulder, ruefully shaking his head. 'Always wanted to say that,' Semester added, still giggling.

'Thought you said it every night with the wife?' quipped Frankenstein from the head of the queue.

'And if the woman didn't keep renewing my Viagra subscription, I might get away with it.'

Proudfoot glanced at Igor. 'Don't think we'd get away with talking in class,' she said.

'Keep it down,' snapped Frankenstein, by way of confirmation.

'Arf.'

242

They crept on, a short stretch of wall that seemed to take much longer than they'd thought. The noises of the others had died away, they seemed once again to be alone in the mist and fog. The killer was out there, somewhere, but they didn't know where. The MI6 gang, one down, and still stumbling around in the dark, looking for clues. And food. The two rescued fishermen, taken from the frying pan and dropped callously into the fire. Barney Thomson lost in the mist

They reached the door. From the small window beside it, a dim light shone. Frankenstein looked over his shoulder.

'Ok. Deep breath. We charge. If he's in there, it's no big deal. Just any old guy in a mask. We all need to tackle him at once, all four of us, we go for the guy. If we stand there like a bunch of lemons, he'll pick us off.'

'I *am* too old for that shit,' said Semester.

'Too bad,' said Frankenstein. 'I'll buy you a pint after. If you're not dead.'

'You have confidence you won't be?'

Frankenstein gave him the look, then turned quickly, sprang up, leant on the handle and pushed the door open, charging in full pelt. The rest of them followed, suddenly on the hoof, hearts pounding. Igor and Proudfoot, Semester at the back.

They careered in wildly, nearly taking the door from its hinges, and stood rowdily in the middle of the small office, low lit by a tiny lamp at the back of the room, a ragtag army, ready to fight.

## 17

## Diamonds

Cudge Bladestone looked up from behind the cluttered desk. Sweating profusely, clothes dishevelled, eyes manic. Fumbling about with a small bag. He pushed back in his seat, swallowed, demonically stared around the four assorted police officers, pathologists and hunchbacks. The four assorted police officers, pathologists and hunchbacks stared back.

'What the fuck do you want?' said Bladestone, after a few seconds of Mexican stand-off.

Frankenstein didn't answer, turned and started to look around the room.

'Come on,' he said hurriedly, 'look for the stupid mask. Anything.'

He moved quickly into the other room. Despite the sweaty, guilty exterior of the man at the desk, the prime suspect he'd had pegged for the man behind the Dostoevsky mask was not sitting there looking like someone who had just severed the head of an MI6 agent. He looked like he was as scared as the rest of them.

A quick look in the other room, Proudfoot followed him, then Frankenstein came back through. Stared angrily at Bladestone.

'What are you hiding?' he demanded. 'Now!'

Bladestone's tongue snaked out to lick nervous lips. No words. Frankenstein took another step towards the desk, leant over him.

Footsteps at the door and everyone turned, hearts at the ready. Barney Thomson stepped uneasily into the light, quickly assessed the situation. Looked at Igor and Detective Sergeant Proudfoot and silently asked the question if they were all right, at the same time waved away the concern on their faces about his bruised and bloodied nose.

Frankenstein watched Barney for a second, was aware how easily someone could appear from the fog, then turned back to Bladestone, Barney now coming to stand at his shoulder.

'Show me what's in the bag,' Frankenstein said sternly.

'Have you got some sort of warrant?' said Bladestone desperately.

'Careful, Frank,' said Semester from behind, a sudden calm and measured voice in amongst the turmoil and angst. 'You have to be able to get a conviction.'

Frankenstein tensed, breath coming in a hard exhalation. Bladestone stared at him, eyes relaxing, just a flicker.

'You police have your rules,' he said. 'Don't you?'

Voice the colour of a snake. Frankenstein imagined whipping a .44 from his back pocket and blasting Bladestone's head off. Clean off.

'We're not all the police, are we?' said a voice from the side.

Everyone looked at Barney. Frankenstein knew what was coming and was glad he hadn't had that plastic deputy badge to hand when enlisting Barney to the force.

'Fucking barber,' muttered Bladestone, and he clutched the bag more tightly to his chest. Barney had had enough death, murder, deceit and lies. He was no action hero, no tough guy, but he wanted this to be over with as quickly as possible. He wanted normality back, a subdued normality, and not this absurd, death-filled, death-fuelled normality which he now called his own.

Two steps, round the side of the desk, and he pounced on Bladestone. There was a flurry of arms and legs, but it was never going to take much. Barney didn't need to defeat Bladestone, didn't need to throw him down or get him in a headlock. He just needed to expose the contents of the bag.

He grabbed at the bag, took a boot in the stomach, another blow to the head, reeled but swung at Bladestone with his right arm at the same time. Caught Bladestone off balance. Pushed himself off the desk, fell towards Bladestone, made another grab.

The two men crashed together over the back of the chair, one pulled one way with the bag, the other in the opposite direction. The contents sprayed out, arching through the air, sparklingly beautiful, even in the dim light of the small desk lamp.

Diamonds.

Bladestone's head cracked off the wall, he crumpled onto the floor. Barney thudded into the wall, then pushed himself away from it, straightening up. Avoided the tangle of Bladestone's legs, looked down at his opponent, who lay on the floor, staring up angrily in defeat.

Frankenstein picked up one of the small diamonds which had fallen on the desk. Held it up to the light, looked through it. Didn't know what he was looking for, but for the moment, it didn't matter. A diamond was a diamond. Some of the story, if not exactly all of it, was unravelling this night, as the fog and the horrible feeling of demonic premonition had foretold.

'Where's the guy in the mask?' he said harshly.

Bladestone's eyes flitted frantically around the five of them, all now gathered above him.

'I don't know,' said Bladestone bitterly. 'I'm as scared of him as you.'

'Who said the fuck I was scared?' growled Frankenstein.

Suddenly the door burst open, thrown back, crashing into the wall. Selma and Deirdre came in, running full pelt.

'He's coming!' yelled Deidre.

The men braced themselves. Barney caught Proudfoot's eye across the room and ran across quickly, through the sudden stramash of people, to put himself between her and whoever was about to come through the door. His mother?

Frankenstein stood firm, expected the MI6 girls to disappear into the back room. However they immediately crouched down on either side of the open door, primed for action, Selma with a short piece of rope in her right hand.

Further commotion through the mist, and then Bernard and The Dog With No Name came hurtling through the open door, wailing in terror.

'Like, Oh my gosh!' yelled Bernard. 'The decapitator dude's coming this way! And he's super-mad!'

Bernard and The Dog With No Name were not stopping to get involved in the action. They burst through the crowd and disappeared into the small back room, which would be little protection at all, if the killer was to find his head.

They waited. A moment's pause. The briefest of seconds. Time suspended. They stood, braced for the apocalypse.

The mist parted, the masked figure in black emerged from the murkiness just outside the door, axe raised, feet flying across the ground.

Frankenstein, first in line, braced himself. Saw the flash of the axe. Noticed, with incredulity, that Selma had thrown an end of the rope across to Deirdre, and the two of them had pulled it taught, about a foot off the ground.

'Oh, for fuck's s...' he began.

The killer burst through the door, immediately his right leg caught in the rope. Deirdre and Selma held firm, the man in black flew forward, crashing down towards Frankenstein and Igor.

The detective and the deaf, mute hunchback lashed out at the same time. The killer hurtled towards the ground and, cast sideways, fell harshly against the edge of the desk. Banged his head with a loud thump, his whole upper body jerked awkwardly, the axe fell harmlessly to the floor. He groaned loudly, one leg twitching, a hand lifted defensively to his head. Frankenstein automatically struck out, kicking him brutally in the face so that the masked head snapped backwards, banging once more off the solid wood of the desk. And then Selma and Deirdre, using all their training and experience, leapt upon the killer with the rope, and quickly tied the legs together, tight aching knots. Another piece of rope was produced from Deirdre's pockets, and this one was tightly wound around the killer's midriff, binding his flailing arms to his sides.

And with that, the masked killer, who had so terrorized the small island community for the previous few days, was perched up against the table, trapped and bound.

Barney Thomson stared down at the beaten figure that he had presumed to be Satan, and wondered who could possibly lie beneath the mask.

Everyone remained breathless with the action of the previous few seconds, waiting for something else to happen, some coda to the event. Bladestone looked down at the captured killer, astonished. Then he noticed that everyone else seemed to have been struck by some kind of stupor. One last chance to get away, he thought, some few diamonds still in the torn bag which he clasped to his chest. If he could just get out into the mist, he would have a perfect chance to get away.

Another short pause, the briefest of hesitations, and then he rose quickly, put his foot on the desk, hoisted himself up, skipped across and jumped down onto the office floor, just three feet from the door and freedom.

Unfortunately for Bladestone's aspirations, Frankenstein saw him coming all the way. As the man's feet hit the ground, Frankenstein delivered a cutting blow to his ankles which pitched him forward with a crash into the wall on the other side. Another head knock, this time he stayed down and looked groggily back around the room.

Another pause, as the room waited to see if this would be the last of the action. Barney turned to Proudfoot and squeezed her hand, Proudfoot who had been in a daze since witnessing the murder of Sergeant Kratzenburg.

'You ok?' he asked.

She nodded. Couldn't speak.

'Can we come out now?' came Bernard's voice from the other room.

'Sure,' said Deirdre.

Bernard and The Dog With No Name came loping into the room. The crowd automatically gathered around the killer, his head slumped forward, bound at the feet and chest, strange little noises coming from behind the mask.

'Time to find out who Fyodor Dostoevsky really is,' said Selma.

Barney swallowed, wondering if the greying old wizened face of his mother was about to be presented to the public. Knew intrinsically that she was gone, the demon was gone.

Selma stepped forward, peeled away the latex at the neck and then with two hands, tugged the Fyodor Dostoevsky mask quickly up and over the head.

The assembled crowd stared in amazement.

'Mr. Andrew the hotel manager!' they all said.

'*You* were the diamond smuggler?' said Semester, who had been so welcomed into The Stewart Hotel.

'Yes,' said Andrew. 'And I would have gotten away with it if it hadn't been for these meddling MI6 muppets.'

Frankenstein scowled. 'Fuck them,' he muttered. 'I was always going to get you, you bastard.'

And then he thought of the murder and havoc this man had wreaked, and forgetting that things were different in this day and age from the innocent times when he'd first joined the police, he stepped forward and kicked Andrew, the mild-mannered hotel manager, viciously in the face.

'Bastard,' he said, as the killer's head bounced back off the desk and slumped down onto the floor.

Barney Thomson, barber, had nothing to say. And while he could not in any way have articulated what had just happened to him this evening, he understood perfectly.

The demon, be it the Satan that waits at the crossroads to hand out eternal damnation in return for missing chords, or some other generic fiend who lives and inhabits every evil deed that is ever committed, was gone.

Not forever, and maybe not for long, but he had left this island for a while and he had left the life of Barney Thomson.

## 18

# Like, It's A Wrap

The fog lifted slowly through the night. Gradually the police reinforcements arrived, the authorities found their way to the island. The various crime scenes were closed down, the bodies of the dead and decapitated were gradually bagged up and removed. By the time the town woke up the following morning, it had what it wished for. The fog was gone, the killer had been arrested, there would be no more murders.

There was a big sky. From where Barney Thomson was sitting, there were large patches of blue, big bulbous white clouds, floating wisps of white and grey away to the south. The sea chopped and swelled.

He was on a bench to the town side of the boatyard, sitting with Proudfoot and Igor and Keanu, watching the sea. They had sat up through the night. Proudfoot had called home, Igor had gone to see Carmichael to tell her of the evening, and had just recently returned, clutching coffees and breakfast, Keanu in tow.

Barney had had his nose cracked painfully back into place, and then had sat through the night, watching the lifting of the fog and the gradual appearance of the day from behind bruised eyes. Hadn't spoken much to whoever was close by, and now the four of them had been sitting for a long time in silence.

Away to his left Barney heard voices. He turned and looked back towards the playpark at the end of the football field. Four people and a dog were walking towards them. The MI6 gang. He felt a slight shudder of surprise, until he realised that the fourth member, the blond man walking slightly ahead of the others, wasn't Fred. Some other, look-a-like officer of the security services, instantly drafted in on Fred's demise, he presumed.

'Keanu,' he said, turning back, and breaking the long silence, 'I have to admit that for a couple of awful minutes there, I had the horrible feeling that it was going to be you under that mask.'

Keanu smiled.

'Cool. But you know, I can dig dressing up in a mask, being someone else 'n all, but cutting people's heads off...? That's a bad rap, man, I could never do stuff like that.'

Barney nodded. The others drank their coffee. Barney looked at his watch, realised that it was time that they opened the shop for the morning. Another day.

The MI6 collective closed in. Barney and Proudfoot shared a glance.

'Hi there!' said Selma.

'Like, hi guys!' said Bernard, 'coffee and doughnuts! Any going spare? Me and The Dog With No Name just had triple syrup blueberry pancakes, but we wouldn't say no to another bite, would we Dog With No Name?'

The dog barked, Igor held up an empty bag.

'This is Fred,' said Selma, indicating the blond man standing next to them. 'He came in early this morning to replace the other Fred who died last night. Help clear up the loose ends.'

Everyone looked at the new Fred.

'Hi, friends!' he said. 'This sure is some weird shit that went down. Glad I missed it, I guess. But hey, thanks for all your help in solving this investigation.'

The four on the bench stared at him. This new Fred wasn't a clone of the old one, not facially, but he had clearly been brought up by the same parents, gone to the same school, shopped in the same menswear department and been rodgered up the backside in the same secret service initiation ceremony.

'How many of them are you?' asked Keanu, and not even he was sure if he meant how many Fred's were there in MI6, or how many officers there were in the whole service.

'That's a secret, old buddy,' said Bernard.

'I'm not your...'

'So, you have what you wanted?' asked Barney.

'We sure do,' said Selma. 'We've been following this diamond operation for three years now, from Sierra Leone, via Amsterdam and Dublin, all the way to the jewellery shops of Great Britain. This was the final link in the chain.'

'Then a couple of weeks ago one of our colleagues on the continent jumped the gun and started closing the line up from the middle,' said Deirdre.

'And, like, everyone knows you can't do that,' chipped in Bernard.'

'Andrew the Mild-Mannered Hotel Manager knew that the whole operation was imploding, so he took himself out of the loop, then secretly intercepted the last trawlerful of contraband diamonds. Just too bad what happened to him.'

'Why did he dress up as Dostoevsky?' asked Proudfoot, asking the question that had been on her lips, while wondering what Deirdre had meant by the last remark. 'And why take the two guys prisoner when he was killing everyone else?'

The MI6 collective looked at each other. The Dog With No Name shrugged.

'When you've been in this game as long as we have,' said Deirdre, 'you'll come to realise that not everything has an explanation.'

'Like sure,' said Selma, 'sometimes life is like an episode of a kids tv show. Not everything adds up, not everything makes sense.'

'Arf,' muttered Igor.

'Exactly, my little hunchbacked friend,' said the new Fred.

A few more looks and then everyone turned and stared out to sea, the waves hurrying into shore. A couple of kids had appeared on the rocks to their right, buckets and small nets in hand, and they watched them for a short while. Finally, when one of the kids shouted, 'I've found the Incredible Captain Death's footprint!' it broke the spell, and the strange collection of people started shuffling about, knowing that there was a day to be getting on with.

'Right fellas!' said the new Fred, in an unusually loud voice, 'we need to get going. Gee, guys, like thanks for all your help, it sure was useful.'

'Like, totally,' said Bernard. 'Come on Dog With No Name, let's see if we can rustle up a peanut butter and sun-dried tomato meringue before we go.'

The Dog With No Name barked. Deirdre and Selma and Fred held up a hand of farewell.

252

'I hate myself for asking this,' said Barney, 'but why has the dog got no name?'

Bernard shrugged.

'Well, the big fella just turned up one day out of nowhere, and I looked at him and tried to think of a name, tried to think of something that would be suitable, but you know, I just didn't have a Scooby.'

He snapped his fingers, and with that the MI6 collective turned on their heels and walked quickly away back towards the football field.

They watched them go, the four people and a dog, speeding away with a youthful rush rather than a swagger.

'What did they mean when they said, too bad what happened to him?' asked Proudfoot.

No one knew, a shake of the head, a shrug of the shoulders.

'They kind of remind me of something but I can't think what it is,' said Keanu.

'Arf.'

Keanu looked round at Igor. Igor was looking at him, eyebrow raised. Keanu smiled.

'You just said that it was time we went and opened up the shop,' said Keanu. 'I got you at last! I am so geeked.'

Igor put his hand on Keanu's shoulder and nodded, then slowly got to his feet and looked at Barney.

'I'll be there in ten or fifteen minutes,' said Barney.

'Arf.'

'See you later, boss,' said Keanu. 'Sergeant,' he added, nodding at Proudfoot.

And then Igor and Keanu walked slowly away, Keanu's hand on Igor's shoulder as he chatted amiably.

Barney and Proudfoot turned back out to the restless, endless sea. Another absurd instance of mass murder in their lives was over, as if it should be commonplace in anyone's life. She checked her watch, glanced along the road. A police car was just coming down the hill from Cardiff Street, and she knew that Frankenstein would be coming to get her. Time, for her at least, to leave the island and get back to what she could salvage of her sanity.

253

'It doesn't explain your ghosts, does it?' she said to Barney. 'It doesn't explain the message on the wall of the café. What are we missing, Barney Thomson? And that beaut of a broken nose you've got there, you haven't said how you came by that.'

Barney stared at the water. It made sense to him now, but he had no desire to explain it to anyone else, or to drag anyone else into his mess. His demons were for him to deal with. Maybe now, at least, he had some of the answers to the mysteries of his life, even if he wasn't entirely sure that he wanted to believe in those answers.

'I don't know,' he said. 'I just want to forget about it for a while.'

'Did you sell your soul to Satan, Barney?'

Barney lowered his eyes, from the sea to the rocks to the grass at his feet. He lifted his hands in a phlegmatic gesture.

Footsteps to their left. Proudfoot looked round, Frankenstein walking quickly towards them across the grass. She squeezed Barney's hand.

'I'm going to have to go,' she said quietly. 'I like you Barney, you're not half as weird as the papers make out, but you know, I just hope that we never, ever meet again.'

He looked at her, smiling. She smiled back, shrugged and then took her hand away and looked up as Frankenstein arrived and stood beside them, although he too was drawn to look out at the sea.

'You ready to leave, Sergeant?' he asked.

She nodded.

'Get you off this stupid joint. Although,' he began, and he waved a hand over the sea, 'now that we've got the nutjob and the darkness has lifted...' and he let the sentence drift off.

'Where is he?' asked Proudfoot.

Frankenstein shook his head. He had managed to get an hour alone with Andrew the hotel manager in the Glasgow police station where he'd been taken in the middle of the night. He had got to the bottom of Andrew's paranoia and greed, he had learned the story of how this disparate crew of ten had come together to form a cabal, each with their own particular finger in the pie. He had learned about diamond

254

smuggling and where the diamonds had been hidden and why the diamonds had been hidden. He had even managed to elicit some names of contacts in the city that they hadn't heard before. An hour of good quality revelations and information.

He had left the room, with two constables guarding Andrew the Mild Mannered Hotel Manager. And when he had returned to the room ten minutes later, Andrew the hotel manager and both of the constable were dead. All strangled.

No one had come in or out, there had been nothing recorded on the cctv which watched over the room.

For all the fear and emotion which he had felt the previous evening, nothing had scared Frankenstein like this.

'Gone,' he said simply. He coughed, looked unnecessarily at his watch. 'Your man's on his way, Sergeant. Probably just off the boat. I'll take you round.'

He stepped forward in front of Barney and held out his hand.

'Mr Thomson, you're officially de-deputised. Thanks for your help.'

Barney stood and shook his hand. Nothing to say.

'I take it you're not going anywhere. I may have the odd question after I've read the sergeant's notes on your discussion.'

'I'll be here,' said Barney, and he sat back down beside Proudfoot. Where else was he going to be?

'That's a hell of a nose you've got there.'

Barney didn't say anything. Frankenstein lifted a hand and then turned and started walking slowly towards his car. He stopped a few yards away and turned.

'Andrew, he was a talker. Quite happy to admit to all sorts, even things I didn't know about. But you know, it wasn't him who wrote that thing in blood on the wall of the café last night.'

He stopped. Barney looked over his shoulder.

'Who wrote it, Barney Thomson?' said Frankenstein, but he knew he wasn't going to get an answer. And so he didn't wait for the reply, turned and started walking across the grass. 'Come on, Sergeant,' he threw over his shoulder.

Proudfoot looked at Barney, some part of her feeling that she was walking out on him and unfinished business.

They stared at each other, nothing else to be said. And then slowly she rose, took one last look at Barney Thomson and the cold grey sea, and then walked quickly after Frankenstein.

Barney Thomson did not watch her go.

# Epilogue

The haircutting was over for the day, although the Closed sign had not yet been placed on the door. The three amigos stood at the window, looking out at the end of the day, across the white promenade wall to the light fading on the water. Occasionally people would walk slowly by or a car would pass or a seagull would land on the wall and look their way.

The day had progressed slowly, the town had returned to normal. The shop had been busy all day, an endless stream of people coming to chat, men and woman. Theories abounded. If the police had set up a tape recorder in the corner of the room, they would have learned much. Andrew the mild-mannered hotel manager and his alcoholism. Andrew and his rising gambling debt. Why Andrew wasn't married. Andrew's decision to take out all the other members of the smuggling cabal to keep all the money for himself. Andrew's fascination with Russian literature. Andrew's fascination, bordering on obsessive man-love, for Colin Waites and Craig Brown, so that he could not quite bring himself to kill them.

Barney had watched them all come and go, cutting hair, mostly keeping himself out of the conversations. He had no questions about the diamond smuggling case. He didn't care about the diamonds. He wasn't sure that he even cared about the blood on the walls, his endless stream of non-existent visitors and ghosts.

For now, at least, it seemed like more than just the fog had lifted. The winds were fresh, autumn would turn to cold winter, the sea would continue to occasionally rage and rumble. At some stage the evil would be back, but for a while, Barney could cut hair, he could share amiable chats with Keanu and Igor, and he could work late when he felt like it, without fear of strange men with beards knocking on his door and asking for obscure haircuts.

The past, however, was still out there. The reckoning of Barney Thomson was still at hand.

A long silence, none of them thinking beyond the moment. Except perhaps Keanu, who felt rather that the whole event had passed him by, and was mulling over the previous few days, wondering if he had missed his chance to make a breakthrough into the public consciousness. He glanced back at his laptop, which lay untouched on the counter.

'That Fred guy,' he began, softly throwing some words into the relaxed quiet of the afternoon.

'Which one?' asked Barney.

'The one that came off the substitute's bench,' said Keanu. 'The doppelganger. He may have been a complete tube, but you know, he nailed the whole business on the head when he said that there had been some weird shit.'

Barney nodded. Igor popped a small bubble with his Winterfresh PestoMint. The latest seagull came and sat on the wall and looked across at them, head cocked to the side.

'Thought I might write a book about it,' said Keanu. 'I mean, the blog thing never really got going, but a book about the case. That might stand a chance. You know, from an insider.'

Barney nodded again. Knew Keanu well, knew that Keanu would never write a book.

'Good idea,' he said.

'You think?'

'Arf!'

'Only one problem,' said Barney.

The seagull lifted its head, turned and languidly took off away across the rocks and the sea. Igor raised an eyebrow, Keanu turned with interest.

'No one will ever believe it,' said Barney.

Keanu shrugged. 'I don't know,' he said. 'People are usually willing to believe stories about men in masks.'

The streetlights came on, the dark of early evening crept along the road. The seagulls mournfully whirled and cried, and the sea, the endless restless sea, sucked and swelled and tossed and turned.

✄

Later, after a lazy drink, a relaxing spot of dinner and some amiable chat across the table, the fellowship of the barbershop split up for the evening and each of the men made their own way home.

Barney walked around Kames Bay, across the sand, keeping his shoes away from the gentle waves. The evening was bright, no clouds, some part of a moon, the stars were out. Barney had relaxed into the day, had come down off the high of another misadventure. Knew that he could relax for a while and was determined that he wouldn't even think about what might come in the future for at least a few weeks. Enjoy the peace of a quiet community by the sea. Christmas with Igor and Garrett and the kids. Worry about the future when the future came.

Round the far side of the bay, he walked along the rocks above the waterline. Occasionally found a small stone to throw into the sea, meandering, doing that timeless thing that he had done decades before. Same spot, same view, same rocks, same sea.

He sat down on a flat rock and looked back across to the town, the eternal fairy lights strung out between the lampposts.

'None of it means a thing,' he muttered to himself, throwing a small piece of seaweed at the water.

Something was washing up on the quiet waves onto the rocks. He stared at it for a while, wondering what it was, wondering where it had been thrown into the water so that it ended up on the rocks at Millport. Ardrossan? Dunoon? Larne? Boston?

From nowhere he felt the crawl of tiny insects up his spine, and he reluctantly leant forward to take a closer look. A step, still watching his shoes against the incoming tide. He reached out to lift the piece of rubbish, then hesitated when he realised what it was.

He swallowed, did his best to dismiss the ill-feelings which swamped over him again, then reached out and lifted the flesh coloured piece of latex rubber out of the water.

He held it up in front of him, extended his fingers to stretch the rubber, and looked into the empty eyes of Fyodor Dostoevsky.

A second, another moment of fear, then he muttered, 'Aw, fuck it,' poked his fingers through the empty eye sockets, turned the mask inside out and threw it as far as he could out

259

into the sea. The mask landed lightly, was taken by a wave, and then was swept quickly beneath the water.

Barney Thomson, barber, took one last look out over the sea, then turned quickly away and did not wait to see if the mask was going to resurface.